THE DEATH

ERADICATE

BOOK TWO
THE DEATH TRILOGY

JOHN W. VANCE

For information contact:
info@jwvance.com
www.jwvance.com

ISBN: 10: 1505724066
ISBN: 13: 978-1505724066

DEDICATION

TO MY BEAUTIFUL AND LOVING WIFE
YOUR DEDICATION AND SUPPORT IS ENDLESS

ACKNOWLEDGMENTS

I have traveled the world many times and one thing that has stuck with me is that nothing happens without a group effort. Yes, I wrote the words and created the story in this book, but this book is more than just the initial words and story. Before this book got into your hands it went through many others. It is those people, some family and friends, others contract professionals that I want to acknowledge.

Thank you to my wife and family. You have been there from day one supporting me and giving me encouragement throughout.

Thanks again to my dear from G. Michael Hopf. You have been there mentoring and kicking me in the ass to fulfill my dream of being an author, Semper Fi.

Thank you Pauline, you have turned my book into something is readable.

Thank you to Roberto for the cover art. Love it, you're a true artist.

And finally thank you Amazon. Without them my dreams might have just stayed that. You gave me and others a platform from which to put our words out to the world.

John W. Vance

Prologue

DAY 14

October 16, 2020
Washington, DC

Horton sat pensively tapping his fingers nervously on the leather satchel he cradled in his lap. A small bead of sweat coursed down his throbbing temple as he peered up at the clock that he swore wasn't working. The small hand indicated he had only been waiting for twenty minutes, but to him it felt like twenty hours. The nervous anticipation was apparent, and he began to worry that the guards would notice his odd behavior.

His phone vibrated in his jacket pocket. He took it out and saw the number was blocked. Believing it was one of his colleagues and the timing wasn't appropriate he hit decline and placed it back in his pocket. A moment later, the phone vibrated again. He again pulled it out and saw the same blocked message. Frustrated by the timing he answered it. "Yes."

"Stop what you're doing this is madness," the voice said.

"Who is this?" he asked.

"Please, we can stop this from getting any further, please for God's sake," the voice pleaded.

Horton became frightened, he wasn't sure who was on the phone but the voice did sound familiar. His eyes darted back and forth to see if the guards were suspicious. "I don't know who this is, but it's too late."

"I will not let you finish this genocide; I swear to you, I will not allow you and the Order's vision become reality."

"Wait a minute, is this Calvin?" Horton asked, suddenly realizing who was on the other end.

"Please don't do this. We can stop this together; I know you're better than this?" Calvin begged.

"FYI, your timing is really bad, but why don't you tell me where you are and we can talk."

"No."

"Calvin, it's too late, but if you want to join us again, I can talk to the others."

"You're sick, you really are. I promise you, your dream of Arcadia will not be realized," Calvin sternly said and disconnected the line.

Horton pulled the phone away from his head and looked at it. "What do you know a blast from the past."

"Sir, no phone, please put it away," a guard said from down the hall.

Clearing his throat, he asked, "Um, any idea on when-?" Just then the elevator doors down the hall opened.

"Mr. Director, please follow us," one of the suited guards said to him, gesturing towards the open elevator doors.

Quickly wiping away the perspiration, he stood and shuffled down the ornate hallway towards the large elevator car not a foot behind the guard.

He paused just before stepping on and took a deep breath.

"Director Horton, is everything all right?" the guard asked, noticing the peculiar pause.

With an awkward smile, Horton answered, "Everything is fine."

A man appeared from the corner of the large elevator, his dark suit and demeanor telling Horton he was someone important, and asked, "Are you feeling okay?"

"I'm fine, just nervous is all," Horton answered, a smile still on his face.

The man looked him over and asked, "You have the vaccine with you?"

"Yes, I do, right here," Horton replied, tapping the dark leather satchel now draped over his shoulder.

"Good, come on," the man instructed, motioning for Horton to step on the elevator.

Horton quickly entered and faced the man. "Sorry, just nervous. Not every day you get to meet the president."

"I wish it could have been under better circumstances for you," the man said.

The elevator doors closed.

A guard that was on board inserted a key, turned it right and hit a button marked B.

"B stands for basement?" Horton joked.

"Actually, it means bunker," the man answered.

Horton looked around the large elevator car and noticed it wasn't what he thought it would be. Somehow he fully expected it to be adorned like the hallway upstairs, but it was a simple stainless steel box. He could feel the speed of the elevator as they sank deep into the earth.

"I'm sorry, but I should have introduced myself. I'm Dan Bailey, chief of staff."

"Hi."

"I'm surprised you never met the president before," Dan commented.

"Um, no, I was appointed under the previous administration, so never got a chance."

"Makes sense. It's not as if the director of the CDC is really a political position."

Horton chuckled and said, "You're right, no politics on my side. Heck, I can't even remember when I voted last."

Dan looked at him and cocked his head.

Horton saw the discerning look and looked away.

"It's truly amazing that there's a vaccine for this virus already," Dan commented.

"Like I mentioned, it was fairly easy to synthesize. We took patient zero into custody immediately, and with her, we've been able to create this."

The elevator stopped abruptly and the doors opened to another hallway. This one did not have the same appearance as the one above. It was nothing more than a well-lit concrete chute.

"Right this way," Dan said as he exited and walked briskly down towards a large metal door at the end guarded by two armed men.

Horton followed right behind.

"Gentlemen, you know me. This is CDC Director Horton on behalf of the president."

The door beeped, clicked, and suction sound soon followed as the door unsealed and began to open up.

When it fully opened, Horton saw a wall and two more

guards.

Dan stepped in and Horton followed.

The large door closed behind them, sucked closed, clicked and beeped.

"The president is waiting for you in his residence," Dan said as he turned left and walked down a hallway that looked more civilized and reminiscent of the hallways in the White House above.

Horton nodded to the stoic, statue-like guards and followed Dan.

After navigating through the maze of hallways, they stopped just outside another large metal door, unmarked but manned with two more guards.

"Let the president know the CDC director is here," Dan ordered.

The guard pressed a button and spoke into a throat mic.

A moment passed and the door clicked and opened fully.

"Madam Secretary," Dan said.

"Hi, Dan, he's right here," Secretary of State Donna Crawford said.

Dan walked in with Horton right behind him.

Horton looked around the room and was impressed by the accommodations given the president even in his bunker. The room they were in was a lounge of some sort, with tufted leather couches, thick plush carpet, and dark mahogany wood paneling with large brass sconces every six feet. In the far right corner was a large fully stocked bar, opposite that was a large square table, its polished top covered with papers and documents, and hovering above it was the president.

President Brown, a tall, lean man with thick curly hair looked over and said, "Director Horton, just the man we've been waiting for. Please come over here."

Horton smiled and rushed over, his hand extended.

Brown looked at his hand and said, "Is this a test?"

Horton raised his eyebrows, then understood the comment. "Yes, correct."

"I believe that was part of your protocol, no handshaking," Brown said.

"Right, yes, sir."

"You have it?"

"Right here, sir," Horton answered and again patted the satchel.

Brown quickly rolled up his sleeve and took a seat.

Dan stepped forward and interjected, "Now you're sure this won't harm him?"

Horton's eyes had grown twice the size as he stared at Brown, his enthusiasm piqued.

"Director Horton, did you hear me?" Dan asked.

"Yes, yes, we've tested it. It works."

"Human trials?" Brown asked.

"Yes, sir. Based on your orders, we administered it immediately upon creating it," Horton answered. He had the satchel on the table and opened. "I even took it myself," Horton lied.

"You realize we can never disclose…"

"Yes, sir," Horton acknowledged, interrupting Brown, but his focus was fully on a small sealed box.

"I'm ready," Brown said, his arm extended and ready to receive the shot.

Horton pulled a syringe from a sterile wrapper and injected the tip into a small vial. He pulled the plunger back and watched as the barrel filled halfway. He sat the syringe down, took out an alcohol wipe, and dabbed the spot he was about to inject on the arm. Once done, he took the syringe and stepped toward Brown. He took his arm, and just before he was about to stab him, he paused. This moment was huge; it was impactful and would finalize phase two of his and the council's plan.

Brown looked up at Horton and asked, "Director, everything okay?"

"Fine, sir, everything is just fine," he said, then jabbed Brown's arm and pressed the plunger down.

"How soon do you think we can mass produce this?" Dan asked, escorting Horton back to the elevator.

"We can start on it within a couple weeks," Horton lied.

"Good."

"Just keep the president and everyone else quarantined down here. I recommend after I leave that no one else be admitted until we get this produced and sent out," Horton instructed.

The elevator doors opened.

Dan put his hand out and said, "Thank you so much for your hard work and dedication."

Horton looked at his hand and didn't hesitate to take it. He shook it firmly and said, "My pleasure." He stepped onto the elevator and watched the doors close.

Just before they could close completely, a hand jutted in and stopped them. The doors reopened and Dan was there. "I forgot to mention, on your way out the president ordered that you go and give the vaccine to the vice president. You can do that, right?"

"Of course I can. I brought enough just in case the president changed his mind," Horton answered, a large grin stretched across his face.

"Good man, thank you again, Doctor, we'll see you soon."

The doors closed and whisked Horton away.

DAY 209

April 28, 2021
North Topsail Beach, North Carolina

For Tess, the long and harrowing drive from Reed, Illinois, now seemed like it was the easy part of her long journey back home. For the past ten minutes she stood frozen in the driveway of her old house, her eyes fixed on the weathered and flaking blue paint. She found it strange that after a little more than seven months it looked as bad as it did. Maybe it was the tall grass and weeds coupled with the trash and debris that littered her street that gave an impression of dingy. Whatever it was, a fear gripped her that was uncommon for her. The answer to what she had been seeking for months sat inside, but was she ready to find it?

Brianna sat in the Humvee, staring too, her eyes unmoving from Tess's back. She wanted to go out and ask her if everything was okay, but deep down she knew why she couldn't move.

Against Tess's wishes, Devin had gotten out and was patrolling the street and the exterior, seeing if there were threats. Upon his return, he found Tess exactly where he had left her. He stepped towards her, but she put her hand up, signaling for him not to approach.

Devin complied and with a look of concern turned his

attention to Brianna, who shrugged her shoulders. He contemplated ignoring her request but knew he would be met with anger if he approached her. Instead he barked, "All clear around the back. I didn't see anyone, but the house has been broken into. Nice spot, by the way."

"Tess, enough. Go inside and find out where your man is," Tess mumbled under her breath.

A quick movement caught Brianna's eye. In the house across the street, she saw a blind move and what looked like a shadow shift.

The Humvee was parked in the middle of the street, perpendicular to the houses.

She leaned across the center console and peered through the side window towards the house. Nothing, no movement, but that didn't mean somebody wasn't there. Now with concern, she shouted, "Devin, I think I saw something in the house across the street, number 17!"

Devin raced towards the Humvee, his eyes glued to the house, rifle at the ready.

Hearing this, Tess finally moved. She turned around and looked towards the house Brianna had mentioned. She thought for a moment, then remembered who lived there, Mr. Phil Banner, a snowbird from New York and his wife. It wasn't unrealistic to think he had survived and was still persevering through all of this.

"That's Mr. Banner's house. He's harmless," Tess said.

Devin craned his head towards Tess and remarked, "Harmless? No one's harmless anymore."

"I'll be right back," Tess said as she took her first step towards her old house.

The salty smell of the Atlantic Ocean filled her nostrils

and instantly brought back happy memories of her and Travis's time there. Like it was yesterday, she thought of the first time she saw the house. He had surprised her by getting the property and had gone as far as blindfolding her so she wouldn't know where it was. A slight grin crossed her face as she thought of that special moment and how she knew exactly where he was taking her.

When one sense is impaired, the others take over. Her ears captured the sound of the grated bridge that took them over to the island, and the seagulls confirmed they were close to the ocean. The sounds of seagulls were gone now, but the old bridge still stood. When he parked the car in the driveway and excitedly got out and opened her car door, her nose and ears confirmed it. The rich salty smell hit her and the lapping of waves sealed it. Before he could get her to the front door, she had blurted out, "Topsail Beach, you got us a place on Topsail Beach!"

She made it to the stairs and looked up the worn wooden steps that led to the front door. Like most homes on Topsail Island, they were constructed using pile foundations so that they would sit up one story off the ground. She had never been a fan of the look; she forgave it so she could have the location.

Taking the first step, she paused and allowed another emotional moment to pass. She blinked hard, looked back up, and said to herself, "Tess, enough, your friends are waiting, go." This was the last bit of encouragement she needed. She knew she was holding things up, and the longer they sat, the more vulnerable they could be. With her newfound confidence, she bolted up the steps and made it to the front door. The screen door was torn and the front main door was wide open. Painted on the door was a large X with a zero above it. She looked at it and wondered what it meant, but soon put that aside. Her mind now wondered how long the door had been open. She stepped in and right away could tell by the condition of the living room that it had been open and exposed to the elements for months.

She wasn't angry at the sight of her house, destroyed by nature and strangers, she was just sad. Sad that the one place that had symbolized happiness and love was now gone and would never come back. She still held the memories, but this was a reminder that the life before was gone too. The shambles of her home was the physical representation and stark illustration of what the world had become.

She pulled the Glock 17 from her shoulder holster and opened the screen door. The large picture windows that overlooked the beach and ocean beyond brought in enough natural light for her to see. The crunching sound of broken glass underneath her first footfall hit her ears; the unpleasant noise was matched by the strong mold odor that hung in the air. She took a few more steps and paused; she could not be too careful. It didn't appear that anyone had been there in months, but after over a month on the road, her experience told her to never take chances. She steadied her breathing and continued on. From room to room she went, only to find the place had been ransacked by people for whatever items they thought had value. Seeing the amount of rummaging made her distraught that she wouldn't find the note left by Travis. All he told her was that he had put it in a safe spot, but where was that? One place she thought it might be was in the safe that had been bolted to the floor, but that was gone, a square hole remained. Her mind raced, and she scrambled from one possible location to the other, but each one proved wrong. With no other options, she fell to the floor in exhaustion and anger.

As she sat looking at the pieces of what had been her life strewn around the room, she strained to think of where he might have put it. She had pored through the photo albums, Bible, his favorite fiction novels; she had gone through every drawer in every room, but nothing. Where was it? Was there even a note? Was it destroyed?

She didn't know how long she had been sitting there thinking when the tap at the door jarred her back.

"Tess, it's Devin. You okay?" Devin asked from the open doorway, his shadowy figure looking large.

"I'm fine. Come in," she answered.

He stepped in, looked around and joked, "You know, you really should think about cleaning the place."

"Nothing."

"You can't find it?" he asked.

"No, nothing, I've looked and looked, but nothing from him that looks like a note that would tell me anything," she said in a tone of deep frustration.

"Well, it doesn't help that the lights don't work," he said, flipping a switch up and down.

She watched him as he flipped the switch, stopped, and stepped further into the condo. He kicked around the garbage that was once prized possessions. He peered into the kitchen that sat adjacent and laughed.

"What's so funny?" Tess asked.

"Did you have a refrigerator and dishwasher, or did…?"

She interrupted him and said, "Of course, some dumbass thought those would be valuable."

"Ha, what an idiot."

"Well, there's no shortage of them around," she said as she stood and stretched. "How's Bri?"

"Good. No other sign from your neighbor. Not sure if she saw something, but she and Brando have it covered out there. Thought I'd come in and see if I could help."

"What time is it?" she asked.

"Past noon, you've been in here a while. We got worried," he answered. He walked over to her and put his hand on her shoulder. He could see the strain on her face, and the hopelessness she was feeling oozed out of her.

"A new set of eyes will be helpful. How about you take the office? First door on the left," she said.

"Sure thing." He walked off and into the room. Instinctually he went to turn on the light, but nothing happened. He looked down after feeling the large faceplate and saw it was a heart. "I have to say, it must have been you who decorated this room."

Tess was busy in the bedroom again. She was now on her hands and knees crawling around, picking up every little piece of paper. "Why do you say that?"

"I can't imagine a big tough Marine putting a heart-shaped light switch on the wall."

Upon hearing that, she shot out of the room and into the office, stopping just at the doorway. She looked down at the heart-shaped face plate and blurted out, "That's it! He hid it behind there, I know it!"

"Behind the light switch?"

"Yes." She looked around the desk for something to unscrew the screws. "Help me find something to get the plate off."

"Really, he hid it there?"

"Maybe, Travis has hidden things behind switch panels before. No one looks there for anything, and this one I gave to him on our first anniversary."

Devin didn't need to look. He pulled out his Leatherman tool and opened it up to the flat head screwdriver. As he handed it to her, he asked, "You gave your man, a Marine, a heart-shaped light switch? Even my metro-sexual self would think that was gay."

"Shut up. It's personal; there's a story behind it," she barked as she snatched the Leatherman out of his hand.

"I'm sure there is. Does that story include role-playing and zipper masks?"

She snarled at him and didn't answer his snarky comments. She quickly unscrewed the panel and removed it. She looked behind the toggle switch and saw a folded-up piece of paper. She squealed, "There's something there!"

"I thought I'd seen everything, but this is incredible," Devin joked.

Her hands were shaking as she unscrewed the switch and pulled it out; with a hard pull, she yanked it out and tossed it. With her other hand she pulled the thick folded paper out. She looked at it for a nanosecond and unfolded it. Each fold revealed the mysterious note wasn't a note but a map.

Devin was looking over her shoulder; the anticipation was riding high. For him it felt like Christmas in some way.

When the paper was fully unfolded, it showed a map of Colorado, and the only mark on it was a circle around an icon of a plane with three handwritten letters, DIA.

"What does it mean?" Devin asked. "Is he at an airport?"

"Yeah, if my memory serves me, DIA stands for

Denver—"

Devin interrupted and finished her thought, "—International Airport."

They both looked at each other oddly.

Devin stepped away and ran his hand through his hair. He turned to her and asked, "Are you sure this is the note?"

She gave him a look that told him it was, but answered, "Travis was being very careful. He must have been worried. For whatever reason he didn't want to tell me over the phone, and by hiding it in here, he's telling me that he knew something bad was coming."

"Do I have to be the one to say the obvious?"

"What's so obvious?"

"If I knew the end of the world was about to happen, I'd just tell you where I was going. I mean, this whole thing, this entire trip is total bullshit, if you ask me."

"Travis must have had a good reason. He must have known that he couldn't talk with confidence over the phone. Maybe he feared for his life, maybe—"

"Still, he has put your life in danger; he could've given you a better clue than this. If you had left North Dakota knowing where he was, you'd be there right now. This is, pardon me for saying, silly."

Tess cut her eyes at him and said, "He had good reason, he had to!" Tess hated having to defend Travis but did so out of obligation. There wasn't a day that had gone by since the outbreak that she hadn't asked herself the same question, but hearing Devin ask it made it different. He didn't know Travis; it was easy for him to judge, she thought.

Devin and Tess's disagreements had been growing in frequency and intensity since leaving Daryl's house, making the journey personally tense.

Devin opened his mouth but stopped short. He knew whatever he'd say would not do any good and only add fuel to the fire. Regardless of how silly or needless leaving the message there was, now they had something to go off of, and they had a very long trip ahead of them.

Tess looked at the map and ran her fingers over it. She then placed it against her chest and closed her eyes.

Devin reached out. He felt badly and wanted to apologize, but Brianna's yell halted his mea culpa.

Tess shoved the map in her pocket, pulled out her Glock, and bolted out the door. Devin was right behind her, his AR-15 at the ready.

When they exited the condo, they had a clear view of what was happening. Half a dozen young boys were around Brianna.

At first they looked harmless, they were children, but upon stepping off the deck and hurrying towards Brianna, who was standing outside the Humvee with a pistol in her hand, they could see these children looked anything but harmless.

Their soiled and torn clothing clung to their scrawny bodies, dirt and grime covered their gaunt faces, and in their boney hands they had bats, pipes and several had guns. They were taunting and jeering Brianna, who had a look of fear on her face.

"Help, Devin, Tess, help!" Brianna cried out again, not knowing they were coming.

"Bri, we're right here!" Tess responded.

The boys, surprised to hear another voice, looked at Tess and Devin coming.

Half of the group turned and faced them. Two held guns, one a revolver the other a 1911.

"Boys, hold up. Put the guns down. There's no need for this," Devin yelled, his rifle raised.

"Listen, boys, whatever you think was going to happen, isn't. If you're looking for some food, we can help out," Tess offered. She held her pistol up in an attempt to show she meant no harm.

Devin quickly glanced at her and said, "Tess, what are you doing? We don't know who they are and what they're capable of."

Not looking at him, she answered, "They're just kids."

"Did you hit your head in there?" he asked, mocking her.

"You look hungry. We have some food we can share, okay?" Tess asked.

Brando was standing next to Brianna, his leg still bandaged from the gunshot wound weeks ago at Daryl's house in Reed, Illinois, but his fighting spirit was very much there. His hair was standing up on end and he growled deeply at each boy.

The boys began to laugh at Tess, and the boy holding the revolver started to laugh so hard his laugh turned to a cackle.

Devin felt very uneasy about the situation before him. He had seen so much since all hell had broken loose seven months ago, but never had they encountered feral children. He tightened his grip on the rifle and took aim on the boy with the revolver. He seemed to be the oldest at ten, and the others seemed to look towards him.

"What's your name?" Tess asked.

The boy with the revolver lowered it and answered, "Alex."

Tess smiled and said, "Alex, hi, my name is Tess. Are you hungry?"

He nodded.

"We can help," she said.

"Tell them to back off Brianna," Devin ordered.

"We'll give you some food, okay, but can your friends back away from our friend?" Tess asked.

Alex whipped his greasy hair out of his face, smiled and said, "Sure."

Just with that simple answer, the other five boys lowered their weapons and took a few steps back.

Devin still didn't trust the situation and kept his rifle firmly planted in his shoulder.

"Hey, lady, what about him?" Alex asked Tess, his finger pointed at Devin.

She looked over and raised her eyebrows.

Devin stepped laterally towards her and stopped just next to her, his rifle not moving an inch, "Tess, I don't trust this," he whispered to her.

She whispered in return, "They're just hungry boys."

"Exactly."

Tess rebuffed his concerns, holstered her Glock, and walked past Alex towards the back of the Humvee. She opened up the rear hatch, pulled out a case of MREs, and tossed it on the ground.

Alex whistled and two of the boys, who looked around seven, ran over and grabbed it.

"Are we good?" she asked.

Alex, while only appearing ten years old, had the bearing and presence of an adult. His dark brown eyes had a deadly and menacing stare.

Devin saw this, but for whatever reason, Tess did not. The Tess he knew before stopped being her the moment they had arrived in Topsail Beach and parked in front of 18 Island Drive.

"You get the Hummer from Lejeune?" Alex asked.

"No," she answered.

"Where you from?" he asked.

"Right there." She pointed to her old condo.

He looked back, cracked a half smile and said, "You're a local?"

"Sort of. So where are your parents?"

"Dead, everyone's dead," one of the seven-year-olds blurted out.

"Where do you live?" Tess asked.

Alex pointed to the house where Brianna had seen the movement hours before.

"I told you I saw something move!" Brianna exclaimed feeling vindicated.

Tess exhaled deeply. She felt for the boys, but she now could see a hardness and desperateness about them. Tapping her intuition that timing was everything and theirs could be running out, she said, "Well, boys, we have to go. Enjoy the food, and please drink extra water when you eat those, they'll jam you up otherwise."

Brianna opened the driver's door, Brando jumped in, and she followed.

Alex's face went emotionless.

Seeing this, Devin slowly raised his rifle, ready for anything to happen.

Tess circled the Humvee and jumped into the front passenger side.

The other boys were looking to Alex for instructions while keeping an eye on Devin.

Alex turned and grinned at Devin.

The Humvee came to life with a rumble.

The anticipation was killing Devin. He just knew this was about to go sideways and didn't want to risk losing by not having the advantage, so he fully raised his rifle and shouted, "Alex, nothing personal, but don't think about it!" He sighted in on Alex's chest and placed his finger on the trigger.

"We're good. Don't shoot!" Alex said. A strange calmness emanated from him, strange because he was so young to display this type of cool behavior.

"Miss Slattery, Miss Slattery, is that you?" a little girl yelled. She had appeared from nowhere.

Brianna swung the Humvee around and pulled up to Devin, blocking Alex.

"Miss Slattery, Miss Slattery!" the girl again yelled. She ran to the driver's side and began smacking the window.

Brianna looked down at the dirty-faced girl who was no more than seven years old. Brianna could see the desperation in her eyes.

Tess looked, and the expression on her face shifted. "Stop the vehicle!"

Brianna did just as Tess ordered.

Tess jumped out of the Humvee and ran around to the little girl with arms wide open. "Meagan, oh my God, Meagan, it's you."

Meagan jumped into Tess's arms and clung tightly. She whimpered, "Don't leave. Please don't leave. We need you. I'm scared."

Tess returned the girl's embrace with the same love she

had received. "I can't believe it's you."

"You're leaving. Please don't leave!" Meagan pleaded.

Tess pulled her away to examine her. Meagan's face was smeared with dirt and grime; her thick long brown hair was tangled and greasy, similar in look and feel to dreadlocks.

Tears began to stream down Meagan's face, and her body began to tremble. "Please don't leave us."

"Where's your sister? Is Melody with you?"

Meagan nodded and pointed. "She's sick."

Tess stood, grabbed Meagan's hand, and said, "Take me to her."

Devin watched the entire scene while keeping a watchful eye on Alex.

"Hey, lady, you're not allowed in there," Alex barked.

Tess ignored him and walked briskly towards the house where the kids claimed they had been staying.

Devin walked over to the open passenger window of the Humvee and said, "Pull down the street and park. Get up in the hatch behind the big gun. I don't trust these little fuckers."

Not debating his order, Brianna did just as he said.

Alex's age and maturity began to show. His temples throbbed, and his teeth clenched as he watched Tess walking towards his house.

While the other boys began to rip apart the MREs, he marched towards the house.

Devin was right on his heels. "Hey, Alex, where are all the adults?" he asked in an attempt to steer the conversation and get more information.

"I told you, they're all dead," he answered as he strode quickly, his eyes focused on Tess's back like lasers.

"There are no adults anywhere?"

"No good ones."

Devin raised his eyebrows, intrigued by Alex's response.

"Hey, lady, I said you can't go in there!"

Tess had reached the screen door. She turned and replied to Alex, "Meagan is my friend and so is her sister. If Melody is hurt, I'm going to help. Plus I don't take orders from children." She opened the door and walked inside the dark and smelly living room. The pungent smell of feces hit her hard, to the point she almost gagged. As her eyes adjusted to the dim light, she looked around the room. Garbage, debris was everywhere; the place was a total dump.

"Where's Melody?"

Meagan escorted her through the maze of garbage to a bedroom. There on soiled sheets lay little Melody. Her tiny five-year-old body was curled up and shivering.

Tess bolted to her side. Brushing away her curly blonde hair, she found her face.

"Melody, hi sweetie, it's Miss Slattery," Tess softly whispered as she petted her head.

Melody opened her eyes slightly and looked at Tess. She attempted to smile but couldn't.

An intense heat radiated off her tiny body. Tess began to look at her more closely to see if she could identify what was wrong with her or what might be causing her intense fever. She pulled the stained sheet back and found a small puncture wound on her calf that was red and inflamed. "What's this from?" she asked Meagan.

"Alex hit her with a rake."

"Nice kid that Alex," Tess murmured loudly.

"Screw you, lady," Alex blurted out. He was now standing in the doorway.

Tess hadn't seen him walk in and really didn't care. She looked around the room. The filth, decay and disgusting smell were repulsive. She needed to care for Melody, and this wasn't the place to do it. She shoved her arms under Melody, who let out a slight whimper, and heaved her up. "C'mon, baby girl, I'm going to take care of you."

Melody was so weak she couldn't hold on to Tess. Her frail arms dangled like small sticks.

Cradling her tightly, she walked to the bedroom doorway.

Alex defiantly stood in the way. "You're not taking her anywhere. She's part of our group," he snapped.

"Get out of the way!" Tess said.

"No!"

"Listen, kid, I don't know what your problem is, but get out of the way," Devin said and touched Alex's shoulder.

Alex shrugged his hand off and pushed him away.

Devin, tired of Alex's behavior, had had enough. He grabbed him by the back of the neck and forcibly removed him from the doorway.

Alex resisted, but he was no match for a grown man.

"Get off of me!"

Devin pinned him against the wall and yelled, "Listen, kid, I don't give a shit if you survived till now. This little girl needs medical attention. Now you can help us or get the hell out of the way. Consider this one less mouth to feed."

"Two," Meagan said as she followed right behind Tess.

Alex stopped squirming and gave Devin a hard look.

Devin let him go slowly and said, "We good?"

Alex didn't answer; he kept staring.

Tess didn't concern herself with the spat between Devin and Alex. Her objective was finding a safe and clean place for

Melody. When she reached the front door, she kicked it open. Once outside, the fresh air filled her nostrils and lungs. Never in her life had she experienced anything as disgusting as the squalor the children were living in. With purpose she marched ahead, down the stairs, across the driveway and into the street. Her first inclination was to go to her old house, but she stopped just short of the driveway and paused. She looked at the house she had once called home and decided she didn't want that either. To her right was another property, similar to hers but with an additional bedroom. Not sure what to do exactly, she looked at Meagan. "How about we go to your house?"

She shook her head. "No."

"Oh, c'mon, it will be fine. It'll be good to have things around you're familiar with," Tess said and began to walk towards Meagan's old house, three doors down from hers.

"No!" Meagan yelled.

Tess stopped, turned and looked at her.

"No, we can't. Mommy and Daddy are there."

This said it all for Tess. Not wanting to waste another minute, she headed directly for the larger house next to hers. While size was important, she prayed the condition of it was good enough.

Devin ran up beside her and asked, "Where are you going?"

"This house will be better, larger," she said as she swiftly traversed the abandoned cars in the driveway. "Please get the door," she ordered Devin.

While Tess and Devin were making their way to the house, Brianna watched with curiosity from the hatch of the Humvee.

The boys who had remained in the street only gave them glances as their attention was still on eating the MREs.

Devin raced up the long set of stairs and stopped just outside the front door. It too had been damaged. The handle was broken off with part of the wood cracked off near the deadbolt, a clear sign that someone had kicked it in. He pushed it open to find a scene similar to Tess's house. Old personal items were broken and strewn on the floor, but to his surprise upon entering, it was in better shape overall. He swiftly cleared each room and came back to front to find Tess waiting for his okay.

"It's clear. The second bedroom on the left looks perfect," he said, motioning down the long hallway.

She rushed past him. Entering the room, she saw exactly what he meant. The bedroom was painted pink and had posters of kittens and rainbows on the walls. She remembered the girl who lived here but only in passing.

Tess carefully set Melody on the bed, but just before she pulled the sheets over her, she stopped.

"Devin, get me some clean water, soap, a hand towel and Advil!"

Devin raced out of the condo.

"Sweetie, find me some pajamas in the drawer there," Tess ordered Meagan.

"Here," Meagan said, handing her a long nightgown with a princess embossed on the front.

"Perfect," Tess said. She began to undress Melody. As she removed the filthy clothing, she was shocked by Melody's physical condition and lack of hygiene.

Just as she removed and tossed the last piece of clothing, Devin entered the room with everything he was instructed to get.

"How's she doing?" he asked.

Tess didn't answer for fear of concerning Meagan; she looked at Devin and grimaced.

"What can I do to help?" Devin asked.

She looked again at Devin and said, "Settle in. We're not going anywhere anytime soon."

Devin nodded and left the room.

Tess gently closed the bedroom door and walked into the living room, a look of pleasant surprise on her face to find it clean and tidy. In the hour it had taken her to wash and attend to Melody's wound, Brianna had cleaned the condo.

"Looks great," Tess exclaimed.

"I had help," Brianna said, pointing to Meagan.

"And look at you, such a beauty," Tess remarked on Meagan's appearance.

"Where's Dev?" Tess asked.

"Out front on watch," Brianna answered.

Tess walked towards the door but stopped for a moment to give Meagan a hug.

The intimate touch from another person melted Meagan, who firmly returned the embrace. She whispered into Tess's ear, "Thank you."

Tess whispered back, "You're welcome, sweetie."

She gave her another hug and exited the room.

Sitting like a hawk on a power line scanning the area was Devin with his AR-15 rifle across his lap. The afternoon sun was hitting him at an angle, casting a long shadow against the condo. Shielding his eyes from the bright sun, Devin wore an old New England Patriots hat he had found weeks before. Devin's dark hair was the longest it had ever been in his adult life. From underneath the hat, it curled and jutted out. He had thought about cutting it, but he just didn't care. This same disregard even went for his facial hair, which had now grown a solid quarter inch. It was lighter than his head hair and had patches of gray throughout.

Tess found his new, rougher look more attractive than the scared and clean-shaven man she had found in Illinois.

"All tucked in. Hopefully, she'll do better now that she's out of that shit hole," Tess said.

Devin looked up, grinned and said, "I was going to ask earlier, but it just seemed the timing was off, but I'm assuming finding these girls changes our schedule?"

"Scoot over," Tess said.

Devin slid over and Tess took a seat next to him on the wooden step.

"Yes, the plan has changed. Not my intention, obviously, but how could I leave these little girls?"

"I'm not debating at all. It would be inhuman for you or anyone to leave them in the hands of the lord of the flies."

"Lord of the flies?" Tess asked.

He cocked his head and asked, "You've never heard of the book *Lord of the Flies*?"

"Should I have?"

"How old are you again?"

"Enough, what is it?"

"So what did you guys read your junior or senior year in American Lit?"

"Whatever."

"*Lord of the Flies* was a fictional book about a group of boys stranded on an island. They created a society of sorts, and soon it turned violent and barbaric."

"Now I understand."

"What the hell was that earlier today, anyway?"

"In regards to what?"

"Giving them food and trying to negotiate with Hannibal Lecter's son."

"That one I get." She laughed. "That, my friend, is called taking care of a situation before it can go badly."

"You know and I know those boys are bad news."

"You're right, but I don't think they're evil like the fucking cannibals we dealt with," Tess snapped back.

"I'm not making this up, but I watched a program about the apocalypse on the Discovery Channel or maybe it was the History Channel. Regardless, they had experts on discussing people's reactions to living in the exact world we have now. Anyway, when the topic turned to children, all the experts agreed that some of the most ruthless killers in situations like this are children."

"So I assume you would have started shooting?" Tess challenged.

"I mean, looking at it now, no, but then yes, you have the advantage of hindsight to validate your position."

Tess calmly said, "You're right about those boys. They probably meant to do us harm, but I know that sometimes people just need things. I gave it to them; they were distracted by it. I also showed I wasn't afraid of them. That confidence was disarming for them, and of course, you had a bead on them the whole time. Will those boys eventually hurt other people? Yes, but it's not my business until it's my business."

"What's your plan now? Those kids are our business since they're our neighbors," Devin said as he stared at the house the kids resided in across the street.

"Lucky we have you to protect us from a ten-year-old and his gang of second graders," Tess joked and patted his leg.

"Glad to see you're taking this seriously."

"Oh, I am, but there's fucking dangerous situations everywhere. At least I know this town."

"I disagree; you don't know this town anymore."

Tess was about to counter but paused to think about what he said. It took only a few moments for it to sink in that he was right. She knew the streets, the lay of the land, but she didn't know the dynamics of who was out there or what they were dealing with.

"I swear, you guys are sounding more and more like my parents, always squabbling. Ever since that final dinner at Daryl's you've been feisty, Tess," Brianna said.

Tess and Devin looked back and saw Brianna standing behind the screen door.

"I agree," Devin said.

"And you, you've been mister trigger happy," Brianna remarked to Devin.

"Just trying to keep us safe," Devin said, defending his recent actions.

"Brianna has that right; what about the guy at the mall outside Salem?"

"He was coming at us fast, and I didn't know if he had a weapon."

"Ha." Tess laughed. "He was limping, not coming at us fast, and he was like eighty years old." Tess said, referring to a situation the trio had encountered a few days back.

"Both you two can go fuck yourselves. I only shot him because he refused to listen to my commands to stop."

"Because the old man's battery was dead in his hearing

aid," Tess joked.

Brianna started to laugh loudly.

"Screw you two, really," Devin said.

Brianna opened the door and stepped out. She looked at the lapping waves on the beach.

Tess turned and looked at the sulking Devin. She patted his leg and said, "Cheer up. We're just busting your balls."

"I can't tell sometimes."

Tess faced Brianna and said, "Beautiful, isn't it?"

Brianna hesitated answering; she looked longingly towards the beach. The sun's rays were shimmering off the water. She gasped loudly and lamented, "I really want to jump in the water."

"Have you ever been to the ocean before?"

"No."

Tess looked at Devin, winked and said, "Then you should go for a quick dip."

"Really?"

"Yeah, why not?" Devin agreed.

Brianna's face lit up. "Let me go see if I can find a bathing suit." She flung the door open and disappeared inside.

"You go with her. I'll hold the fort down," Devin said.

"Holler if Melody wakes up," Tess said, then went inside to gather her belongings for the beach excursion.

Brianna fell onto the sand, giggling; a large toothy grin graced her face.

A large shadow cast over her. "Was that fun?" Tess asked.

"Oh my God, you have no idea. I've always wanted to

swim in the ocean. It was amazing, thank you," she said, then sat up and gazed at the seemingly endless sea.

"I'm glad you enjoyed yourself," Tess said.

"I wish I could feel like this all the time."

"I wish we all could."

"I'm sorry about your house. Was it really messed up?" Brianna asked.

"Yeah, but I found what we came for."

"I'm so sorry I forgot to ask. With those boys, Meagan, Melody, all of it, I didn't…"

"Nothing to apologize for."

"When do we leave?"

"Not sure. Here, need a towel?"

Brianna took the towel and began to dry off her long blonde hair. The joy she felt inside from this brief respite was priceless, and she was happy to hear they would be staying put for a bit. Life on the road was hard and unpredictable. She understood there were no guarantees, but having a temporary home gave her a small sense of security.

"So you knew the girls before?"

"Yes."

"What happens now?"

Tess sat on the damp sand and leaned back onto her elbows. She cocked her head and stared at the deep blue sky above. "First thing we need to do is make sure Melody gets better. When she is, we make for Denver."

"Never been there."

"You've never been anywhere, have you?"

"Nope, what we've done is the most I've ever traveled in my life. I just wish I could have seen all of it under different circumstances."

"You and me both.'

Their short and peaceful break was shattered when they heard Devin hollering, "Tess, come here now!"

They both sprinted for the house. When they reached the beach front of the house, they discovered the reason for Devin's alarming call. Alex and his entourage were there.

"Lady, we came to talk," Alex said sternly.

Tess almost burst out in a fit of laughter seeing Alex act tough and formidable. She knew he couldn't be trusted and that he had the potential for being deadly, but seeing a ten-year-old trying to intimidate an armed adult was somewhat comical to her.

"It's a free country. Go ahead," Devin said.

"We need more food," Alex answered.

"I think the closest store…" Devin said but was interrupted by Tess.

"We can't spare anymore right now, but…"

"Give us more food," Alex barked.

"If you'll let me finish, please," Tess chided him. "I propose tomorrow we, you and me, go looking for food."

"No."

"If you want more food, you're going to have to go find it," Tess lectured.

"No."

"I'm not going to argue with a ten-year-old."

"I'm eleven."

"Whatever." Devin smirked.

"Alex, we can't spare any, and in fact, we also need to go scavenge. Listen, there has to be plenty of food around here. There's no way you hit every one of the thousands of homes on Topsail Island."

"The food is all gone," Alex answered.

"You know this how?"

Alex lowered his head and winced. The fact he'd have to show weakness ate at his immature mind, but he resisted telling her the truth. "Because we know."

Tess stepped towards him and said to another boy, "What is it? We can help, but we can't if we don't know what's going on."

The boy, not a day over eight, replied nervously, "The men told us."

Alex elbowed the boy hard and snapped at him, "Shut up!"

"What men? Alex, just tell us; we can help you," Tess urged.

Alex kept his head lowered and mumbled something unintelligible.

"Tess, this is useless. The kid's a retard!" Devin blurted out.

Alex lifted his head and shot Devin a nasty look.

Tess took a couple steps closer. Now she was within arm's length of Alex, who looked anxious about her proximity to him.

"Alex, we can't give you any more food, but we can help you get more. Please let us help you."

After an uncomfortable pause Alex lifted his head and confided in her. He told her that a group of men, approximately a dozen, had come through several times. They had gone door to door scavenging food. He told her about the older teenage kids that had been with them from the start and how the men had taken them away.

"How many did they take?" Tess asked.

"Four."

"Anything else?"

"They told us not to go anywhere. We weren't allowed to scavenge. They took what food we had and said this was their territory. They told us to stay put, that if we went scavenging, it was the same as stealing from them."

"How long ago was this?"

"Two weeks ago."

Tess looked at Devin. His only response was a raised eyebrow.

"How can you help us? Those men were mean. I don't want them to come back and hurt us."

"We will take care of you. We'll give you each an MRE for tonight, but tomorrow we go looking for food," Tess said, her tone lowered. She reached out and rubbed Alex's shoulder. This time he didn't flinch.

He nodded and said, "Okay."

"Devin, you heard the deal. Get these boys another box of MREs," she said and turned back to Alex. "Tomorrow we go out and find some food."

"What if they come back?" Alex asked.

"Well, it's an easy solution. If they come back, we'll kill them," Tess replied.

Outside Livermore, Colorado

As she sat rubbing her belly, the soft wind gently blew Lori's thick brown hair. Once again she found herself enjoying the old wooden rocker on the front porch of their new home. She and Travis had discovered the abandoned ranch house following their narrow escape from Horton and his minions at the Denver International Airport. Her afternoons on the porch were the only moments she felt any peace and she was grateful for them. She had given up on getting any real sleep; thankfully the house not only provided sanctuary but came fully stocked with food, water, medicines, firearms and melatonin, a natural sleep aid, which she took regularly to help her get what little sleep she could. When she did close her eyes and drift away, she would soon be met with recurring nightmares.

Travis had been a Godsend for her, for without him she didn't think she and her unborn baby would have survived. Immediately upon finding the house, he set to making it perfect for her. The first task was securing it as best he could. He created a safe room and stocked it just in case Horton or other undesirables came knocking. His inventory of the stores came back positive, but they weren't infinite. They'd be able to survive for approximately nine months; then they'd have to resupply. Another positive of the property they came into possession of was that the previous occupants had a garden and a large supply of seeds. By Travis's estimates, the house sat on approximately ten acres; this was a rough count as he walked the fenced property. On these ten acres there was the main ranch house, a single-level three-thousand-square-foot wood-sided house; the outbuildings included a two-thousand-square-foot barn and two smaller sheds. The metal barn was full of equipment, including a tractor, three quads, three snowmobiles, countless tools and other items that could come in handy. It was like they had hit the lottery when they stumbled upon the place. Even the men's clothing they had found fit him properly, allowing him to get rid of his Marine uniform. However, Lori was realistic and knew what good fortune they had would not last forever.

The issues that hadn't come up but needed to were her pregnancy, the status of her husband, David, and son, Eric, and his fiancée. He hadn't talked about her much, but she felt he had to be consumed with her condition. She had decided that today would be the day they'd begin to hash out these issues and begin to make a plan to figure them out.

One of the reasons she had been successful professionally was she wouldn't let things lie. If something had to be taken care of, she'd set to doing it. The past weeks had been a nice vacation from reality, but they couldn't sit there forever, and if her baby were to be given a chance to survive, she needed the vaccine, R-59

As the sun was meeting the horizon, ending another day, she decided they would have the *talk*.

"I'm so tired," Travis said as he plowed into the large plate of pasta she had prepared him.

She sat across from him at the small round dining table centered in the large open kitchen and just played with her food. She was nervous about discussing the topics but knew it had to happen. Lori had a way about her that sometimes could create drama when there was no drama. She was fully aware of this trait, so she thought long and hard about how to address the sensitive issues.

"Um, Travis, I think we need to talk," Lori said as she swirled pasta around her fork.

The yellowish orange glow from the candles created

bouncing shadows, and many would have found the scene almost romantic in its nostalgia, but for Lori it was disturbing in an odd way.

She watched as the shadows grew and subsided along with the flames' movements.

Travis heard her and murmured, "About what?" his mouth full of food.

"I didn't want to talk about these things while you were busy getting the house ready and setting us up, but we need to discuss what might be some touchy things."

He looked up from his plate for the first time and said, "I'm a big boy, go ahead."

With an awkward smile, she said, "First, my husband and son. I'm obviously concerned for them. Have you thought about what we can do to help them?"

He wiped his mouth off with the paper napkin, took a large drink of water, and said, "I have thought about it, and the reason I haven't wanted to talk about it was because I don't think there's much you can do for them."

"Nothing?"

"No, think about it. Everything you told me about the chancellor makes me think he has either killed them or is holding them close, hoping he can use them if you ever return. That's what I would do. He has no leverage against you except your family. There's no advantage for him to kill them, but that's not to say he hasn't because…"

"Because why?"

"Because you pissed him off."

Lori exhaled deeply. "I had no choice. I had to run. I couldn't just wait around to get them. It's all my fault if anything bad happens to them. I didn't mean for this to happen, it just did. How was I supposed to know?"

"Lori, don't beat yourself up. Of course you didn't mean for this to happen; it just happened. You have an obligation to protect your unborn child."

"Do I? I mean, sometimes I think I'm taking a huge risk here. What if, what if I have a miscarriage? Then this whole thing is for what? Nothing." She began to cry and then realized that she was trying to upset him, but she was the one who was.

"You had your reasons; you made the decision. You can't go back and try to make the decision again. The only thing we can do now is find a way to make it all work. I'm glad we're talking about this stuff. To be honest, I was thinking about a good time to bring it up. I just didn't want to upset you, but it looks like I already did."

"No, no, it's not you, it's me. I'm hormonal."

"Oh, I thought that was just being a woman," he responded in an attempt to lighten the mood.

"Ha, ha, funny guy," she said, a slight smile on her tear-covered face.

"There she is, I like your smile."

"I'm so frustrated; I don't like not having a plan. I hate feeling helpless. I want to do something for David and Eric."

"At the moment I don't see what you can do that wouldn't risk the baby."

"Okay, let's talk about the baby. I need that drug. I need to get my hands on the R-59. How are we going to do that?"

"Of course, me and my infinite wisdom have come up with a possible plan for that," he said, leaning back and showing a bit of bravado in his arm movements.

"You're being corny."

"You see, that's one of the differences between military and civilians. You civvies get so worked up over stuff. We're so used to sphincter-clenching situations that we can make fun and laugh them off. In fact, us warfighters love action; hence why we join."

Ignoring his little diatribe, she asked, "What's your plan?"

He leaned in, placed his elbows on the table, and said, "There is one thing Marines pride themselves on and that is the love of their brother Marine. When we fight, we fight for the man next to us. I just need to get to one of my good friends and I can get the vaccine."

He paused and grinned.

She waited for him to continue, but he didn't. "That's it?"

"In a nutshell."

"That's not a plan, that's a concept."

"Oh, you want operational details?"

"Yes!"

"You don't need them; in fact, I'd rather have you not be in the know."

"Don't be stupid. I don't want you risking your life if you don't have a plan, so please indulge me."

"Since you insist," Travis said and began to detail his plan. He told her about a good friend, another captain he went to officer candidate school with, who was part of a unit that provided physical security assistance to the DHS's FEMA camps in Region VIII.

Hearing this, she asked, "How do you know where he is specifically, and how do you know he has R-59?"

"I don't know exactly where he is, but I know he operates from a forward operating base south of Rapid City, South Dakota. As the camps grew, they pulled assets from the military to provide support. His light armored unit was tasked with providing additional security."

"Do you know exactly where this base is?"

"I have a good idea."

"How do you know you can make it?"

"I don't."

"How do you know he'll help you?"

"I don't, but do we, do *you* have a choice? I have to go and get that vaccine for the baby. Fortunately for us, we have time, but I need to leave soon."

She raised her eyebrows.

"As you know, I have a fiancée out there somewhere. Now that I'm retired, I need to go find her, but I feel obligated to you as well."

Lori reached across the table and took his hand. "Travis, I've been thinking, and I just don't feel right that I'm here with you while the love of your life is somewhere out there."

"I don't like it either, but these are the sacrifices we military types make when we join. I gave an oath to defend the country, and now that country is gone. Next thing I know, I'm here with you. I have an obligation to make sure you and the baby are safe."

"I should go with you."

"No, it's not safe out there."

"But how? I can't stay here by myself."

"Lori, I'm almost done making this place run on its own. I won't be gone that long. Once I return with the vaccine, maybe then we can talk about you joining me as I look for Tess, but I don't feel right having you come with me now."

He placed his other hand on top of hers and squeezed it. He enjoyed her company and found her attractive, but his endearment for her had changed from a simple attraction to one of responsibility for her care and well-being. He would never tell her, but he didn't look at her as a woman he should attempt to covet, but one he needed to protect.

Lori bit her tongue; she was so use to getting her way and arguing her point of view ad nauseam till she got it. He had been so helpful and gracious; how could she argue with his plan? And she thought he was right; staying there was the best option for her baby.

The clunk of a car door closing startled them.

Travis whipped his head in the direction of the noise and listened intently.

"Did you—" she started to ask.

"Sshh," he snapped, and then blew out the candles.

Several more car doors slamming echoed from outside.

He bolted from the table, grabbed a pistol and her arm.

"Huh?"

"To the safe room!"

She just let him take charge.

They ran down the hallway and darted into the first door on the left, an office. He slid open the closet door, shoved the hanging clothes aside, and pushed against the paneling. A four-by-four-foot piece popped out from the force of his push; it was being held by a magnetic hinge.

"Get in!" he ordered.

She did just as he commanded and crawled through the opening. The safe room was a small three-foot-wide by seven-foot-long space. He had created it by taking space from the office closet and the adjacent bedroom's closet. He had built faux walls using materials he had found in the barn. Once inside, a person could hide relatively comfortably. In the floor of the space there was a trap door that led to the crawl space beneath the house; there he had created a route to escape. Both the room and the crawl space had food, water, firearms, flashlights, blankets, extra clothing and toiletries—specifically an item that Travis was all too aware was often overlooked in the field, toilet paper and a bucket to go in.

"Everything you'll need is in here for up to a week. I'll come get you when it's all clear," he said, placing the paneling back up.

"Hold on," she said urgently.

He stopped and looked at her cuddled up inside. "What?"

"Be safe."

"I always am," he answered, gave her a wink, and sealed her in.

She put her head between her knees and began to pray.

Travis put everything back to make it look like a closet and went to the main living room window to look out. Once there, he saw two pickup trucks near the barn in the dim light of the rising moon but no sign of anyone. His heart was racing, and his instincts told him it was a matter of moments before he encountered someone. He knew the best way to survive this type of situation was to lay in wait. His Marine Corps training had taught him that the odds for a defender were nine times better than someone on the offense. With this knowledge, he took up a position in the far bedroom. As he sat in the darkness, he longed for a pair of night-vision goggles, but he used his other senses and listened intently.

His ears perked when he heard unintelligible talking down near the barn. He imagined they were just scavengers and probably didn't want a fight, but if it were to come to it, he was determined to win.

As he patiently waited for them to come to the main house, he thought about Lori and their discussion earlier, soon his thoughts turned to Tess. Not a day had gone by that she didn't cross his mind. He missed her and in some ways wished he hadn't gotten entangled with Lori, but he just went with his gut. Like he told Lori earlier, he put it out of his mind, because you can't relive the past, you can only learn from it.

Unaware of how much time had elapsed, the moment he knew would come came and it came with a crash. The front door burst open in an explosion of force. The sounds of broken glass and wood reverberated down the hall. He steadied his breathing and positioned the shotgun across the footboard of the bed. The Remington 870 pump-action shotgun had a twenty-inch barrel with an extended tube. He was ready for whatever they could bring, and was confident he'd be successful.

The voices of the people echoed off the walls and down the hall.

Lori sat shaking in her safe room. When she heard the door explode, she quickly scrambled and grabbed the revolver that she had seen sitting on a box. The small room was so dark she couldn't see anything, and the sensation of being immersed in darkness added to her fear. She focused on steadying her breathing and remaining calm.

By the voices, Travis identified the people as men and their number being around four at the minimum.

They bantered back and forth, laughing and crashing through the living room. When they reached the kitchen, they became quiet.

Travis could see their flashlights bouncing off the walls,

floors and ceiling and didn't have to guess the reason for their silence. They had reached the kitchen and seen the plates of fresh warm food there.

"Is someone here?" a man asked, hollering down the hall.

Lori tensed when she heard the man call out. She again prayed, but this time her prayer was exclusively for Travis's safety.

Travis could hear the men talking among themselves quietly; he figured they were deciding what to do.

"Hey, we know you're here. We see the warm food. Come on out. We don't mean harm. We're neighbors of the Branson's, the owners of the place," the man called out.

Travis didn't believe the story.

"There's two of you and five of us. Come on out!" the man cried out.

Lori pressed her lips together and gripped the pistol tightly.

"I'll tell you what, we're gonna just leave you guys, we don't want trouble, but we'll be back tomorrow to say hello," the man said.

More unintelligible back and forth chatter between the men was followed by the shuffle of feet. A moment later Travis heard the trucks' engines roar to life.

Unsure if they had actually left, Travis stayed put.

Hours had gone by since Travis had heard the trucks leave. Feeling he could explore, he slowly stood and carefully exited the room. With controlled effort he took one step after another down the carpeted hallway. At the edge of the hall and living room, the moon's light provided enough illumination for him to see the room was empty. He pulled a flashlight out and turned it on; the light splashed across the room and verified that he was alone. He examined the damaged front door and the ransacked living room. An image of Lori sitting alone and terrified in the darkness of the safe room flashed in his mind. He rushed to the office, cleared the closet, and began to open the panel when she screamed out.

"Travis?"

"It's me, sorry, I should have warned you." He popped the panel and reached in for her.

She breathed a long sigh of relief and grabbed his arm. When she went to stand, she realized her legs were asleep. The painful pins and needles made it difficult for her to exit the small space.

"You all right?" Travis asked.

"No, I'm not all right."

He helped her clear the tight opening and carried her to the back bedroom and placed her on the bed.

"Sorry you had to stay in there so long. I just didn't know if they had left when I heard the trucks leave."

"It's okay. I figured you were being careful."

He got her some water, and while she rested, they talked about the events of the evening, and the specific point that the men would return in the morning came up.

"What should we do?" she asked.

"We have two options. Stay and confront them; they could be harmless or they may not. Second, we flee, to where, I don't know."

"Why didn't they come looking for us?"

"Because they're smart. They suspected we were lying in wait for them. I wouldn't go looking for someone I didn't need to."

"How can we hold off five men? What if they come back with more?"

"Or they may not come back at all," Travis proposed. "That might have been a blanket threat; they may never come back for fear of their own lives. We do have an advantage here."

"I think we should leave."

Travis sat on the edge of the bed and looked at Lori; the tea-light candle shined on her smooth face and glimmered in her eyes. At that moment he felt a weakness and wanted to kiss her. He resisted the urge, but wondered why he had that feeling suddenly hit him. Was it because she was vulnerable? Was he really drawn to her? What about Tess? He stood up suddenly and said, "Let's discuss this in the morning. Get some sleep," and he left.

Lori was shocked by is abrupt exit and lay there wondering what was wrong. Too wired and scared to sleep, she got up and went to find him. She found him sitting in the large armchair in the living room with only the moon's light to see.

"Is everything okay?" she asked.

"Fine, just thought you could use some sleep."

"You sure?"

"Yeah, I'm fine," he answered, then promptly shifted the topic. "I moved the heavy baker's rack in front of the front door. I'll also sleep out here, just in case."

She placed her hand on his shoulder and said, "I know I've said this before, but I don't think I can say it enough, thank you. You saved my life, and you continue to save it. I don't know what we would do without you."

"You're welcome."

"I don't know how to repay you."

"Stop, there's no need to repay anyone. But seriously you need to get some rest."

"Travis, I'm not a child. I know when I need to rest."

"So I was thinking."

"Isn't that a difficult task for Marines?" she joked.

Ignoring her, he continued, "I think we leave tomorrow morning, take the old minivan parked out back, and go."

She sat on the coffee table and stared at him.

"Are you fine with that plan?" he asked.

"Yes, I say we leave and go find your friend together, and from there we go find Tess."

He leaned forward and placed his head in his hands and sighed. "But when I say we leave, I then think that it's more risky on the road than here. I'm confusing myself."

"Don't confuse yourself. We leave tomorrow, first thing. Pack what we can and go."

He faced her and said, "Then that's the plan. We leave and head towards Rapid City."

She again touched his arm and in a soft tone said, "We're in this together. We'll find your friend, get the vaccine, and then find your fiancée."

"And what about David and Eric?"

Without hesitating, she answered, "I'll have to have faith that the chancellor won't kill them. When the timing is right, I'll go find them."

"What will you do if he's killed them?" Travis asked.

"Then my search is over. My baby and I will go and live out our days somewhere safe."

"That's it?"

She gave Travis a hard look and answered, "Trust me, if he's killed them and I have a chance to return the favor, I will."

Denver International Airport

Horton held the phone away from his ear, not because it was too loud, but because he didn't want to listen to another word the caller was saying. He was tired of being told what he needed to do or that he needed to do it differently or what he had done was wrong. He had imagined greater autonomy when he was given the chancellorship years ago. He never thought the council would micromanage the entire operation. What upset him the most was the loss of Lori. It wasn't so much he couldn't find another mate; it was that his failure to stop her was a huge embarrassment that had almost cost him his position. There was no urgency in finding her, as what secrets she knew were useless now. Their plan for the cleansing was underway, essentially the cat was out of the bag, but finding her was not operational, it was personal.

During the weeks that had passed since her escape; he had executed the operation known as the cleansing. The plan was moving forward, but killing tens of millions by firing squad was not a quick process. His desire was to selectively kill. He wanted to keep the best and brightest, those with skill sets that could be used. He also was determined to allocate time to ensure all those in the camps had their DNA sampled. If they passed, they would be spared. The way his system worked was simple: there was the elite class of which he was part of, the warrior class, the chosen class and the working class. If your DNA was unsuitable or you had no value, you were considered a liability and disposed of. However, his selection process was slowing down the cleansing in North America, and that didn't bode well with the council, hence the phone call.

He looked around his adorned office while the person on the phone droned on. He loved and admired the artwork he had collected, not just the unique paintings but the sculptures. Being in a position of power gave him certain luxuries and privileges; one of those was collecting the finer things from the old world. He had his people scouring the old museums to pull together a collection that would rival anyone's.

The voice on the phone began to yell louder, jarring him and pulling him back to the present.

"Yes, I'm here," he said into the receiver. "Yes, I understand, right away, thank you and bye." He looked at the now silent phone, and just before he placed the receiver on the base, he threw it across the room in a fit of anger. He stood and walked towards a cabinet and opened the veneered door. Inside were a dozen crystal decanters with the most select whiskeys and scotches. He pulled a short stubby decanter out, grabbed a glass, and made for the tufted chocolate leather couch. He sat down, poured a glass and relaxed. He no more than took a sip when the door bell chimed. He grunted and yelled, "Yes, what is it?"

The door opened and his new chief of staff, Roger Wilcox, was there. "Sir, the people you requested are here."

He rubbed his eyes and thought; not having a clue, he asked, "Who did I request? Please remind me."

"Sir, David and Eric…"

His eyes opened wide; the names jogged his memory. He jumped to his feet and barked, "Good, good. Bring them in ASAP."

Roger nodded and closed the door. A moment later the door opened again and in came David and Eric.

Horton walked over to them with his hand extended and said, "Gentlemen, thank you for coming. I appreciate it."

David looked wearily at Horton but took his hand. He understood the politics of things and how important it was to keep up good relations, especially with the chancellor. "Mr. Chancellor, what can my son and I do for you?"

"Please come in and take a seat. Drink, food, anything?" Horton asked.

David and Eric shook their heads.

Everyone sat in the front lounge. An uncomfortable silence and awkward looks occupied the first moments, but Horton quickly remedied it by coming out and speaking his mind. "David, do you know where your wife is?"

"Excuse me? I didn't know she was missing," David said, a look of surprise on his face.

"Yes, she had a breakdown of sorts and just up and left. We imagined she might have gone to see you at Camp Sierra."

David looked at Eric and turned back to Horton and said, "No, we haven't seen her. Is she okay?"

"Unfortunately, I don't think so. As you know, she's pregnant, and I don't know what happened, but she just had a complete meltdown and fled the base. We're obviously concerned for her and the baby's well-being. She was a vital part of our design team for Arcadia."

"When did she disappear?" Eric asked.

Horton opened his mouth and was about to tell the truth,

but he cut himself off. Thinking the truth would sound odd, he lied. "A couple days ago. We've been looking for her since, but nothing. She just up and left."

"You think she went to find us at Sierra?" Eric asked David.

"This is all my fault," David said in a somber tone.

This comment piqued Horton's interest. "Why do you take responsibility?"

"The way we left things, I, um, I wasn't the nicest person. I'm sure you're aware of the accusations I made about you and her."

"I am, but I don't pay that any attention. I did notice her emotional state had begun to slip around that time. We had the hardest time getting her back to work. Then she began to have delusions, and next thing we know, she's gone."

"Is there anything we can do?" Eric asked.

"Yes, there is," Horton answered.

David and Eric looked desperate to help.

"I need you two to stay here, under our care. We will find work for you. We'll send for your things."

"But don't you think she's going there to look for us. Wouldn't it be better if we stayed there?" David asked.

"You asked if you could help, and that is the best way. Stay here."

David and Eric exchanged looks and then nodded in agreement. "Very well."

Horton wanted to just tell them everything, taunt them with the truth and then have them killed, but he held back. His anger with the council drove him to do the exact opposite of his emotional instinct. They might hold some value if he happened to find Lori; he could use them against her. His orders from the council were to move past his own personal desires for revenge. but deep down he couldn't control himself. He wanted to defy the council. He wanted to find her just so he could see her watch her family die in front of her eyes. Never in his life had he felt so emotional about someone. He couldn't explain the draw she had on him, but her rejection of him was legend, and the troubles she had caused him deserved retribution. After all the years of disciplined patience and planning he had endured, he couldn't look at this pragmatically. Finding her and exacting payment was a fire that burned brightly in his chest.

Day 210

April 29, 2021
North Topsail Beach, North Carolina

Tess woke up thinking about her and Devin's vigorous discussion concerning the boys and the deal she had struck without his input.

Devin was very leery of Alex, and something told him they couldn't trust him.

She insisted that the way to a hungry boy's heart was through his stomach.

He disagreed, but the deal was set, and Devin gave in but insisted she consult him before she made anymore rash decisions.

She agreed.

A whimper from Melody's room tore her away from her thoughts; she jumped out of bed and ran into her room.

"I'm here, sweetie," Tess said, coming up to the side of the bed.

"It hurts," Melody whimpered.

The mere fact she was talking was an improvement from yesterday.

"Where does it hurt?" Tess asked.

"All over, but my neck and here," Melody cried, pointing to her jaw.

Tess felt her, and her fever was still present. She opened a bottle of Advil and dumped one in her hand. "Here, take this."

Melody lifted her head and opened her mouth.

Tess popped in the small capsule and gave her some water.

"I'll be right back. You need to eat something," Tess said and left as quickly as she had come. She walked into the living room and found Devin asleep on the couch.

"Dev, wake up," she said, pushing him

He shot up and looked around, his eyes as wide as saucers. "What is it?"

"I think I know what's wrong with Melody.'

Wiping the sleep from his eyes, he said, "Huh, what?"

"Melody—I think I know why she's sick."

"Infection."

"Kinda but this is specific."

He swung his feet off the couch and sat up. As he stretched, he curled his toes into the thick Berber carpet and yawned. "Go ahead."

"Tetanus."

"Are you sure?"

"No, but I remember the girl's parents didn't believe in vaccines. It makes sense. She was hit in the leg with a rake. I bet if I took a look at that rake, it was probably old and rusty and God knows the germs and other shit around. I'll ask them, but I'm willing to bet she has tetanus."

"Who gets tetanus?"

"People who aren't vaccinated."

"How do we cure it, antibiotics?"

"I don't know exactly, but I think you can't do anything about it but let it run its course, and I don't know how long that is."

"That's it? Just let it run its course?"

"As far as I know. But to make sure, I'm going to stop by a bookstore in town and find a medical book."

Devin scratched his head and stood up. He looked down at her and asked, "I guess that makes me babysitter for the day?"

"That's right, you're the manny."

"Wonderful," Devin said as he tiredly staggered towards the front door. "Very well, I'll be on diaper duty, but now I'll go see a man about a horse," he said as he exited the condo.

Tess smiled as she watched him leave. She enjoyed his sense of humor; it matched hers in many ways. Again a feeling of attraction hit her, but she quickly dashed the idea as she thought of Travis. Not wanting to think about anything remotely romantic, she went to get ready for her long and busy day.

Devin leaned in and grimaced. He wanted to be the third person instead of Brianna, but Tess insisted he needed to stay to protect the girls. It wasn't that he disagreed with her, he just was concerned they might encounter the group Alex had mentioned, and knowing that Brianna and a snot-nosed kid was Tess's backup gave him concern.

"Wipe that grouchy look off your face and keep your radio on," Tess reminded him. "We'll be back before sundown."

"You guys be careful," he said.

"Always," Tess said, a shit-eating grin gracing her face.

Devin stepped away from the Humvee, gave a wave to

Brianna behind the .50 caliber, and said, "If you find Twinkies, I'll do your night shift for two weeks."

Tess started the Humvee and drove out of the driveway and headed north.

Brianna turned around and yelled, "If I find Twinkies, I'm eating them, and don't forget to feed Brando."

Devin waved again, this time with his middle finger.

Brando was sitting next to him and whimpered as he watched the Humvee drive away.

Devin looked down and said, "I'm worried too, boy. I'm worried too."

The drive into Jacksonville followed the route they had used coming into town. As she navigated the roads and streets by memory, she peppered Alex with questions, most of them personal.

Alex continued his stubborn behavior and refused to answer.

The city of Jacksonville resembled every other city or town they had encountered, vacant and ransacked. Mother Nature was quickly taking back the roads, parking lots and sidewalks. Sprouting out of every crack and crevice were tall weeds and grasses. Covering like a blanket in some areas were large piles of leaves. She and the others had discussed a few times how long before the signs of modern society would be wiped clean. Was it a thousand years, ten thousand? Those conversations often pivoted to the ultimate question of whether humans would survive and prosper again. This latter question began to concern her as she and the others took notice of how few people they had come across since leaving

Reed, Illinois. It's as if no one was immune east of the Mississippi. They had seen a few people here and there, but the numbers didn't match the estimates of survivors. She had heard early on that approximately ten percent of the population had survived, but where were they?

Tess's first destination was the Barnes & Noble store; there she also hoped to scavenge food and water from the café attached to it.

She backed the Humvee up to the front entrance and took hope that their first stop might be a success from the fact the glass doors were still intact.

"Bri, take watch. Alex, you're coming with me," Tess ordered.

Alex pulled his small J-framed Smith & Wesson revolver out of his pants pocket and gripped it tightly. He stood next to the doors, anxiously waiting for Tess.

Tess scanned the parking lot for any movement. None seen, she headed for the doors, rifle in hand. She peered into the darkened store and smiled. "Looks surprisingly promising. I don't think anyone's been here before."

"It's a bookstore, that's why," Alex said.

She looked at him curiously and asked, "Is that a joke?"

"No, it's the truth. This town is redneck; rednecks don't know how to read."

She slung the rifle and double-checked her gear. Pulling the Glock from the holster on her tactical vest, she press checked to ensure it was loaded. Confident in her equipment, she donned a headlamp and stepped up to the glass door. She pulled out an ASP baton and extended it with a whipping motion.

"That's cool," Alex said, his eyes wide open with

excitement.

She raised it above her head and with a powerful downward thrust brought the ASP down against the door The force of her impact shattered the glass and after several more hits the the bits and pieces fell to the ground. She turned on her headlamp and stepped through the door and into the store.

Alex followed right behind her.

"Head to the café. Look for anything we can eat," she ordered.

He walked off into the dimly lit store.

She headed into the interior of the store in search of a medical book.

It took her minutes to find the exact books she needed. Tucking them in her backpack, she headed towards the café. As she drew closer, she could hear Alex rifling through cabinets and drawers. She caught sight of his flashlight beaming off the walls and ceiling. Then all movement stopped.

She approached and heard the sound of plastic wrappers and smacking lips. She peered over the counter and saw him. His cheeks were round and stuffed with muffins.

Too busy eating, he hadn't noticed her approach. When the beam from her headlamp splashed down on him, he jumped. His mouth half open, crumbs fell from it onto his dark T-shirt.

"Save some for us," Tess teased.

"Sorry," he mumbled.

"It's all right, I know what hungry is like. Just don't get

sick."

He nodded and held out a tightly wrapped poppy seed muffin.

She took it and looked at it carefully. The last thing she wanted was to eat mold. She tore the packaging and pulled out the firm but surprisingly edible muffin. "Got to love preservatives."

"It's good too," he said.

She took a small bite. The sweet and lemony taste was a shock to her taste buds. The overall taste was a bit off, but it appeared to be safe. Again, she looked at it and with a shrug took a huge bite. "You're right, not bad."

"Here, there's chocolate too," he said, his arm outstretched.

She took it and said, "Let's pack this stuff up. I'll go get some bags from the checkout area," she said and walked away. As she was heading to the checkout counter, she thought of Brianna and how she'd love to have the chocolate muffin. She exited the store to find her attentively manning the machine gun.

"Bri, here, catch," Tess said and tossed her the muffin.

"Yummy, chocolate, awesome!" she exclaimed. Sinful joy glimmered in her eyes at the thought of devouring the decadent offering.

"Anything?"

"All quiet."

"Good, we'll be a bit, but looks like we found a lot of stuff."

Tess headed back in and walked to the counter. There she found the bags and other items that could come in handy, batteries and candy.

As she began to stuff the plastic bags, something caught her eye. She walked over and picked up a My Little Pony board game. She thought of the girls and how she remembered them liking the characters. She opened the bag and slipped in the game. Then small plush toy ponies came into view; she grabbed those as well. She looked forward to surprising the girls with the gifts. Seeing them smile and be happy was a vision she wanted to hold, but that wouldn't be. Her radio crackled to life, breaking that vision.

"Tess, this is Bri. We have visitors."

Tess bolted, hollering to Alex as she headed for the entrance, "Stay put. We might have trouble!" Within seconds she was outside and saw a truck parked in front of the Humvee. The two passengers, both men, were out and heavily armed.

"Whatcha doin'?" one man asked, his Southern accent shining through. An AR-15-style rifle was slung over his chest. His thick dark shoulder-length hair protruded from a weathered beanie.

Tess raised her rifle and pointed it at him.

This aggressive posture caused the other man to raise his weapon.

"We're just grabbing some things. We mean you no harm!" Tess yelled.

"You see, this store here is ours. I don't seem to have you on a list to come and take what's in it," the man barked.

"I don't think you're a rep from Barnes and Noble, so why don't you and your friend just take off!"

"That's not going to happen. You must not be from around here, but this town is controlled by James Renfield."

Tess could see the impossible situation they were in. She

didn't want to have this turn ugly, but she predicted one of the next things the man would demand was the Humvee and the machine gun. If he just allowed her to leave, she would, but if he had further demands, she'd have to take this to another level.

"We don't know a James Renfield, but we'll leave. It's that simple," Tess answered.

A crooked smile appeared from beneath the man's thick beard. He cocked his head to his colleague and asked rhetorically, "Just leave, she says. Now, should we just have her and her pretty little friend leave?"

"Nope," the other man responded, his rifle pointed at Tess.

The whole while this back and forth was happening, Alex was watching from the shadows in the store.

Brianna pivoted the machine gun and aimed it directly at the second man. "This pretty little thing knows how to use this, and I won't hesitate to push this trigger."

"Ha, ha." The man laughed.

"Alex, come out here. We're leaving," Tess yelled.

Hearing her, Alex immediately responded and left the safety of the darkened store.

The man watched Alex slowly walk and get in the Humvee. "I know you, boy, don't I?"

Alex slammed the rear door and didn't answer.

"I know that boy. We know that boy, don't we?" the man asked the other.

"Yep."

"He was with those other kids we ran into over on Topsail. Oh boy, those teenie girls were something else. They're a bit loosened up now, but wow that was some ass!"

the man yelped.

Anger grew inside Tess; the pressure her finger was applying was becoming greater. What the man mentioned verified Alex's story. These were the men that had come into the neighborhood and stripped them of their food stocks and taken the teenaged kids.

"Which one was it that you sampled?" the man asked the other.

With that question, Tess was convinced this situation was going to end bloody. She applied more pressure.

The man turned his creepy gaze on her and smiled. His hand slowly migrated to the pistol grip of the AR.

Tess ran the optimal scenario through her head. She'd squeeze off the first few rounds and quickly sidestep, creating a moving target for the man who had his sights on her.

She applied more pressure and was about to squeeze the trigger when her peripheral vision spotted the movement of something to her right.

Out of the alleyway appeared a large white-tailed deer, a buck with eight points.

The deer stopped and looked at them; it was just as startled as they were to see it.

The men looked and were dumbfounded.

That was it, Tess thought, the distraction they needed. She looked at the man, who also realized the opportunity the deer had given them. She squeezed hard, the rifle roared, and a single 5.56mm round exited the barrel. Within an instant it hit the first man squarely in the chest. The impact of the shot forced the man backwards till his body hit the quarter panel of the truck. He looked down at the hole in his chest, looked at her, and then fell to the pavement.

Tess moved just like she envisioned.

The second man took several shots but missed.

Brianna pressed the butter trigger of the .50 caliber. It roared to life; a short volley of rounds blasted out of the long barrel and ripped the second man apart.

Tess advanced on the first man, but Alex had without notice jumped out of the car. He walked up to the first man, who was still alive but squirming in pain on the ground.

"Where's my sister?" Alex asked, and then kicked the man in the ribs.

The man looked up at Alex. He went to respond, but he coughed up a small pool of blood.

Tess went to sidestep Alex, but the boy stopped her.

"Where's my sister? You took her. Is she alive?"

"Fuck you!" the man responded, his shaking left hand reaching for a pistol.

"No, fuck you!" Alex screamed, and then shot the man in the face.

Tess jumped, startled by Alex's lethal response.

Alex looked at the man for a second. He then spit on him and walked back to the Humvee.

Tess didn't say anything; she was in shock by what had happened. She glanced at Brianna and then back to the dead men. She looked around and knew that the gunfire would draw others. They needed to flee. However, Tess couldn't leave their car and guns.

"Bri, get behind the wheel. You're driving the Hummer; I'm taking this," she said, pointing at the truck. Not wasting another moment, she gathered up the weapons and tossed them in the truck as she climbed in. Taking one last look at the grisly scene, she started the truck, and with Brianna following, she headed back for Topsail Island.

Outside Livermore, Colorado

Travis and Lori had spent the greater part of the early morning packing everything they thought they'd need into the minivan. The rush to leave such a perfect spot tore at them, but Travis could not risk having those men return with far greater numbers. He was confident he could hold them off for a while, but it all depended on the numbers. He knew the road didn't guarantee safety, but neither did the ranch now.

He pulled up to the end of the long driveway and stopped. He looked both ways, then into the rearview mirror.

Noticing the long pause, Lori asked, "You good?"

His focus still on the mirror he answered, "Yeah, I just hate leaving the place. It was perfect."

"It wasn't that perfect."

"No, it was. I just wish there was another way."

"This is it. I need the vaccine, and I couldn't stay there by myself. This is the best idea. We have to go. It was great for when we needed it. Look, I promise you we'll find another place, even better."

Travis just hated having to take her on the road, but she was right. Leaving her there after what had happened last night was not an option. "Okay, let's do this," he said and turned the wheel hard to the right. As he began to accelerate to crest a hill, several large trucks came over, heading the opposite way. Were those the men? he asked himself.

Lori craned her head to get a better look and exclaimed,

"That's them, isn't it?"

Travis put his full weight down on the gas pedal and his eyes on the rearview mirror.

"They're turning, they're turning!" Lori cried.

"They're coming after us?"

"No, they turned down the drive. I saw them turn left down the driveway. It was those guys, and they did have a lot more people coming this time."

Travis glanced at the rearview mirror, but it was too late, they were over the hill and heading away at over ninety miles per hour. "I guess our timing was impeccable."

"No doubt." She sighed.

With that threat literally behind them, they relaxed and enjoyed the ride. Together they watched the rolling hills unfold before them as each mile melted into the next. Their conversation started out discussing the task before them but soon turned personal.

"What does Tess look like?" Lori asked.

"Hot."

"Hot?"

"Oh, I can describe her, like her hair and wonderful breasts, but all I see is just hot."

"Wonderful breasts? Guys and breasts."

"No, really, I think she's incredibly hot, but it's much more than her looks. I mean, is she beautiful? Absolutely, but I just love her attitude, her strength, the way she's attentive. For me, how someone is—you know their personality—enhances their looks. Tess was already a solid eight, but who she is makes her a ten to me."

"I don't think David would describe me as a ten."

"He wouldn't? He's crazy. You're definitely a ten."

Lori blushed when Travis made the comment. She had resisted exploring this before but decided to test the waters by asking a probing question. "Remember when you ask me to sit with you at the cafeteria?"

"Yeah."

"Why did you do that?"

"I told you before; you looked lonely and kinda lost."

"Nothing more?"

"More like?" Travis asked, but he knew exactly what she was fishing for. The conversation excited him a bit. He gripped the steering wheel tighter and sat up straighter.

"Were you flirting with me then?"

Travis shot her a glance and smiled.

She hit him on the arm and said, "I knew it, you were."

"I'm only human, yeah, you're beautiful. What man wouldn't?"

Lori held back from honestly answering his question. For her she knew the type of man who would was looking and was not completely settled down. She put her finger in her mouth and bit down ever so gently. Flirtation was in the air, and it didn't help that she was nearing her second trimester, because for her sexual desire was heightened then. Needing to divert the topic she started, she asked, "How long will it take to get there?"

"All depends, in a perfect world, we can arrive in a couple days, but I don't think that will happen. We'll need to refuel in a couple hours, and I want to find a safe place to crash, somewhere off the main road."

"Makes sense," she replied, her tone changed. The

flirtatious conversation was fun, but now she regretted it and felt guilty. Her thoughts now focused on David and Eric.

Sensing a shift, he asked, "You all right?"

She answered, "Yeah, just thinking about David and Eric. If anything has happened to them, it's my fault. I put them in that situation. I should've known something was wrong."

"You did."

Tears began to flow from her eyes.

"Hey, I thought we discussed this before. It doesn't make sense to beat yourself up."

"Easier said than done," she said as she wiped her face.

A loud beep sounded in the car.

"What's that?"

"Fuel light, but the gauge says we have a quarter tank." He hit the dash. The force from the impact jarred the gauge, and it floated down to below empty. "Shit."

"We have a can, right?"

"Yeah, but only five gallons."

Travis pulled over and quickly poured in the five gallons. He looked around, but there was nothing but rolling plains surrounding them. They thought it best to take small highways and county roads. He remembered that DHS had set up roadblocks and checkpoints on major highways before, and running into them was something he wanted desperately to avoid. The winds chopped and gusted, but thankfully the temperature was moderate. By his calculations he was close to the point he'd begin to head due north, and with a good five hours of daylight left, they'd be halfway by nightfall. Not wanting to waste another minute, he got back in and began the trip again.

"We'll try to find some fuel at the next town," he said.

"Okay."

The fuel light alarm sounded again.

He stared at the light and smacked the dash again, hoping the gauge would read something better than empty. "This is impossible," he barked and pulled the minivan off the road again. He jumped out to inspect the vehicle; he had a suspicion what it might be.

Lori didn't like car trouble before, but now it was more than an inconvenience. It could spell death for them. She overheard him cursing; this told her something was terribly wrong.

Travis opened the door. A gust of warm fresh air rushed in. He sat down and slammed the door shut. "Just as I thought. Fuel tank is leaking, rusted and looks like it has a small puncture."

"Oh no."

"Now I think I know why they left this piece of shit."

"What are we going to do?"

Travis started the minivan, put it into gear, and sped off. He looked at her and replied, "Keep driving till we find another vehicle or run out of gas."

North Topsail Beach, North Carolina

Devin paced the driveway, not saying a word. The conflict Tess and Brianna had just fought frightened him. By the sounds of it, this group sounded eerily similar to Mayor Rivers' gang back in Reed; he just hoped they weren't cannibals too. The thought of having to deal with another group of barbarians didn't thrill him, especially considering it was only the three of them and a bunch of kids.

Tess also told him what Alex had done.

He wasn't shocked; he'd seen the lethal potential Alex had the minute they met him.

"I know what you're thinking. I know that walk," Tess said to Devin.

He looked at her but didn't answer.

"We can't leave just yet. They'll discover their bodies, but there's nothing that ties them to us. It's impossible. I'm sure they'll chalk it up as some random gang violence," Tess explained.

Devin stopped and asked, "Are you saying that to reassure me or you?"

"You."

"You're confident they won't track you here?"

"They're not going to know it's us."

Devin pointed at the truck and asked, "But you're not confident they won't stop by here randomly and see that?"

"Stop panicking. We'll park it in a garage."

"Stop panicking? I'm not, I'm just worried!" Devin snapped.

"Get a hold of yourself. We didn't have a choice!" Tess fired back.

"Both of you, enough! All you ever do is argue with each other. I'm tired of hearing it, just stop!" Brianna yelled.

Tess and Devin were shocked by her loud and vocal response.

"We don't argue," Devin said.

"Yes, you do, all the time! Just kiss her and be done with it," Brianna fired back.

"What?" Tess asked her mouth wide open at Brianna's comment.

"That's right; I've seen the tension between you both since we left Reed. I also see how you two look at one another."

Tess was flabbergasted, and Devin remained speechless. He looked at Brianna, who was now standing, both feet solidly on the ground, firm in her conviction.

"Now that makes things very awkward," Devin commented.

"I'll be right back; I'm going to park the truck. When I get back, let's begin our discussion on just what we're going to do," Tess said and stormed off.

Devin watched her go; he then turned his attention on Brianna, who was staring at him.

He began to think about everything, and Brianna was correct about one thing, at least one thing he was willing to admit to. That being he had become someone who complained all the time. He also had to admit that he and Tess found themselves in constant debate and disagreements. He admitted to himself that it was not only him but her as well. There were countless incidents where she would just start in on him, just for making a reasonable comment. For some reason they had a hard time not having a conversation that didn't devolve into a fight. He found Tess attractive and had thought of her sexually, but what man didn't think about sex all the time?

He stepped up to Brianna and said, "I apologize. You're right about the fact we fight a lot. I will do my part to not do it anymore."

Brianna held her stern look for a brief moment but finally

relented and said, "Fine, but trust me on this, she likes you. When the timing is right, give her a kiss."

Devin's face turned red as he blushed. He said, "I don't think I'm going to do that."

Brianna put her hand on his shoulder and said, "I might only be seventeen, but I know when girls like boys. Believe me, she likes you." She patted his shoulder and walked up the stairs and into the condo.

Tess walked up just then and asked, "What's going on?"

Startled and embarrassed, he said, "Nothing."

"Hey, she's right, we need to stop bickering and work together. So for my part, I want to say I'm sorry," Tess said.

"Me too."

"I had a chance to look through those medical books. I believe my amateur diagnosis might be right."

"That's good, so what do we do?"

"Bad news is nothing but provide comfort. I think we should continue to give her antibiotics just in case, but we have to let the tetanus just run its course."

"We can't find the vaccine and give it to her?" Devin asked.

"Too late for that. We'll give her fluids, IV if we have to, and monitor and make her comfortable."

"Can she travel?"

"I think we'll be fine here till she gets a bit better. I don't know if she'll travel well. She needs rest."

Devin wasn't happy with staying, especially after the confrontation earlier today, but there wasn't any security on the road. In fact, the road was more dangerous. He nodded and said, "Let's bunker in, then."

"I want to move the other kids out of that shit hole

they're in."

"There's not enough space."

"Yes, there is; some of us will sleep in the garage. I'll take Alex with me, and we'll grab every blanket, pillow, and sleeping bag we can find. I need you to dig two more latrines in the front yard, put up some poles, and hang tarps for privacy."

Devin took mental notes of his responsibilities.

Alex came down and said, "What can I do?"

"You're coming with me," Tess said.

As she entered each house along her old street, a surreal feeling came over her. She tried to explain away the feeling, but it was hard to process. For the first time since the outbreak she felt like she was breaking into houses. She knew the people who owned these houses; they were her neighbors, her friends. Before now it seemed like she was living in a nightmare. Everything she had encountered was outside her past experiences and knowledge. Now she was immersed in a world she was intimately familiar with but it was destroyed, it was dead. She first experienced this feeling when they had driven across the bridge to the island, then struck her when she first saw her street and then at her house. Now going in and out of her neighbors' houses brought it out of her again.

"You're quiet," Alex said.

"Oh, sorry, lot on my mind," Tess responded.

They were walking towards a large house at the far end of the street. One she was familiar with, especially during Halloween.

"These people had the best decorated house during

Halloween," Tess remarked.

"I know, they gave away full-sized candy bars, not the snack size," Alex said, a slight grin on his face.

"I loved houses that did that, always the best."

"The man would dress up too. Last Halloween he was dressed like a vampire. He'd have a large plate with all the candy bars lined up."

"What's your favorite candy?" Tess asked.

"Reese's Peanut Butter Cups, hands down!" Alex answered, his grin expanding.

"Mine too, love them. In fact, last Halloween my fiancé and I ate all the Reese's out of the candy we were giving away. God, we were so bad. I think I gained ten pounds."

"Your house had cool decorations too. I loved the boiling pot with smoke, oh, and the large spider, that huge one, bigger than me."

"I love Halloween," Tess said and put her arm around Alex's shoulders.

They were now standing at the front door of the house. Alex looked at her and said, "I loved it too, but it's gone now. It's all gone."

Tess rubbed his shoulders, put her attention to the task at hand and said, "Well, kid, ready to go to work?"

"Yes, ma'am."

Outside Pine Bluffs, Wyoming

The minivan sputtered and jolted until it came to rest on the side of the road. The hopes of finding another vehicle never materialized, but the sign for the small town of Pine Bluffs, Wyoming, provided hope, literally, or that's what the sign had painted on it. The town's name, Pine Bluffs, was crossed out and the word HOPE was stenciled below it in bright yellow paint.

Unable to carry most of their things, Travis buried them near a small dry creek bed a hundred feet off the road.

"What do you think?" Travis asked, pointing to the sign. He cinched down a strap on his large backpack and adjusted it so it hung evenly.

"We don't have a lot of options," Lori answered. She too donned a small pack.

"Let's go see what Hope is all about," Travis said and began to walk further away from the road.

"Where are you going?"

"Not safe to walk the road. We'll walk parallel to it but a thousand feet or so off it. I don't want some marauder coming along."

"Makes sense," Lori replied and jogged up to him.

Gone were the rolling hills, replaced by a long flat and dry plain. The sun was quickly receding; soon the warm rays would disappear, but the protection of the darkness would be welcome.

Both remained silent during the slow march towards Pine Bluffs. Their attention focused on each step over the uneven ground.

Travis dug through his memory to recall the name Pine Bluffs. He hadn't traveled north but knew some commanders who had. Nothing popped into his mind, and why would it, really? he thought. There were tens of thousands of towns across the old United States. Unless something happened here that was important, it would be just another small town out of the many.

After two hours of drudging along, dim lights came into view. This told them two things. The town was just ahead, and people were there.

Travis pulled a set of binoculars out of his pack and surveyed the dark silhouettes of the town buildings.

"You see anything?" Lori asked above a whisper.

"Yeah, there are definitely people there. Nothing like the glow of a cigarette to give one away," he replied.

"What should we do?"

"Go find us some wheels."

"Are you sure?"

"Yes, I'm sure. Do you want to walk the rest of the way?"

Lori was nervous; her imagination ran wild with visions of being captured, tortured and a myriad of other horrible acts that could befall them.

"C'mon, it'll be easier in the dark," he said, standing and putting his pack back on.

"Maybe I'll stay here," she said.

"No, you have to come; I'm not going to drive over here."

She stood begrudgingly and said, "Fine."

"Wait, how do you feel?"

"Tired, my feet hurt, my back hurts, and I…well, I just feel like shit," she answered.

"I guess we can take a short break. We have all night. Might be best to go for a vehicle in the wee hours."

Lori dropped her pack and sat back down. She began to

dig through the pack and pulled out a thin blanket.

"Well, you didn't need to be told twice," he joked.

"I'm tired. You can't forget, I'm pregnant."

"I haven't forgotten." He took off his pack and placed it next to hers. He then took a seat on the ground and leaned back.

Lori looked into the star-filled sky and struggled to remember the constellations she'd learned as a child. "Is that Orion, the three bright stars in a line?"

"Yep, that's it."

"How do you get a hunter from three stars?" she asked.

"Oh, that's just his belt. Go down and you see two stars, there and there, and over to the right is an arc of stars. That's his bow." He had taken her hand and lifted it, using it to pinpoint the stars.

"I see."

"And over there is Taurus. Orion is shooting his bow at it. See the V shape?"

"Travis, what will happen to the world?"

He sat for a bit, not knowing how to answer her question. It was commonplace for him to be motivated and inspirational, but deep down he felt the world was doomed.

"Is this trip worth it? Are we just putting off the inevitable?" she then asked.

"God no, we have to try."

"Do we? Why not be like some people and just take the easy way."

"You mean kill yourself?"

"Why do I want to bring a baby into this world? We're too afraid to even walk into a town renamed *Hope* for fear we'll be attacked. Who wants to live like this?"

"Why don't you get some rest? I'll stay up," he said, deliberately avoiding the conversation.

"Here, take some of this. You must be chilled," she said, offering him part of her blanket.

He was chilled, and as the evening wore on, the temperature would continue to drop. He already felt a bit chilly from the cool breeze that was coming in from the northwest.

"Thanks," he said.

She squirmed towards him. "Don't get any ideas," she joked.

"Wouldn't think of it."

Laying her head against his shoulder, she closed her eyes.

He wasn't sure how much time had gone by, but by the sound of her deep breathing he could tell she had fallen asleep in a matter of minutes.

As he looked above at the dazzling tapestry of stars, the brilliant streak of a falling star caught his attention. He closed his eyes and, much like a child, made a wish. Pressing his eyes tighter, he wished he, Lori and her baby would survive to see a world reborn, a world where they weren't afraid but one that held promise and peace.

Day 211

Pine Bluffs, Wyoming
April 30, 2021

The early morning air had a chill that hit Travis. He was beginning to feel the early stages of fatigue overcoming him, so getting up and moving around both helped him stay awake and stay warm.

Lori was still asleep. He wanted to go find a vehicle, but that would require him to wake her, something he didn't want to do. However, the sun would be rising in a few hours, and he wanted to find a vehicle and get back on the road.

The continued observations of the town proved that it was occupied, but with who and how many was the ultimate question. He needed to get closer to get better intelligence on what they could be dealing with.

After one last scan, he looked over his shoulder at the now snoring Lori. He hated to have to do it, but he couldn't risk just leaving her there. He strode over to her and tapped her foot.

She stopped snoring but continued to breathe heavily.

He tapped her foot harder.

This made her roll onto her side, but she was still asleep.

"Damn, woman, you sleep like a rock." He laughed and kicked her a bit harder.

She opened her eyes and said, "Everything okay?"

"Good morning, sleepyhead, sorry to wake you, but you've gotten a good six hours. I'm getting tired and soon the sun will be up. Time to go snoop around town for a vehicle to take."

She sat up, stretched and yawned.

He started packing up what little gear he had out while she stood and began the same process.

After some small talk and a quick summary of exactly what their plan was, they set off. Based upon his observations they were a little less than a mile away, so within twenty minutes he'd know if the town held promise.

After fifteen minutes they reached a three-foot-high wooden fence. It resembled something more decorative than functional. They scaled it and continued till they reached a small grove of trees. He pulled out his binoculars and looked north towards a light.

"Ha, just what I expected. It's a roadblock."

"What do we do?" she asked.

"We keep going, but now we know they have manned roadblocks, something we can't forget once we snag a car."

He stuffed the binoculars in his jacket and got up to stand when she grabbed his arm. "Hold up."

"What is it?"

"I don't want to take someone's car that needs it."

"Exactly how will we know that?"

"If it's parked in front of a house, I'd say no, but sitting on the side of the road, well, then it's fair game."

"Now you've made what was already difficult practically impossible," he griped.

"Not impossible, more challenging. Just don't want to leave a family without a car."

"I can't make guarantees."

"I trust you'll do the right thing."

He grunted and stood up. "Enough happy talk, let's go."

She followed behind him as they ran from the cover of the grove to a series of small metal buildings. The darkness was providing great cover, but within a few hours that protection would be gone.

"What I'd give for a set of NVGs."

"What's that?"

"Night vision."

"It's so dark out, there could be a truck not thirty feet away and I swear we'd walk right by it."

What should have taken them mere minutes was taking them three times as long. Once on the other side of the metal buildings, they found themselves next to a large field.

"Not too much further now, I think," Travis said.

Hiking across the field improved their time, and soon they were at the edge of town.

Other than the two men he had seen at the roadblock, not another person could be seen, but that didn't mean they weren't there. While the darkness shielded them, it also provided the same cover for anyone and anything.

"I can't see a damn thing," Travis groaned, the binoculars still pressed against his eyes.

He pondered what they should do. His training told him to be cautious, as he didn't know a thing about the town. Not wanting to walk them into an ambush, he turned to her and said, "Here's what's going to happen. I'm going to go by myself. I know exactly where you are. When I find a—"

"No way, you're not going alone."

"Listen, I don't know what's out there. I can't risk both

of us walking into something bad."

"That's not our deal. Now make sure your pistol is handy and sit tight. If I take longer than need be, make your way back to those metal buildings. There you might be able to find shelter till I come for you."

She grabbed his arm tightly and said, "Not happening."

"This is not a time to argue. You have a way of doing that a lot, but do this and I can move faster, and I don't think I'll be gone long."

"What if you don't come back?"

"Then that proves my point; it was too dangerous."

She relented and said, "Be careful."

"Always," he replied. He stood and sprinted off into the black of night.

North Topsail Beach, North Carolina

Tess woke suddenly. She reached out and felt for Meagan, who was breathing heavily. Unsure of why she woke so abruptly, she rolled onto her back and closed her eyes. Sleep was a privilege in this world, and she never took it for granted. Especially after surviving on her own during the time she'd spent on the road. Having a group of people to share the burden of watch made life easier. Just as she was about to doze off, she heard chatter in the other room and then crying. This brought her back from the edge of sleep. She sat up, interested in identifying who was in distress. Suddenly it stopped and the chatter began again.

She jumped up, and before she left grabbed her pistol.

Going anywhere, even in the safety of a house, the tools of protection needed to be taken.

Once in the hallway she heard the chatter. It was coming from the living room. She walked into the space and the conversation stopped. She looked but found it impossible to see anything. The heavy breathing of the other children, now camped with them, filled her ears.

"Everything okay?" she said above a whisper.

No response.

She imagined it was a couple of the children, and just when she was about to abandon her investigation a small voice chimed, "I miss my sister."

Tess turned and asked, "Who is that?"

"Becky."

"No, who's talking?"

"Brady, it's Brady."

She remembered Brady was one of the younger boys, six years old and never let you forget it. He was short and little for his age and often mistaken for much younger. Tess specifically remembered Brady because of the way he introduced himself. *"Hello, I'm Brady. I'm six years old."*

"Brady, what are you doing awake?" she asked.

"It's my fault," Alex said.

"Is everything fine?" she asked.

"Yes," Alex answered.

"No," Brady responded, then squealed out in pain. "Ouch!"

"I told you to keep your mouth shut!" Alex exclaimed.

The increased volume caused the other children to stir.

"Sssh, you're going to wake the others. Both of you, get up, come with me, outside," Tess ordered.

The boys listened and promptly got up.

Outside they found Devin perched at the top of the stairs, rifle at the ready. "I think Brianna is relieving me but not for an hour."

"These two were being loud, and apparently something is going on," Tess explained.

"Boys will be boys," Devin joked.

Tess sat the boys on the stairs and asked, "Brady, were you crying?"

He hesitated but relented after Tess's hard stare. "Yes."

"Why?"

"My sister, I miss her."

"Okay, that's understandable. Now, Alex, what did you mean by keep your mouth shut?"

He wouldn't answer; he wouldn't even look at her.

Tess looked at Brady, and just before she could ask, he blurted out, "He said our sisters are probably dead or worse."

"Why would you say that?" Tess asked.

Alex leered at her and barked, "It's the truth and you know it. You saw those men; they're horrible."

"That doesn't mean they're dead."

"They might as well be."

"Why do you say that?"

"Because we're not going to save them."

"You think we're not going to help you find your sisters?" Tess asked.

"We are?" Devin asked.

"Boys, I promised to help you, and that includes finding your sisters."

"Tess, wait a minute. You can't make that decision for all of us," Devin fired back. He had already expressed his displeasure with her making unilateral decisions, and this was the last straw for him.

"We can't leave these boys' sisters in those men's hands," Tess replied.

"That may be what we all decide, but you need to have us all agree. You have to stop acting like a queen."

"Fine, what do you think we should do?"

Alex and Brady watched the argument like spectators at a tennis match.

Tess and Devin went at each other. The intensity of their exchange woke the children inside and prompted Brianna to come out.

"Seriously!" Brianna shouted.

Tess and Devin stopped and looked at her.

A couple of the kids got upset and started to whimper.

"Now look at what you've done!" Brianna hollered and slammed the door.

Tess and Devin looked at each other with regret written all over their faces.

"Hey," Devin said but was cut off.

"It was me, all me. You're right. I need to stop just making decisions for everyone."

"We both need to stop it and just talk things out like adults," Devin added.

The boys remained quiet and watched as Tess and Devin expressed their apologies for the uproar.

"What should we do?" Tess asked.

Devin wanted to come back with a joke or snarky comment because that was his personality, but he resisted. He looked at Tess and at the boys. To him, she was right, he couldn't in good conscience leave their sisters captive. "We go."

Alex jumped up, excited about what he was hearing, "Really?"

Devin looked at him then back to Tess. "Yes, we go get your sisters. That's what we're going to do because that's what good people do."

Brady stood and took Tess's hand. He squeezed it and looked up at her. He then grabbed Devin's hand with his other and smiled.

"Devin's right, that's what good people do, and that's exactly what we're going to do."

She felt happy and had purpose beyond finding Travis. It wasn't that she didn't want to be with him, it's just that in this hostile world now full of barbarians and savagery, they had decided to set a new tone. They were going to be those people who helped others; in a world full of bad people, they were going to be the good ones.

Pine Bluffs, Wyoming

From house to house he went; the cars he did find that were suitable for hotwiring were parked in driveways. He kept on going without trying because of the promise he made to Lori, but when he came upon an old Chevy S-10, he stopped and decided enough was enough. He ran up to the driver's door and closed his eyes to say a quick prayer, "Please be unlocked." As if God answered them, he lifted and it clicked, the door was unlocked. "Yes, thank you." He opened the door fully and sat behind the wheel. Not hesitating, he looked quickly just in case there was a set of keys. Nothing. "Sorry, Lori, but time to get to work," he said, turning on his headlamp, and with a short screwdriver he pried off the steering wheel column case. He ducked under the dash and began to look for the ignition wiring when he heard the crunch of soles on pavement. He jerked from underneath the dash, looked towards the door, and found himself face to face with the barrel of a shotgun.

"Stop right there!" the woman shouted.

"Don't shoot, please."

"Get out of my truck now!" she ordered.

"Please don't shoot," he pleaded, his arms raised.

"Easy and slow, don't make any moves or I will shoot you," she said.

He did as she said. He slid out from the truck and stood, his back against the open cab. His headlamp light shined down on her.

She backed away from the light and hollered, "Help, I need help!"

Different scenarios ran through his mind. Should he run or should he stay? He thought of Lori, who was counting on him returning. If he ran and got shot, well, that would guarantee he wouldn't return, but if he escaped? So many what ifs but not enough time to run them all through. His instincts told him to run; by staying their presumptive captive, he may never return. With his decision made, he lifted his head slightly; the beam from his headlamp hit her in the eyes.

She flinched angrily and stepped to the side, just to the side of the not fully open truck door.

Travis saw this as his moment and aggressively pushed the door fully open, hitting the shotgun. The force of the impact caused her to fire the shotgun. Fortunately for Travis the barrel was no longer pointed at him.

His actions and the accidental discharge made her drop the shotgun.

Travis took off towards the street away from her. He glanced behind him but didn't see her. When he turned back around, he ran directly into another person.

Both of them fell down.

Travis went to jump up, but the woman was on him, barrel of the shotgun again positioned at his head.

"Just stay down!" she yelled.

He moved, but she jammed it behind his head and racked the slide. "I said stay down!"

Travis obliged.

The man he had run into got up and walked over.

Travis could barely make him out. He was tall and muscular and was also armed, but with a pistol.

The man leaned over and looked into Travis's eyes. "Just who do we have here?"

"I need a vehicle, that's all, nothing else," Travis responded.

"Where are your manners, son? We ask for things in this town, we don't take them," the man said.

Travis recoiled from the man's harsh bad breath.

"Janine, your choice what we do with him," the man said.

"Take him to see the magistrate," she replied.

"Very well," the man said.

The blow to the head happened so quickly that Travis didn't see it coming. All he felt was the blunt force; then everything went black.

Lori lay trembling, her eyes useless against the dark so she let her ears communicate the situation as best they could. It first started with the woman's cries for help, then came the shotgun blast and more yelling. Following that came what sounded like a herd as townspeople rushed to the scene. Images of Travis dead and dying flashed before her eyes. She wanted to go to him, but she could be walking into a situation that was untenable.

Soon the sun would be up and she'd be a sitting duck out in the open. She needed a place to hide, a place that she could plot how to help or save Travis. The metal buildings came to mind and without further delay; she rose and ran for what she hoped was safety.

Denver International Airport

Horton loved to get his day started early; he received an incredible feeling of accomplishment if by mid morning he had completed what most people would have in a full day. Today would be another one of those days where he'd not only accomplish much, but today would signify a turning point for him.

He looked at a map of North America and marveled. So much had been achieved in such a small amount of time. He just wish he could get past the phase he was in and back on track to building his new capital Arcadia.

A tap at the door signaled that his next meeting was about to begin. He strode back to his desk and sat down, but not before he called out, "Come in."

The door opened and in came a man he had only heard about. Thomas Wendell briskly walked in and stood at attention in front of his desk. "Assistant Director Wendell at your service, sir."

"Director Wendell, please, no formalities needed, especially from someone as notable as you," Horton said.

Wendell was a tall man, almost six foot four inches, and his broad shoulders made him look formidable. His clean-shaven square-jawed face showed the physical scars of a lifetime of law enforcement work. With more than thirty years as a law enforcement officer, Wendell was finishing his career as a mid-level administrator for FEMA when the Death struck.

Wendell took a seat and asked, "How can I help?"

"First, how can I help you?" Horton asked. He leaned and put his elbows on the desk.

"I don't follow?"

"Director Wendell, you've surprised us with your abilities. When we gave the orders to begin the cleanse, you outperformed everyone. In fact, you've already achieved your goals," Horton said as he looked at a piece of paper on his desk.

"Just doing what was ordered."

"I believe in rewarding people for doing a job above and beyond. You see, I brought you here to ask what we can do for you, you know, a way to say thank you."

Wendell looked surprised. He wasn't expecting to hear this.

"You look a bit shocked, but I can tell you that you'll see that's how we do things here. Let me first ask you something personal; can I do that?"

"Yes, sir," Wendell replied, a look of uneasiness on his face.

"When the order came down to begin cleansing the undesirables, why did you comply?"

"Because it was an order."

"Bullshit."

Wendell looked down, briefly searching for the right thing to say.

"Don't tell me what you think I want to hear; tell me why you did it. You didn't have to, hell, we had others in your position who said no, and we removed them till we found the one person who would. So tell me again why you chose to fulfill our order and do it so efficiently?"

He looked up and assumed since he was there he might as well be honest. He knew the power they had, and if they had wanted him dead, he would be, so why not just open up. "Because when I saw exactly what you were doing, I agreed with it. It made…well, it made sense. The people you had us cleansing were of no need to the system. In fact, they would only stress what vital resources we have. They were those with no skills or those that needed others to in order to live. You were ridding the world of the undesirables."

"Bingo, give this man a prize. That has been our mission the entire time. Of course, some good people, not many, died along the way, collateral damage, but you see what we're doing is saving the planet. We are restoring order to a broken ecosystem. The people we have removed will now allow us to focus our collective efforts to restore the planet to its natural state and create equilibrium. Before we focused our system on helping them, we didn't want to unleash the Death, but…"

"I'm sorry, what did you just say? You released the Death?" Wendell asked, stunned by Horton's smug confession.

"Yes, there was no pathogen from that asteroid. That was just a helpful ruse to unleash it."

Wendell shifted in his chair, a bit more uneasy than before.

"Thomas, can I call you that?" Horton asked.

Wendell nodded, then said, "Actually, Tom is good."

"Tom, follow me," Horton said, motioning for Wendell to rise.

Wendell did as he asked.

Horton walked him over to a side conference room of his office. The walls were adorned with large three-by-five-foot high-definition images of nature. The first image he stopped at was a large waterfall; the colors of blue, white and foam green were intense. He looked at Wendell and asked, "Beautiful, right?"

"Yes."

"What about that one?" Horton asked, pointing to a scene of a savannah in Africa.

"Yes."

"Look at all of them. What do you see?"

"I see pictures of nature."

"You do, but you see something more. You see a world as it should be, not destroyed for greed or progress. Imagine this, an unspoiled world where the parasite that is mankind isn't present in vast numbers, where we manage the herd. You see, man has destroyed this world; we will restore the world. We will restore the balance. You have been a big part of this, but your part is only just begun."

Wendell faced Horton and asked, "What is it I can do?"

Horton grinned and said, "A lot, but we will discuss this over dinner, you and your family."

"My family? They're back…"

"Mr. Wendell, your job will require you to be here, so I took the liberty of bringing them here. I hope you don't mind. They are being settled in right now. I picked a nice residence for them. Your daughter will be able to complete her high school here as well."

Wendell's face turned ashen. He gulped and said, "You honor me, Chancellor."

Gripping his shoulder more firmly, Horton replied, "Remember, this isn't about the one, this is about the many. What we do will save this planet, just know that. I have big plans for you. Welcome to the core."

"Thank you, sir, I will do my best."

"I know you will. So I'll see you later."

"Yes, sir," Wendell said and began to walk away.

Horton called out, "Oh, and tell your family welcome from me."

Wendell stopped, turned and responded, "I will." He headed for the door with a look of fear on his face.

Horton walked back to his desk and picked up the phone. "Please have Dr. Cook contact me immediately. Tell him I need an update on the new serum from patient zero." He hung up the phone and rocked back and forth in his chair, pleased that each small piece of his puzzle was coming together.

Pine Bluffs, Wyoming

When Travis came to, he had a throbbing headache and found his accommodations were exactly as he imagined they'd be: a small cell in the local jail. He rolled off the bed and rubbed the lump on the back of his head. In his life he'd only been knocked out a few times; this time was the worst. The light shining in from a small window at the end of the narrow hallway outside his cell told him he'd been out for a few hours at least. His mind raced to Lori. He wondered where she was and if she was okay. He then shifted his thinking to what might happen to him. He stood up to walk but felt a bit of vertigo and promptly sat back down.

He looked around his new home and knew that his fate might be sealed. Having no expertise in jail breaks, he'd have to use the only thing he had left, his silver tongue.

Staring at the plaster ceiling, he mumbled, "Trav, what the hell ya going to do?"

A loud clang echoed down the hall.

He sat up, anticipating who was coming.

A man appeared at the door to his cell and said, "Good, you're awake." He took out a set of keys and unlocked the door. "Don't think about trying anything. You can't escape from here."

Travis did have the thought, it was instinctual for him, but he dashed the thought. He imagined the man was correct; there was no escape. Then he thought to himself, 'Yet.'

"Down the hall and out the large metal door," the man instructed. He was short and chubby, something not seen often seven months after the outbreak. With the scarcity of food many people lost the excess body fat created from living the American lifestyle. His face was adorned with a thick white beard, almost Santa Claus-like in appearance. If Travis were to guess, the man looked in his late fifties.

Travis did exactly as he ordered and made it to the door.

The man unlocked it and said, "Straight through, second door on the left."

The hallway in front of him looked like any other small local governmental office building, tile laminate floors, drop ceilings and plastered walls where framed posters of McCruff the Crime Dog were hung next to pictures of sponsored Little League teams.

He entered the room and found two people, a man and a woman. Both were middle-aged, but these two people were dressed in semi-professional attire. The man, in his forties, wore a clean pair of khakis, brown boots, and his green polo shirt was tucked in. The woman was wearing an almost similar outfit, khakis, light brown hiking boots, but a thin sweater replaced the polo shirt. Her hair was pulled back into a long ponytail while his hair was cut short and combed to the side.

Travis took a seat in a metal chair opposite them at the small table in what looked like a briefing or interrogation room.

"Thank you, Sam," the woman said to the old man.

"I'll be right outside," the old man responded and closed the door.

Travis's mind raced with different stories to tell. He thought about giving a sob story about traveling with a pregnant woman, but that would tell them about Lori and possibly put her in jeopardy, so he quickly dismissed it. Telling them he was a lone wanderer wouldn't win him any points either. Stealing a car from someone was akin to stealing a horse in the Wild West; he just hoped the consequences weren't alike too.

The woman leaned on the table and said, "My name is Carolyn, and this is Franklin. We're town leaders."

"Hello."

"We normally would say welcome to our town, but that's not the case here," she said.

"Can I have a start over?" Travis asked.

"Unfortunately that's not going to happen, and that saddens us," she responded.

Travis didn't like what she just said. He asked, "What's going to happen to me?"

Carolyn looked at Franklin, who took the lead. "What is your name?"

"Travis."

"Travis, our little town has survived because we have rules and laws that we all live by. We run a tight ship here and have zero tolerance for crime, such as theft."

Now Travis's mind was going a hundred miles an hour. The thought of just fighting his way out started to sound appealing. If he was going to die, why not die fighting?

"However, we are also a practical people and believe that the punishment should fit the crime," Carolyn added.

"I don't mean to be rude, but can I explain myself?"

"Of course you can, but we don't know what explanation you can give that warrants attempting to steal a car," Franklin said.

"What was I supposed to do, ask?" Travis said mockingly.

Carolyn and Franklin looked at each other, and Franklin

continued, "We're a fair people, so we'll give you time to offer your side of the story and to ask for forgiveness from the woman you attempted to steal from."

Travis felt his fate was sealed, so he just wanted to get it over with. He didn't want to agonize over it too much, so he said, "Let's get this show going, then."

"If you were in need of a vehicle, why didn't you just come into town and ask for help?" Carolyn asked.

"Serious? Ask for one?"

"Yes, ask. We would have helped you out," Carolyn answered.

"I don't believe it," Travis blurted out.

Franklin stood and lifted the metal blinds up. The bright light of day splashed across the room. "Travis, please come and look."

Travis stood and walked to the window. He gave Franklin an odd look before seeing what he was showing him. When he peered through the blinds, he saw the main street of town, people walking, coming and going in relative peace. A few of the shops along the street were open, with customers shopping and browsing, and a couple cars passed with their drivers waving to those walking the sidewalks.

"What do you see?" Franklin asked.

Travis replied, "A town."

"But not like any town you've seen since the outbreak, I'd wager."

"How do you keep—how did you?"

"The covenant."

"How do you?"

"Welcome to the town that will be the model for a new America. Welcome to Hope."

Lori found sleep was impossible, so she spent the hours awake planning how she could help Travis. However, not knowing what exactly happened to him was an issue. She thought about just leaving, but she vanquished that thought immediately. Travis was like family to her. She cared for him and couldn't abandon him if he was in need.

The rumble of a car outside the main building startled her. She peered out the window but saw nothing.

The front door of the building she was in opened.

Panic set in, and without thinking she ran out the back door right into a chain-link fence. Looking both ways, she decided going left was best, not because of anything specific, it just seemed like the best way to go. When she reached the end of the alleyway, she remembered that she had left her backpack. Not willing to get caught going for it, she pressed ahead and came to the edge of the far building and large gravel parking lot. She peeked out, and to her left about a hundred feet away saw the car she had heard, a blue sedan, but no one was around. To the front of her was the parking lot and beyond was the road. Her indecision was becoming a liability; unsure of what to do, she remained frozen in place. With her back firmly planted against the cold metal siding, she closed her eyes and prayed for an answer to her dilemma.

Lost in her prayers, the sound of the car starting brought her back. She poked her head out and saw it pulling away towards the road. She exhaled deeply and squatted to the ground, relieved that her prayers were answered.

"That was close," she muttered.

She jogged back to the main building using the alleyway and opened the back door to find out her prayers hadn't been answered. Standing there like a massive tower was a huge man;

he looked down and asked, "Who are you?"

Lori screamed, turned and tripped over herself. Her body slammed the ground hard, her head hitting the exposed edge of the concrete foundation. She rolled onto her back. Blood was flowing from the cut on her head and her vision was blurred. She could feel the almost dreamlike sensation that presaged passing out. She blinked hard to clear her vision, but she saw double.

The man stepped out and looked down at her.

She tried to move, but the darkness was overtaking her. The last thing she saw before the darkness came was the man reaching out for her.

North Topsail Beach, North Carolina

Devin and Tess walked the street, discussing the new objective of rescuing the older kids from the clutches of James Renfield and his men. They wanted to be free to say what they wanted without hurting anyone's feelings, specifically the children.

After being confronted by Brianna twice in as many days about their inability to calmly talk, they took to heart her direct and truthful criticism and pledged to work together without the conflict.

"Before we get into the nuts and bolts of just how we'll find these kids, I wanted to confess something," Tess said.

"Go ahead."

Tess stopped and said, "You've been right the entire time."

He stopped and looked at her. Tess appeared

downtrodden. The upbeat and confident woman he was so use to seeing wasn't there right now. He saw a fragile woman standing before him. "What was I right about?"

"You have no idea how painful this is to say." She laughed.

"Oooh, now I'm excited to hear what it is."

The laughter quickly subsided and a more serious look gripped her face. "You've been right about Travis and this entire journey here. I agree that him not telling me straight out was stupid, silly. Yes, I can come up with excuses for his inability to tell me, but he's always been a by-the-book person, and you know something, I can respect that, but the moment I needed him not to be, he still was. He could have told me somehow. He could have gotten word to me if he tried, but I know him, and he was just following orders, being that ever-obedient Marine. It pains me to say this, believe me, I needed him and I felt he let me down. I needed to know so much that I risked my life to find out, and even then, his message is bullshit," she said, her emotions were at a peak and the octaves in her voice had risen a few notches. She reached into her pocket and pulled out the paper Travis had left for her and continued, "I came all this way to find this—this doesn't tell me anything. That day we found this, you again questioned why he would do this and I argued with you. The thing is, you were right and I was just defending a man I love but has let me down. I feel embarrassed. I feel…"

Devin took a step towards her and said, "There's no need to feel embarrassed."

She put her arm out signaling for him not to approach closer. "You see, I needed purpose, and finding this stupid map that says nothing gave that to me."

He wanted nothing more than to hold her and comfort her, but clearly she needed this moment to vent.

"I've thought a lot about this, and you were right, but where I'm grateful to Travis is the journey to find this map has given me you and Brianna. You two are amazing and wonderful people. You're my family."

"I feel the same way."

"So I'm grateful to Travis; he gave me purpose and helped me to find two people who have helped me survive this fucked-up world. But now we have these children. They need us, and you know what they give me? They give me purpose, a purpose greater than finding Travis. I now know what this was all about. Travis started this quest, but it was so I could be here with you and Bri to help save these children. I can't think of a greater thing than that. This is my new purpose, and I hope that you're in this with me till the end."

Tess's speech hit him. Holding back from allowing his emotions to flow, he simply answered, "I'm in till the end."

She reached out, took his hand and squeezed it. "Thank you."

"So how are we going to save these kids?"

"Something else I'm grateful that Travis gave me is knowledge and training. So with respect to him, I'll quote one of his favorite sayings, '*The most important six inches on the battlefield is between your ears.*'"

"So we'll outsmart them?"

"That's right. It worked for us in Reed, and it'll work here."

"And like in Reed, it doesn't hurt to have a .50 caliber to help say fuck you," Devin joked.

"No, it doesn't." She laughed. "C'mon, Dev, let's go find

where these assholes live so we can get these kids back."

Brianna and the kids watched Devin and Tess as they strolled along the road. She wondered what they were talking about, but suspected it had to do with finding the older children but done at a distance in case they had any further disagreements. By their body language she could see Tess was emotional and Devin was for the most part reserved. When she heard them laughing accompanied by a buoyant stride, she felt at ease. The increase in their combative behavior towards each other had reached a tipping point for her. She was tired of hearing it and demanded they stop, specifically in front of the young children.

Tess walked up, a slight grin upon her face and a glow about her. "Everyone gather around."

The kids rushed from the top of the stairs down to the driveway and encircled her.

Devin took a seat on the hook of the Humvee and awaited Tess's briefing.

"As you know, we're committed to finding your brothers and sisters, but in order for us to begin, we need to know where they might be. So raise your hand if you have an idea of where they were taking them."

Alex was the first to raise his hand.

"Yes, Alex," Tess said.

"I heard one guy mention the farm."

"Okay, the farm, that's clue number one. Anything else?" Tess asked.

The kids looked at each other, hoping for an answer.

Brady blurted out, "I heard the same thing."

"So the farm, that's what we have," Tess said.

"Tess, did you ever search the truck?" Devin asked.

"No, let's do that."

Devin and Tess went to the truck and began to inspect it. She pulled everything from the glove box and center console. He took out every piece of trash he could find on the floorboards, under the seat and thrown on the dash. Once they finished, they stood over the heap of papers and garbage.

Many of the kids volunteered to help but were rebuffed. Tess and Devin needed to ensure that every item was examined, and to do so meant they had to keep control of everything.

Morning turned to afternoon as they attempted to decipher each item. When they finished, three things stuck out, a local map with circles, a set of keys and the registration for the truck.

"Looks like we have a lot of places to go recon," Tess said, referring to the dozen circles on the map and the address on the registration.

"I'd see if the address corresponds with one of the circles," Devin commented.

"Exactly, but these keys, they're not house keys or car keys. What are they?" she asked, holding up the keys. One was a brass Schlage door key. The other was unidentifiable; it was small and stainless with a black rubber end.

"Well, the brass key is for a door. The other, not sure, a locker of some type?" Devin said.

"The key chain, does this large rope ball mean anything to you?" Tess asked.

"Nope, looks like a big rope ball. I don't think anything specific when I see it."

"Alex referenced a farm. Besides the address from his regs, we need to see if one of these circles is a farm. I'm betting that if one is, then that's where the kids are."

"I don't see a Blackthorn Street marked on the map anywhere, so the registration address doesn't jive," Devin said, his eyes focused on the city street map.

"I guess we need to plot the routes and do this the hard way, go from one circle to the next," Tess said.

Devin looked up into the early afternoon sky then to her and said, "There's no better time than now."

"You and me, Bri stays to hold the fort down?" Tess asked instead of stating.

"Nice of you to ask," Devin remarked.

"Just trying to hold up my end of the peace treaty."

"Sounds like a plan. Let's get our gear and get going," Devin said with a smile.

Pine Bluffs, Wyoming

Lori slowly opened her bloodshot eyes and panned them across the room, from right to left and back. Blinking heavily, she hoped to clear her blurred vision. As her eyes adjusted to the light, she focused on where she was. It was a small bedroom, and by the way it was decorated, it was a child's room. On the wall were posters of superheroes, and dangling from the eggshell-colored ceiling were models of jets and spaceships. She wondered what time it was. Looking for any sign of the time, she found a digital clock on the nightstand, but it had long since stopped working. The blinds were drawn tight, but enough light crept in from the outside to help her see. Unsure of where she was or when it was, she rested back into the bed and tried to remember any details.

As she searched her memory, she soon found the exact moment and then remembered her last vision, the man reaching for her on the ground. The image frightened her, not because she was afraid he had hurt her but that he might have raped her. She quickly tossed the blanket and sheets off her and found that she was dressed in a nightgown. She pulled it up and discovered she was wearing panties that weren't hers. Her panic grew as she discovered more and more new things. She pulled down her underwear and examined herself. Everything seemed fine, no bruising or abrasions, and she didn't feel any pain from her groin. This gave her comfort, but she still wished she could remember what had happened to her after she had blacked out. She reached up with her right hand and touched a bandage on her head. Strange, she thought, that someone would find her snooping around their property and after she hurts herself they take her in and bandage her up. It wasn't impossible for people to be kind, it's just that she hadn't experienced much of it since the outbreak.

Across the room sat a small brown cushioned chair. Lying on the seat were her clothes, folded neatly. On the floor in front of the chair were her backpack and boots. On the small dresser next to the chair, she saw items from her pockets; however, noticeably missing were her knife and pistol. It made sense, whoever had taken her in didn't know who she was and therefore couldn't trust her. She didn't like that her weapons were gone, but she would have done the exact same thing.

She was about to get up when a light tapping at the door

stopped her. She got back in the bed, covered herself up, and responded, "Yes."

"Are you decent?" a female voice asked.

"Yes."

The glass door handle clicked and turned. The white five-panel door slowly opened.

Lori sat erect in the bed. Her anticipation was running high on who would appear from the other side.

A young woman, approximately in her mid-twenties, stuck her head in and asked, "Are you awake? Can I come in and check your bandage or get you anything?"

Lori's instincts told her to be grateful and sweet. The old adage of winning people over with honey versus vinegar was going to be her approach. "Hi, please come in."

The woman did just that and fully stepped into the room. "You hungry?"

"I'm not terribly hungry, but can you answer some questions for me?"

"Sure."

"Where am I?"

The young woman was shy and had a hard time making eye contact with Lori. Her thick brown hair was worn like most women post-outbreak, pulled back into a tight ponytail. Her clothes, jeans and a sweater, were clean and in good condition.

"You're in my house."

"Where is that? What town am I in?"

"Pine Bluffs but we now call it Hope on the account that this place is a sign of hope for all wandering and lost souls," she said, reciting a line from the town's new charter.

"Hope, yes, I saw a sign on the road miles back."

"Oh, was that your minivan, the blue one we found on the road abandoned?"

Lori's eyes grew large with the question; she hesitated to answer but again thought it best to provide what information she could. "Yes, that was mine; the gas tank had a leak."

"How's your head?"

Lori reached up and touched the bandage again. "Good, I suppose. There was a man; I think he might have brought me here."

"That's my daddy."

"Am I free to leave?" Lori asked, now probing to pinpoint her status.

"Of course, you can leave anytime. Your clothes are right there."

"And my weapons?"

"We gave them to the magistrate; he holds onto them."

"I see. Did your father tell you where he found me?"

"Yes, at his old workshop."

"That's it?"

"Yes, that's what he told me. Is there more?"

"No, I was lost, looking for—"

The woman interrupted her and said, "No need to explain. You're safe with us. We're here to help."

Lori felt an odd feeling about the woman and the town. She kept running the same question through her mind, 'What kind of place is so nice?' It just didn't add up. Every other person or group they had encountered hadn't been so. Why was this place different?

"How about that food?" the woman asked.

"Sure."

The woman went to leave, but Lori stopped her. "Excuse

me, I didn't get your name."

"Sorry, how rude of me. My name is Tiffany."

"My name is Lori, thank you."

Tiffany left the room and gently closed the door, leaving Lori to ponder her situation.

Lori jumped out of bed and went to the window. She pulled the curtains back. The sun was still high in the sky, but what day was it? The view from the window gave her some information on her location. She was in a first-floor room that faced the backyard. The wind was blowing the clothes and linen on the line in the yard. An old swing set lay rusted and broken in the far corner of a six-foot wooden fence line. Beyond that open fields stretched as far as she could see, and in the far distance an old power transmission line stood looking like a relic from a time gone by.

Thoughts of Travis came, and she wondered where he was and if he was even alive. Needing to know, she would have to navigate her current development with care.

A tap at the door drew her back. She said, "Come in."

Like before the door opened slowly, but this time it wasn't Tiffany. It was the large man she'd seen before her fall. Startled that it was him, Lori hurried to the bed and climbed in. "I thought you were Tiffany."

"Sorry to startle you, not my intention," the man said as he stood just inside the doorway.

"Thank you for helping me," Lori said.

"You're welcome. I felt bad about scaring you at the workshop. I seem to be good at that. Twice in one day."

Lori saw tenderness in the man's hazel eyes. His bulky and muscular stature was at odds with his soft-spoken demeanor.

"You're probably curious what I was doing there?" Lori asked.

"I'm sure you had good reason."

"Excuse me, Dad," Tiffany said, a large tray in her hands.

"Go ahead, sweetheart," he said, stepping to the side so she could walk in.

Tiffany came in with the large tray.

Lori saw a large steaming bowl of grits, but what most impressed her was the flower in the small vase.

Tiffany placed the tray at the foot of the bed and said, "I hope you like grits with butter."

Lori stared in amazement at the large scoop of partially melted butter. "Where did you get butter?"

"Oh, from the Briers' farm," Tiffany answered.

"Looks great," Lori said, her stomach responding positively to the food.

"If you're feeling better, the magistrate wants to meet you," the man said.

"So this magistrate is the leader of your town?" Lori asked, her attention still on the food, a large spoon in her hand.

"Yes, he's our elected leader. He's a good man who's given us everything."

"Given you everything?"

"He'll explain everything when you see him later," the man said.

Lori couldn't resist the urge to eat; she took a heaping spoonful and blew on it.

"Really good," Lori said as she ate the grits. "I wasn't the biggest fan of grits before, but this is really good. The butter is so creamy, and it's seasoned nicely."

"Just salt, pepper, butter and fresh goat cheese," Tiffany said, happy to see Lori eating and satisfied.

"And the goat cheese is from the Briers' farm too?" Lori asked.

"Yes, ma'am."

"I'll let you finish your meal. Let's plan on leaving in an hour. The magistrate will want to see you before the trial," the man said.

Lori lifted her head from the bowl and asked, "Trial? Trial for what?"

"A thief we caught last night," the man answered.

She knew exactly who they were referring to.

"I'll let you finish," the man said.

"What's your name?" Lori asked.

"My God given name is Daniel, but everyone calls me Brick."

"Thank you for everything, Brick," Lori said.

"You're welcome," he replied and left.

While Brick and Lori chatted, Tiffany had left and returned with a stack of clothes. "Here, these are your size, but more importantly they're clean. I'll wash these for you, okay?"

"Um, sure, thank you."

Tiffany exchanged the clothes and left.

Lori tossed the spoon on the tray and pushed it aside. Her appetite had vanished the second she heard Brick mention a trial. There was no debate that the thief was Travis. Knowing he was alive was good, but how could she save him from what was no doubt going to be a conviction.

The drive from Brick's house to the town center gave Lori a perspective of the town that neither she nor Travis was aware existed. The pillars of local power were centered in the old Pine Bluffs city office building, and in order to access it you had to pass through another checkpoint. However, this other checkpoint was positioned just in front of a large twenty-foot-high gate. She hadn't seen anything like it before.

"Is the entire downtown walled in?" Lori asked Brick.

"Not all of it, just eight square blocks."

"Totally walled in?"

"Yes, ma'am."

As they drove through, she stared in amazement at the wall and gate that had been constructed.

"It was quite easy to build; most of it incorporates existing buildings. All we had to do was build walls on the streets in between them and secure the building accesses."

"Very impressive, it's like a fort, then."

"Yeah, you could call it that."

"Why do you live on the outside?"

"A few of us do. Most live inside the walls now, but I found it impossible to leave the old place. Too many memories for me and Tiff."

Lori had not met a Mrs. Brick, so she assumed she must have died from the Death. She turned and watched as the massive wooden and steel-framed gate was wheeled back in place and secured. An old truck was connected to the gate on the inside so when they opened or closed, all they needed to do was drive the truck forward or backwards. As an architect, she marveled at the ingenuity of the townspeople. Along the exterior rooftops she saw armed men patrolling and sandbagged positions for the men to take cover if attacked.

"Um, Brick, how many people are left in town here?"

"Oh, about five hundred."

Inside the walls, the town lost its abandoned feel and took on something more idyllic. People were walking on the sidewalks, chatting and laughing. Children were running and playing in a large playground. Opposite them a massive garden was thriving on two old vacant lots.

"You guys have done all this?" she said, marveling at what she saw.

"Didn't happen right away. We had trouble at the beginning like many did. The magistrate took control after the mayor and sheriff died. He was the one who pulled us together. We have him to thank for all of this," Brick said, a sense of pride in his tone.

They made a left turn, and a half block away she saw wooden gallows erected in front of the old Pine Bluffs city office building. Her heart skipped a beat when she saw them. This was evidence that the justice they served went as far as killing the convicted.

"Who's that for?" Lori asked, pointing at the large wooden structure.

"Those souls who get convicted and sentenced to death. They find their last moments standing up there."

"How often does that happen?" Lori asked.

Brick didn't answer; he pulled the car into the rear parking lot and parked it. "We're here."

She waited, hoping he'd say something, but he just didn't. He got out of the car and walked around to her side. He opened her door and held out his hand.

This was a clue to her that he was done chatting.

He walked her inside the building. The contrast she saw

from her care at Brick's house to the heavily manned and armed group at the town headquarters was drastic. Inside the halls of the office building bustled with activity, people came and went, all with purpose. The few that took notice of her gave her stares that extended past the normal glance. She imagined the gossip of a new person in town ran through town as quickly as the virus had spread.

Brick instructed her to sit in a lobby while he informed the magistrate that she was there.

She was still unsure of the story she'd give. Back and forth she went from telling the truth to telling a bold-faced lie in an attempt to save her from whatever judgment Travis would receive.

Wringing her hands, she wished Travis was there to tell her exactly what to do. She wanted to do the right thing, but what was that? She had a life inside her that needed to be considered, and owning up that she was a party to the theft of a car could lead to something horrific. Clasping her hands, she began to pray for an answer.

Down the hall she heard the front doors burst open.

She couldn't see who was coming, but the murmuring and chatter indicated it was someone important. Like the sound of a dozen hooves on pavement, the group got closer. She thought this must be the magistrate with his entourage, but it wasn't. When the group reached her, she saw Travis handcuffed and encircled by four other men, all heavily armed.

Travis saw her and slightly shook his head. He stared at her hard and kept shaking his head.

She wanted to run to him, but she froze. The gesture he kept making with his head was a signal. He was speaking to her, but what was he saying.

As quickly as he had appeared, he was gone, taken to a back room.

All she could think was he wanted her not to stand and acknowledge him. All he did was stare intently and shake his head. That was it, she thought, he wanted her to remain silent.

Brick came back and said, "The magistrate can see you now."

Lori was staring at Brick but not moving. She was terrified of what was about to happen.

"Lori, you okay?"

"Ah, yes, I'm fine, sorry. Sometimes I zone out," she quickly said and stood.

"This way," Brick said as he escorted her down the hall and into a large office.

She walked in and stopped just a few feet inside. In front of her was a large mahogany desk with a massive window behind it. Two fabric chairs sat just in front.

A man stood and said, "Lori, hello, please come in. I promise we don't bite here. Take a seat."

She hesitated.

Brick nudged her and said, "Go ahead, Lori. The magistrate is a good man. He just wants to meet you. He has a few questions, is all."

Lori walked the few remaining feet and sat down in one of the cushioned seats.

The magistrate waited till she sat before he took his seat. With a broad smile he said, "Lori, very nice to meet you."

"Hi," she replied.

"Brick tells me he found you at his workshop just outside town," the magistrate asked.

"Yes," she answered.

The magistrate was a young man, much younger than Lori had guessed he'd be. If she were to guess, she'd say he was in his mid-thirties. He looked as if he was average height, with a lean build. His light brown hair was cut and styled very conservatively much like others she'd seen so far.

"So how did you come to being there?"

Lori thought of giving a short or terse answer, but it made sense to give him greater detail. "My car ran out of fuel. I saw the signs for your town, but who trusts towns these days? Needing fuel but wanting to stay away from people, I went looking in places I thought were vacant."

The magistrate leaned in and asked, "So you saw our sentries but chose to avoid them on purpose?"

"Of course."

"Why?"

The question irritated Lori, so she answered it honestly, "Is that a serious question? You're asking as if you've never been on the road before. Have you been out there trying to survive?"

He cocked his head and answered, "I've seen my share."

"Have you? To ask that question makes me wonder."

Brick stepped forward and placed his hand on her shoulder and said, "Miss Lori?"

"I'm fine, Brick," she said.

The magistrate sat back in his chair and rocked for a second. A grin appeared on his face as he looked at Lori. "Do you have anything at all to do with the man we caught trying to steal a truck last night?"

This was the question Lori was waiting for. Everything boiled down to how she answered. Once again Lori was faced with making a decision that would be transformative in her life. Her heart was racing, and she knew without any doubt how she responded meant everything. Reflecting back to Travis and how he responded to seeing her, she knew how she needed to respond. "Mr. Magistrate, I don't know what you're referring to."

"I'm referring to a young man who came into town last night. He attempted to steal a truck but was stopped. So you're telling me you know nothing of this incident?"

"No."

He looked at her closely, examining her composure to filter out anything that would give him the truth.

"Mr. Magistrate, I realize the timing is strange but not unexpected. My car ran out of gas; I came looking for more fuel and food."

He kept looking at her, then looked at Brick. "What do you think?"

"She seems honest to me, sir," Brick answered.

"I have nothing to hold you, and your trespass against Brick here, well, let's say he's not seeking justice for that. So without charges, I need to let you go."

The magistrate's response to her gave her hope for Travis. She had thought the worst would happen, but her fears were dashed. Maybe the magistrate would be lenient on him as well, she prayed.

"Was this a trial?"

"Yes and no. You were already cleared by Brick, but I needed to meet you to confirm. I needed to make sure your incursion into our town didn't mean to fundamentally harm us or our people. You see, we do understand how the world works today. We know people naturally will come looking for food, fuel, medicine or whatever, like you. We offer those things to travelers like yourself; all you need to do is ask. We have created a place for anyone to find the thing that will enable them to survive. You see, we changed our name to Hope because we give that. The only thing is that you need to ask for it, not take it."

She thought his response seemed reasonable. This new world was harsh, and if he meant what he said, then his town truly provided hope and a sanctuary from the realities out there.

"Why didn't you go to the FEMA camps?" she asked, the question coming from her spontaneously.

He recoiled from her question.

"We are a self-sufficient people. We don't need the government to protect us," he responded.

"No need for supplies?"

"No."

"Good, you can't trust them."

He smiled and asked, "Why don't you trust them?"

She wanted to tell him everything she knew, but now was not the time. While the magistrate seemed legit, she wasn't prepared to put all of her trust in one person just yet.

He was intrigued by her comment, so he pressed, "Why would you say that?"

"I've been to those camps."

"Have you?"

"Yes."

"And now you're on your own?"

"Yes, on my own," she quickly blurted out. She had now created her story and had to stick to it. Showing any sign of hesitation could give her away.

"What happened? Why did you leave?"

"I'd rather not discuss it. It's very personal."

"I'd appreciate it if you did."

Lori didn't like his last comment but understood where it was coming from.

The magistrate didn't flinch; he sat waiting for her to respond.

"Since you must know, my family was separated from me and I was raped."

Not showing a glimmer of emotion, the magistrate said, "I'm sorry to hear that. I can see why you wouldn't want to stay."

"I'm glad you approve," Lori said sarcastically.

"Please don't misinterpret my line of questioning. We have fought and worked hard to have all of this. We are generous, but please don't mistake what kindness and mercy we show as weakness. I can assure you that would be a mistake."

"So I'm free to go?"

"Anytime you choose. If you want fuel and food, we can provide some to get you going, or you are more than welcome to stay."

"Stay?"

"Yes, we understand that in order for our town to continue to flourish, we must grow. We need more people."

"Let me think about that. Is it fine if I stay in town while I make my decision?"

"Of course. Brick, do you want to be responsible?"

"I will house her, magistrate."

"Great!" the magistrate said standing and putting his hand out.

Lori stood, took his hand and shook. "Thank you. Oh,

two other things."

"Sure, what is it?"

"What's your name?"

"Magistrate, call me magistrate."

"Oh, okay," Lori blurted out. She found it odd he didn't use a real name. She turned to leave when he stopped her.

"Lori, you had a second question for me?"

"Yes, thanks, I'm so absentminded these days. I wanted to get my weapons back."

Still standing, he put his hands on his hips and answered, "We'll be holding on to those for the time being."

"I thought I was free to go. I'm not being convicted of anything. I think that grants me the right to get my possessions back."

"Lori, you're thinking of the ways or laws from the past. Hope doesn't work like that. You're welcome here, you can roam around freely, but until we get to know you without any doubts, we'll be keeping your weapons."

"So you don't trust me?"

"We trust, but we also verify. I'm sure you can understand. We have a lot to protect here."

Not liking the idea that she wouldn't be getting her weapons, she stormed out of the magistrate's office with Brick following right behind.

"Lori," Brick called out, walking a few feet behind her.

She stopped and waited for him, then replied, "Is he always so smug?"

"He's a good man. He's doing what's best for us."

"If I'm not guilty of anything, I want my weapons," Lori charged.

"Not my call, but I agree with the magistrate. If you want

your weapons back today, we can provide them for you at the far checkpoints on your way out of town."

"Such bull."

"I can assure you, you're safe here. There's no need for your weapons."

Lori thought about what he said. It wasn't that she wanted them strictly to protect herself from them. It was more for being able to use them if she could get Travis freed.

Some commotion broke out down the hall.

Brick and Lori turned to see people pouring out of the holding room where she'd last seen Travis go.

Several people pushed past them, heading towards the activity. Lori stopped one of them and asked, "What's going on?"

"Public trial starts in five minutes," the woman said excitedly.

Lori knew what that meant. She looked at Brick and said, "I want to stay for that."

He looked at his watch and asked, "Aren't you hungry? C'mon, let's go home and get some lunch."

Lori wasn't paying any attention to him. She was focused on the ever-growing crowd down the hall.

Brick began to walk towards the exit away from the crowd. He didn't have the time nor desire to stick around for the mayhem that encircled a trial.

Lori knew what it was and had to see. She darted away from Brick and down the hall into the mass of people.

She then caught sight of Travis, his tall build towering above the others. They were escorting him outside the front doors. Taking her place in the crowd, she slowly shuffled out the front. There she was amazed by the crowd that had gathered. She couldn't believe the size and the setup that had all come together in the hour she'd been inside.

To the right of the gallows sat a long table with several chairs. Just in front of that was a single chair. Lori imagined that was Travis's chair. What frightened Lori most of all was that his trial was being conducted next to the ominous-looking gallows. She thought this could only portend his death.

Travis was escorted to the single chair and instructed to stand.

The loud crowd suddenly became silent.

Lori craned her head and saw the magistrate exit the front, flanked by Franklin and Carolyn. They approached the long table and stood at their chairs, the magistrate taking the center.

The magistrate raised his arms in the air and said, "Let us all bow our heads and pray that God will give us and this man the justice that is deserved." A short pause followed, then he said, "Amen."

Travis was pushed into his chair.

The magistrate and Franklin sat. Carolyn remained standing.

She called out, "This man before you is accused of attempted theft. Last night Janine McDonough caught him attempting to hot-wire and steal her truck right from her driveway."

Lori shook her head. None of this might have happened had he just listened to her and not tried to steal a vehicle from someone's house.

"Janine McDonough, please step forward and tell us your account," Carolyn instructed, then took her seat.

Janine stepped from the crowd and walked to a spot in

between Travis and the table. She looked at Travis, but this time the look of anger was gone. A feeling of sympathy came over her as she saw this man sit and await his conviction.

"Janine, please go ahead," Carolyn pressed after watching her stand and look at Travis for what seemed like minutes.

Standing tall, thrusting her shoulders back and clearing her throat, she began, "I heard some noise outside. I stepped out to investigate, and that's when I heard the noise again. It was clear to me that someone was in my truck. I had a gun, my shotgun, and slowly approached. I was scared and didn't know how many people might be out there or who it was. All I knew is I didn't want Carl's truck taken. He loved that truck, and I still needed it. So putting aside my fear, I approached the truck. The door was open, and I saw someone inside."

"Is that man here?" Carolyn asked.

Janine looked at Travis and answered, "Yes."

"Where?"

Janine pointed at Travis. This caused the crowd to mutter and talk.

"What happened next?" Carolyn asked.

"I hollered for him to stop and get out of the truck. He did just that, but he kept blinding me with his flashlight. I stepped aside out of the light, and that's when he hit me with the truck door. The shotgun fired and he ran."

The crowd muttered louder.

"I didn't know what happened next, but I think he ran into Brent in the street. All I know is he's on the ground, and Brent asks me what I want to do with him. I, of course, told him that we needed to bring him before the magistrate."

"Can Brent Sharrod please come forward?" Carolyn called out.

Janine turned to leave, but Carolyn stopped her.

"Janine, please stay put."

Brent stepped out of the crowd and walked up alongside Janine.

"What is your story?" Carolyn asked.

"I was on patrol; I heard a scream for help. I ran towards it, and this guy here ran full force into me. I asked Janine if she wanted to bring him here, of course she said yes, and I then struck him."

The whole time the accounts were being told Travis sat unmoving and staring straight ahead.

"Why did you hit him?" the magistrate asked.

"Sir, I hit him because I thought he was a threat, and my intention was to knock him out, which I did, so I could bring him here."

"Very well, continue."

"That's about it," Brent said.

"Janine, anything else to add?" Carolyn asked.

She looked at Carolyn and then to Travis again. "Nothing to add."

The magistrate looked at Travis and asked, "Do you have anything you'd like to say? This is your time to challenge their testimony."

"I didn't know I was taking her truck. I wouldn't have done it otherwise. I am sorry. I didn't mean to scare you. I'm a good man, just made a bad decision," Travis said somberly. He finished by looking directly at Janine and said, "I'm sorry."

"Very well. Thank you Janine and Brent for your courage and testimony today. You may be excused," Carolyn said.

The two walked back into the crowd.

The magistrate stood and proclaimed, "Seven months

ago, an evil descended upon our Earth and gave us the Death. This was not from the heavens but from the hands of man. Out of the ashes I found you and gave you a new system by which to live. This system requires a code to live by. That code states we must love one another and treat them with care. This code also deals with justice. It must be handled swiftly, fairly and appropriately. Will the accused stand?"

Travis stood.

"What is your full name?" the magistrate asked.

Sweat was streaming down Lori's face, and her body was shaking in anticipation of what was about to happen.

"My name is Travis Priddy."

"Travis Priddy, you have been accused of attempted theft of a coveted piece of equipment. Vehicles are no longer a novelty but a necessity, and in many ways can determine if one lives or dies. By your own admission you did this. So based upon the covenant and codes of Hope, I hereby find you guilty and sentence you accordingly. For attempted theft, your sentence shall be death by hanging."

The crowd grew loud as everyone began to discuss the outcome.

Lori felt her knees begin to give out. She swayed and was about to collapse when Brick steadied her.

The two men who had escorted Travis out came up alongside him and took him only a few feet away to the base of the gallows

Travis had given in to his fate and didn't resist. There wasn't a thing he could do, and he knew it.

A third man appeared; he was wearing black clothes and donned a black hood.

Lori continued to watch and couldn't believe what she

was seeing; the third man looked like someone from the middle ages.

He sauntered over to Travis and stopped just a foot away.

Travis looked at his dark brown eyes peering from the hood. "Make the rope slack, will ya?"

The hooded man spoke; his thick raspy voice replied, "It will be."

Travis lowered his head as he was walked up the stairs to the thick two-inch rope that dangled.

The executioner asked, "Do you want a hood?"

"No, I want to see the world before I go."

"Very well," the executioner said. He placed the noose around Travis's neck and, just as he said, kept it loose. He walked to a lever and grasped it.

"Stop, stop! Please stop!" Janine screamed and came running out of the crowd.

Everyone began to chatter loudly.

Janine ran towards the gallows yelling, "Stop, don't!"

"Janine, this is entirely inappropriate!" Carolyn hollered.

"I invoke the victim's code!" she cried out.

"Too late for that, carry out the sentence" Carolyn responded.

"No, stop!" Janine screamed.

"Wait! Everyone please wait a minute!" the magistrate bellowed. He stood and looked at Janine. "Why, why do you wish to invoke the victim's code? You had your chance, but you presented this case before me knowing what would happen if he were convicted."

"I can see this man is not bad, but desperate."

The magistrate's facial expression changed from shock at Janine's abrupt display to a contentment most often seen on him. "What would you have us do?"

"I'd…um…I'd have him let go. Let us show mercy."

"That, we cannot do. You had your choice at the moment to do that. You know your rights and freely gave him up for us to judge. You know how the covenant works, Janine. If we deviate from it, then our world, the one we all can agree was in turmoil, will return to that. The covenant gives us peace because it gives us a system to follow."

"Please show mercy this once," Janine begged.

"Where is this coming from? Is it because you lost your husband and son?" he asked.

The magistrate's assumptions were like a pinprick strike at her heart. Janine had lost both her son and husband. Not to the Death but to the barbarism that followed. Their story was similar to Travis's.

"Magistrate, I believe in the covenant, but I also believe this man can do good if given the chance. You tell us that we need more people so that we can grow and flourish. Our town grows, but every time our hunting parties go out, they come back with fewer able-bodied men. We need more people. We need more men."

"Or do *you* need a man?" Carolyn sniped.

Ignoring Carolyn, Janine again begged, "I believe this man can be of help."

"And how could you even come to a conclusion like that?" the magistrate asked.

"Because he's a Marine," Janine replied.

"Marine? How do you know that?"

"The night of the attack, we searched him. On his right arm is a tattoo, a Marine Corps tattoo. Brent can confirm this," Janine replied.

The magistrate looked to Brent, who said, "It's true, his upper right shoulder."

"Mr. Priddy, are you a Marine?" the magistrate asked.

Travis thought about how he should answer. Since it seemed like it could benefit him, he remained honest to a point. "Yes. I was a captain in the Marines, an infantry officer."

"Hmm, an infantry officer could be useful. Answer me this, are you a master tactician or an excellent marksman?" the magistrate asked. He had now walked from behind the table and was standing at the base of the gallows.

"I'm great at both," Travis replied.

"Pick one."

Travis didn't know where this was going but answered the one he thought would spare him. "I was one of the top tacticians in my class at OCS."

"So you're better at war planning and tactics than you are a shooter, correct?"

"Correct."

"Good," the magistrate said and walked back to the table.

"You're not going to let him go, are you?" Carolyn asked, her face scrunched in frustration at the situation.

"Janine, I agree with you. This man will be more valuable to us, but there are two conditions. One, he has to agree to stay, and second, you must house him. If he steps out of bounds, we will then carry out *this* sentence fully, no mercy. You will also be subject to the same punishment if he flees. Do I make myself clear?'

Janine looked at Travis and then back to the magistrate. "Understood, I agree."

"Mr. Priddy, oh, wait a minute, we should call you

Captain Priddy. Do you agree that *this* sentence will not be carried out?"

"I agree."

Hearing this, Lori almost exploded with excitement.

"I protest. Franklin, say something," Carolyn barked at her colleague.

"Let all of you here be witnesses. I hereby commute the sentence given to Captain Priddy. You have heard the reasons—"

"This is not how the system works. Magistrate, you are deviating from the covenant!" Carolyn exclaimed.

Many in the crowd began to stir and shouted their protests.

The magistrate stopped speaking. He couldn't be heard, and he didn't like being interrupted. He stood waiting for everyone to quiet down.

Franklin, seeing an opportunity to be on the magistrate's good side, called out, "Everyone, please stop talking. Let him finish!"

The crowd grew silent again.

The executioner removed the noose and walked to the side.

The two guards took Travis and escorted him from the gallows and back to his chair.

"I know that the covenant is sacred, and I am not abandoning it completely. I will not hang this man, but he should still receive a punishment for his crime that is fitting."

Janine looked oddly at the magistrate as she didn't know what he was doing.

"Janine has agreed to care for this man, and he has agreed to be a part of our community in exchange for not killing him.

However, I am sworn to uphold the covenant and must still sentence this man to a punishment that fits the crime."

"What's going on?" Travis asked.

"Captain Priddy, your life has been spared, but you must still be punished for your crime. Not to do that would jeopardize everything we've worked so hard to accomplish."

A smile began to spread across Carolyn's face as the magistrate continued to speak.

Lori's previous panic attack started again as she feared the worst was coming.

"So I decree that Captain Priddy's punishment will be the amputation of his left hand."

The crowd howled in excitement at the news.

"You said I—" Travis protested.

The guards grabbed him, but this time Travis resisted; however, they were too strong for him as they dragged him to the side of the gallows. There sat a large log, the top stained with blood and showing the hack marks of past sentences. They pushed him to his knees, grabbed his left hand, and placed it on the top of the log.

"This was not the arrangement!" Travis screamed.

"Captain Priddy, I said I would commute the sentence of death by hanging. You must still be punished. It is our way, it is our laws, it is our covenant."

The executioner reappeared, but now holding a large axe.

"This is madness!" Janine hollered.

Lori looked and wanted to do something but knew anything she did would not matter. Travis's fate was sealed, and he'd want her to remain silent.

Travis looked at the axe, the edge gleaming in the sunlight. He then looked at the executioner, who stood ready to carry out his gruesome task. "Please make it a clean cut," Travis pleaded.

"I will," he said as he raised the axe high.

Travis lowered his head and closed his eyes.

The crowd continued to howl with excitement at the spectacle.

The executioner held the axe high in the air and with a swift and forceful blow brought it down on Travis's wrist.

Denver International Airport

The candles flickered, casting long shadows across the large dining room. Horton tossed the linen napkin on the table and leaned back in his cushioned high-backed dining chair. A pleasant expression graced his face as he looked at Wendell and his family sitting around the table.

"How was everything?" Horton asked.

"Very good, thank you," Mrs. Wendell replied.

"Good, I personally loved the dessert, nothing like a mousse done right. My chef is the best. I'm blessed to have him."

"The pudding was the best," Wendell's young daughter blurted out, a bit of chocolate on her chin.

"So glad you liked it," Horton said, smiling.

Wendell had left earlier feeling apprehensive; that feeling still lingered. The hours in between his meeting and the dinner were torturous for him. One horrific image after another entered his mind, and having his family sent there unexpectedly scared him the most. He was willing to suffer, but the thoughts of his family being harmed sent chills down his spine. Deep down he knew what he was doing for the chancellor and the order was nothing short of genocide, but surviving himself was his top priority.

Horton stood and said, “I want to thank you all for coming. If you don’t mind, I need to meet with your husband a bit longer. I’ll have one of the guards escort you back to your residence.”

Mrs. Wendell smiled and said, “I hope to return the favor, and by the way, our accommodations are amazing. I’m honored that you thought of us. I just know Tom appreciates this and will do his best in his new position.” She reached out and touched Wendell’s arm and caressed it.

“I’m sure he will. Till next time.”

Mrs. Wendell and her daughter stood and left.

“Let’s go to the lounge and have a drink,” Horton suggested.

Wendell watched his family leave before joining Horton. While he was still extremely nervous, the fact that he had survived dinner meant something positive for him. He entered the lounge and found Horton looking at a map on the large leather ottoman.

“Sit down. I want to show you something,” Horton said.

Wendell did just that and looked closer at the map before him.

“Nice family you’ve got there,” Horton said.

“Thank you.”

“Now let’s get to why I’ve called you out here,” he said, waving his hand over the map. “This map is the area I’m responsible for managing. You know it as North America, but that is the name of old. It is now called Arcadia, and our capital, which will sit here, will hold that sacred name too. Now everything we've accomplished started out as an idea many years ago. A group of us came together with a vision for a better world. It took us many years to put it all together, but we finally executed that plan seven months ago. Now that vision is being jeopardized by some in that group who have maintained their greed and lust for the pleasures from the past. I need to build a new core that will ensure the vision is completed, and I think you can be part of that core group. You see, you did as you were told and you believe in our plan."

"Chancellor, what is it that you need me to do for you?" Wendell asked, getting right to the point.

"I've been accused of being too verbose, and I can see that critique is holding true. Tom, I need you to continue the cleanse, but I need you to cleanse some traitors."

"Who are these traitors?"

Horton hesitated saying it, but after all, he felt he had the leverage on Wendell with his family being at the DIA. "We are going to remove the other chancellors."

"But, I, um, I'm not a killer. I don't think I'm the right person for this."

"Yes, you are, without a doubt. You killed every person I asked you to."

"But I never killed anyone before."

"Tom, I don't expect you to actually kill them personally. I expect you to create a team that will accomplish this."

Wendell sat hunched over the map, his mind lost in thought of the new responsibility he had just been given. Not only did the task seem extremely difficult but impossible. "How do you want this to happen?"

"Glad you asked. I'll give further details later, but assemble a team of six people. I need them ready to deploy in thirty days."

"Can you give me any more details outside of this? Something that will help me pick the best candidates for the job?"

Horton paused and thought it a good question, "Just between us, this mission will be a suicide one. You should expect these people to never return."

"Oh."

Horton stood and said, "Great dinner tonight. I expect we'll have more over the coming months."

Wendell stood and responded, "I hope so, sir, and thank you for the honor of fulfilling the dream that is Arcadia."

Day 224

May 13, 2021
Pine Bluffs, Wyoming

Travis sat on the porch, staring at the rotting wooden fence that ran the perimeter of Janine's property. The wicker rocking chair had become his daily sanctuary from his new life, but even when he would lose himself in thought, the phantom pain from his absent left hand would remind him of his new existence. It was hard for him not to feel like a prisoner even though Janine did her best to make him feel at home and comfortable. All he did each day since his sentence was carried out over two weeks ago was mope around and sit out back staring. He did think of Lori, but his mind was eased that she had taken shelter with a loving family and her true identity or connection to him was still secret. Immediately after losing his hand, he worried for her, but as each day passed he came to realize that Lori was a very self-reliant person.

He looked down at the white gauze bandage tightly wrapped around his lower arm and stub. He couldn't lie to himself, he missed his hand, but it was gone and not coming back. Deep down he fought the depression that was ravaging his mind, but he found it very hard. It wasn't just the loss of his hand but the fact that he believed he had failed. He had failed Lori, her unborn baby, and the deepest pain he felt was that he felt he had failed Tess. Never before had he ever believed that he'd never see her again till now. Even when things had gotten tough, he'd still held out hope that they'd see each other again. But now he was trapped in a sick and twisted world that had cost him his hand and could cost his life or the lives of others if he didn't obey the rules or what the people of Hope called the covenant.

"Hey, you hungry?" Janine asked from behind the large screen door, a large tray in her hands.

"I'm fine."

She nudged the door open and stepped outside. "Listen, grumpy pants, you need to eat."

"Please don't patronize me. I'm not grumpy, I lost my fucking arm," he barked, holding up his bandaged stump.

She walked around him and forcefully placed the tray down on a small side table. She placed her hands on her hips and glared at him.

He looked down at the tray. On it sat a plate of scrambled eggs, sausage and a glass of milk, all fresh. He glanced up at her and said, "I'm not hungry."

"I put my life on the line for you, not to mention I saved your life. I could have let them hang you. Is that what you wanted? Let me tell you I saw a glimmer of something decent in you, and when you looked at me, your eyes told me that you were sorry. Now get over it, suck it up and deal," she barked and stormed off.

He watched her and at that moment was tempted to respond, but his injured ego wouldn't allow it.

She stopped at the door and turned towards him again. "And take a damn bath, would you?"

He held up his stump again.

"I know, you lost your hand."

"No, I'm giving you the middle finger."

"What a child. I obviously made a huge mistake," she snapped and stormed inside.

He laughed to himself and looked down at the plate of food. He had lied about not being hungry, he was, and the aroma from the food was only increasing his appetite. However, not eating became one thing he could control, a rebellion of sorts.

"There's a set of clean clothes on your bed. I suggest you put them on after you bathe."

"Just please leave me alone!" he hollered back.

She stormed back outside and said, "Unfortunately for me, my fate is connected to yours. Unless you want to go out smelling like a dirty rag, I suggest you eat, bathe and get dressed." She looked at her watch and said, "And do all of that in forty-five minutes."

"What's happening in forty-five minutes?"

"The magistrate is having you picked up; he's putting you to work. Finally time to start paying back the debt you owe for your miserable life."

Travis wanted nothing more but to resist and not go, but he couldn't. Janine was right; her fate was tied to his. Like Lori before, he had another person attached to him. He didn't ask for it; it was just his life. He laughed at how never before had he had such occurrences happen, but for whatever reason, God had chosen him and given him the burden.

Begrudgingly he put on the clothes and admired himself in the mirror. Apparently, Janine's husband, Carl, and he were the same size. What were the odds of that? he thought. But that was where their similarities ended. For Travis, Carl had zero taste or style, but he imagined a man who would live in the middle of nowhere didn't care for such a thing. It had been years since he had worn Levi's 501 jeans, and the red flannel shirt was nice but reminded him more of something he'd have worn if he had been living in Seattle during the heyday for grunge rock.

He stepped out of his room to find Janine waiting. "They fit nicely. Glad to see you in something besides pajamas and a robe."

He couldn't stop himself and smiled slightly. "Yeah, they fit perfectly."

"I know it. Carl was lean and broad up there," she said, pointing to his shoulders.

"I see you ate too," she commented.

"Yeah, the eggs were good."

She took a step towards him and said, "I know you didn't ask for this, but I didn't ask for it either. For whatever reason, we were meant to meet."

"I know."

"How's the arm? Need a fresh bandage?" she asked, looking at his arm.

"I'm good. It's healing nicely. You did a good job with cauterizing it."

"Saw that in movies. I know I shouldn't admit that, but it seemed like the best way to ensure it didn't get infected."

"Well, if an infection was coming, I'd have one by now."

Janine pushed loose strands of her long brown hair behind her ears. If she could describe herself, Janine would say she was tiny with a big personality. She was five foot two inches tall, curvy and 'top heavy' is how she'd put it. She was not a native of Pine Bluffs but had moved there after meeting Carl. She was born and raised in Oklahoma City and had met Carl one night. He had been stationed at Tinker Air Force Base. They fell in love and moved back to Pine Bluffs, his hometown. After the outbreak, they felt blessed, as none of them had died. But the blessings they had counted came to an abrupt end a month after in a scene that was so horrific it had prompted her to step forward to save Travis's life.

Travis's almost brutish stubborn and selfish behavior since his hand had been cut off had prevented them from talking. He had wondered what her story was, but he'd vanquished the thought when he looked at his stub, but her persistence was beginning to wear him down.

"I've been wanting to tell you—" he said but was interrupted when a loud bang on the front door echoed down the wood-floored hallway.

"Tell me later. Don't keep the magistrate waiting," she said and ushered him out.

Outside, he met one of the guards who had been with him the day he had lost his hand. "This way."

Travis followed him to a black Ford Expedition.

The guard opened the rear door for him and said, "Get in."

Travis did and found he wasn't alone. Sitting across from him was the magistrate.

"Captain Priddy how's the arm?" he asked smugly.

The arrogance behind the question made Travis want to punch him in the face with his bandaged stub, but he let it go. "Much better, I'd thank you for asking, but, oh yeah, you were the one who had my hand cut off," Travis sarcastically responded.

"I didn't cut off your hand, you did. Your actions caused your punishment, and until you come to grips with that and hold yourself responsible, you'll never be able to grow as a person."

"Enough of the self-improvement lesson, where are we going?"

"To my office, we have much to discuss."

North Topsail Beach, North Carolina

Devin pulled the Humvee over a few blocks away from their house. He exhaled heavily and rested his head against the steering wheel. He gazed out the windshield towards the ocean and watched the waves move towards the shore. So often he was amazed at how the world around him, the wind, the seas, the trees, weeds and grasses kept on living, even thriving after the decimation of the human species. Each wave that came in took no notice that mankind was gone for the most part and would continue to go on lapping the beach for many eons.

"What are we stopping for?" Tess asked from the hatch. She bent down and asked again, "What's up? Why did we stop?'

"I'm frustrated. It's been two weeks now, and we're no closer than we were when we started."

"We can't quit."

"I'm not quitting, I'm just venting. We've checked every single site, all abandoned, nothing, no one. Not even any encounters with Renfield's people. Where did they go? It's like they vanished."

"Do you suppose these guys were just full of shit?"

"That doesn't make sense. Alex knew the one man. He said there were more."

"Maybe there was then."

"I just don't know what we're going to tell him and the others. They're counting on us."

"Maybe their territory is vast. Maybe they're headquartered somewhere far away."

"Could be."

"Maybe the map is nothing more than locations they were ransacking or held some importance."

"Like what? They were all random. There was nothing there that told me anything or gave us clues. This entire thing is so frustrating," Devin bellowed and gripped the steering wheel tightly in anger.

Tess reached out and patted his shoulder. "Settle down. I need you thinking clearly, not in full rage mode."

"Where is everyone, though?" he exclaimed.

"Good question, make no sense at all."

"Everywhere else we went we found some survivors, but none here, unless…"

"Unless what?"

"Maybe the government had mandatory evacuations and took everyone away, literally everyone."

"Those marks on all the doors, I know where I've seen them before. I've seen them in footage from hurricane disasters. EMS or police will mark doors, letting whoever comes behind them know the house had been checked and what was inside."

"You're just now figuring this out?" Tess joked.

"I didn't hear you chiming in, oh, brilliant one."

"If they were evacuated, where were they taken?"

"The base."

"Well, that partially answers some questions but not all. One is why weren't the kids taken away, and where are these Renfield people?"

"The keys, it has something to do with the keys," Devin stated.

"They look like lawnmower keys or something, or a golf cart."

"We're spinning our wheels here. Let's go back, get some food and keep talking," Devin suggested.

"Poor Alex is going to be heartbroken."

"I'm heartbroken too," Devin said. His mind raced to find an answer, but he was starting to believe that the teens were gone and would never be found. While he didn't want the children to suffer more than they had, he began to start planning what their next step would be once they gave up the search.

When Brianna saw the Humvee pull into the driveway, she raced down the stairs barking unintelligibly.

"Why are you yelling?" Tess asked from her position in the hatch.

Brianna held up the radio and said, "I've been trying you guys all day!"

Devin looked at the radio and pressed the transmit button and spoke in the receiver. "Test, test." He heard his voice come from her radio and finished by saying, "You know these things have a limited range."

"It is what it is. You guys need to come with me!" Brianna exclaimed.

Seeing the stress on her face and her urgent plea, Devin and Tess didn't hesitate. They jumped out of the Humvee and followed Brianna.

"Alex, Alex!" Brianna yelled.

Alex popped his head out of the house.

"Take watch. I'm taking them to the beach."

Alex signaled with a thumb up that he had the watch.

"Bri, what's going on?" Devin asked, finally jogging up next to her.

"We had a little surprise wash up on shore," she answered.

When they crested the small dunes before the beach, Tess could see a body sprawled out, the waves lapping up against it, slowly nudging it.

"Is it one of the kids?" Tess asked.

"Yes, I mean, not one of ours, it's Brady's sister," Brianna replied.

They walked up to the bloated corpse and stood above it looking down.

Devin was instantly repulsed. He had the weakest stomach of all of them. He pulled up his shirt to cover his nose.

Tess knelt down and turned the body on its back.

The naked body was swollen. Chunks of her face had been fed upon by fish. Her eyes were bulging out of the sockets, and the cause of death looked apparent as a horizontal gash across her throat gaped open.

"Has Brady seen this?" Tess asked.

"Yes, he found her."

"Oh my God," Devin blurted out.

"Why were the kids down here playing by themselves?" Tess chastised Brianna.

"Alex was watching over them. He took a few of the boys down here to go swimming."

"That's so irresponsible," Tess continued with her reprimand.

"Ladies, enough, we need to deal with this. How is Brady?" Devin asked.

"He's clearly upset, hasn't come out of the back bedroom since he came back."

"Bri, we need to bury her and have a ceremony. We have an hour or more of light left, so let's get on this right away. Run up to the house and get that large blue tarp in the garage and two shovels," Devin said.

"Okay," Brianna said.

Brianna marched off towards the house.

Tess stood up and looked out to sea. She tore open the pouch on her hip and pulled out a set of binoculars. Putting them to her eyes, she scanned the horizon. "There's two scenarios here. She was either dumped in the river or dumped far out at sea."

"She was dumped out at sea, no doubt about it."

"Why so certain?" Tess asked, lowering the binoculars and looking at Devin.

He dug into his pocket, pulled out the key, and said with confidence, "Now I know what this key fits, a boat."

Denver International Airport

Horton was usually not the person waiting, but when Dr. Mueller asked for more time, it meant you had to wait, regardless of your status or position. As he waited, he looked around the sterile stainless steel walls of the underground secret facility he had built for the doctor. Everything that was happening there had to be kept quiet so much that Dr. Mueller and his staff never left the facility. While Horton was building the facility, he also constructed living quarters and all the comforts and amenities anyone could ever desire.

Dr. Mueller had been the man heading up synthesizing a new strain of the Death using Cassidy Lange's blood. What set Cassidy apart from others who had been immune was that she had contracted the Death, but her body had created antibodies and fought it. From all of their tests during the preoperational stage, they hadn't found anyone who had lived after showing symptoms. Once symptoms appeared, you were dead within days. Cassidy Lange was a unique case. She was not only the first person to spread the virus but also the only one they had discovered that should have died but didn't. She wasn't immune in the traditional sense. Her body had reacted the same way as someone not immune, but instead of killing her, her body fought back and killed the virus. It was from her that they had created R-59, a permanent vaccine unlike the other one they used for support personnel. He had kept R-59 quiet from the Order but planned on unveiling it, and in this unveiling he'd unleash something else that would ravage the remaining population of the world.

"Chancellor Horton, sorry to keep you waiting. Please

come in," Dr. Mueller said, waving him into his office.

"It's not a problem, Doctor; I know how busy you are. If you weren't, I'd be asking you why."

"I won't even wait for you to sit down. We have it; we have created it," he blurted out with childlike excitement.

"The other virus?"

"Yes, and its antidote. I call it Lazarus," Mueller said, holding up a vial.

"Lazarus is the antidote?"

"Yes."

"I'm not liking the sound of that."

"Yes, well. Let's say you practically die, then come back. You essentially experience what patient zero did, but this second virus is worse. You see, I took the Ebola virus, and I—"

"Stop. Don't bore me with the details. I'd rather not know, except how quickly does it kill once it's released?"

"Come see!" Mueller said, rushing out of the office and into his lab.

Horton followed him in the large space. Mueller's team was so busy they didn't take notice of Horton entering the space.

Mueller walked him through the lab to a hallway lined with large windows on both sides. He flipped on the lights and pointed to the first window on the right.

Horton cautiously walked up and looked through the thick protective glass. There he saw a woman in a white gown crawling on the floor, a trail of blood behind her. She was moaning and crying for help, but those pleas were heard but not heeded.

"There's so much blood," Horton gasped.

"Like I said, I took the Ebola virus and combined it—"

"Don't bother, please. So when did you give this woman the new virus?"

"Yesterday," he said, looking at his watch, then finished, "About twenty-two hours ago."

"So it's just as quick as the Death but clearly more gruesome," Horton said. He was repulsed by what he saw.

"It's a beautiful killer. So far not one person, not one, has survived it except those we also gave Lazarus to. When we administer Lazarus to a sick patient they have a ninety-five percent chance of survival. Fifty percent have shown minor symptoms of the Bloody Death, even if we give that to them first. Good news is, all survive, and not a person has died. It's more of an inconvenience."

"Did you just call it the bloody death? No names, okay, this isn't a product we're peddling, and by the time it does its job, there won't be that many people left," Horton said, his full attention on Mueller.

A bloody hand slapped the glass, startling Horton. He stepped back and swallowed hard. "If you give me this now, the Lazarus, I have a fifty percent chance of showing symptoms like that but won't die?"

"Pretty much."

"Dr. Mueller, I thought you were ready, but having a fifty percent chance of bleeding out my ass doesn't sound pleasant. I need you to perfect it. Get working on it immediately, and don't call me down here till it's a much higher rate."

The sick woman again slapped the window, her groans and pleas muffled by the thick glass and walls.

"And for heaven's sake, unless you're going to save that woman, put her down."

Mueller looked up briefly and made eye contact. The pain of being reprimanded hurt him. The vision he'd had in his mind when he called Horton was that he'd be singing his praises for doing such a wonderful job. Unable to contain his feelings, he muttered, "Yes, sir."

Horton looked at the woman one last time, then back at Mueller, a great look of disgust on his face. "And hurry up, we're running out of time," he barked then stormed off.

Pine Bluffs, Wyoming

After spending three hours with the magistrate and his security team, Travis was surprised by the sophistication and level of detail that had gone into the protection of the town, which included the physical security, barriers and the 'hunting parties' that were sent out weekly. For an unknown reason, the magistrate opened up and gave specific details on how the town ran. Travis assumed he wanted to win his trust, but for someone new to town and a 'convicted felon', he thought it odd to disclose so much. He described that in order to remain in town everyone was given a responsibility and had to perform it. Contribution to the whole was critical, and if the whole found one person not working out, they could banish them. Travis laughed to himself when he heard this detail; it reminded him of an old television show called *Survivor* where people were also voted off by the group. While he found that part humorous, if only for its coincidence, he actually respected it. It brought back memories of the Marine Corps and how each Marine had a job to do, each person had a role to play to ensure the completion of the mission. When he thought deeper about this and what mission had meant for him, he could easily make a connection that the town's mission was to survive. But they had gone further than survival; they were thriving and, from what he had seen so far, outside of his situation, were also generous.

The more the magistrate told him, the more he got engaged. He had started the meeting with a disregard for the man but now the magistrate's charm was wearing on him. He didn't know his story, but he had a way about him that set him apart from most other people. He was bright, well spoken and confident. Travis, also an extremely confident person, was finding the magistrate's enthusiasm intoxicating.

Like a school child, Travis raised his hand and asked, "How did you do all of this? I ask because…" He stopped short of offering too much information of his most recent past.

"Structure and systems, plain and simple," the magistrate answered. He had been pacing the floor of the large conference room in front of a whiteboard where he had been drawing and writing notes to help illustrate how the town functioned.

"People do like structure," Travis replied.

"Of course they do. For instance, you're a Marine."

"Was a Marine."

"Whatever, but you understand the need for structure and systems. It gives people certainty. What I have to do as their leader is ensure these systems function as best they can but also keep people busy. Nothing is worse than an idle person."

"Idleness is the parent of mischief."

"Idleness is also the heaviest of all oppressions," the magistrate said.

"Hmm, haven't heard that one."

"Victor Hugo."

Travis like how quick-witted the magistrate was. He cracked a slight smile and decided now was the best time to get at the heart of what he was really doing there. The entire time had been monopolized by the magistrate. "What am I doing here? I have to ask; you don't know me. In fact, all you know of me is that I tried to steal a car and you cut off my hand."

"We know you're a Marine," Martin, the head of his security, blurted out.

"But do you really know if I am?" Travis asked.

Martin looked at him with an odd look but neglected to answer.

The magistrate stepped over to Travis. He looked at Martin and the other man and asked, "Do you mind pulling the vehicle around? Time for us to show Captain Priddy his new job as part of our community."

"Magistrate, don't you think it might be a bit early for that?" Martin asked.

"Martin, please go pull the vehicle around."

Martin and the other man stood and left, closing the door behind them.

"Captain Priddy, I know I can trust you, because I know everything about you."

"How could you possibly know everything about me?"

"Trust me when I tell you this. Now come with me," the magistrate said.

Travis stood and turned, but the magistrate stopped him

and said, "One more thing before we go. I'm really sorry about the hand, but if I didn't punish you in some way, I could have had a revolution to deal with. I didn't want to have to kill you much less maim you. Hearing you had military experience is valuable to me, but that wasn't enough red meat for the masses, so to speak."

Travis looked down at his stub and reflected on everything that led to him losing it. "A good friend told me not to steal from others' houses, and you know what, I did. Look what it got me."

Both men grinned and left the conference room.

Travis had already thought he had been shocked by what he had learned. What would come next would be unimaginable.

Lori hadn't been able to sleep since her arrival in Hope, but a restful night's sleep had been something elusive for her since she had arrived at Camp 13 months ago. The fatigue was wearing on her, though, as was the concern for all she loved, including Travis. With their situations set in the town of Hope, she needed to find a vaccine to save the baby. That was her main concern, and with their attempt halted, she needed to find another way.

Her stay with Brick and Tiffany had been surprisingly pleasant. They were the most accommodating hosts, and she appreciated their kindness. At moments she had felt the urge to tell them about her pregnancy, but she just wasn't quite ready for that. Lori found it hard to trust people anymore, and even though their hospitality had been amazing, she couldn't commit to being fully honest. In the two weeks since Travis's sentence was carried out, they had gone out of their way to help and asked nothing in return, but that was about to change for her.

To keep her thoughts from traveling too often, she had found solace in crocheting. Tiffany had shown her the technique, and within days she had become quite good at it.

Her day had gone as planned, and by mid-afternoon she was relaxing in an old green La-Z-Boy rocker recliner, stitching what she hoped would be a scarf.

Brick walked in and said, "Lori, sorry to disturb you, but it's time for you to go to work."

She lowered the needles and leaned back, surprised by what he had just said. "What do you mean?"

"The magistrate called on the radio. It's time for you to earn your keep here."

Lori looked at Tiffany.

"It's in the covenant. All must labor so that all will have their place," Tiffany said, reciting another line from the covenant.

Not liking what she was hearing, she asked again, "What exactly am I going to be doing?"

"I'm not sure, but he'll be here to pick you up in thirty minutes."

"But I, um, I'm not ready," Lori said, jumping up from the recliner and tossing the hook and yarn on the chair.

"Better hurry. You don't want to be late for the magistrate."

Lori rushed to her room.

A loud knock at the front door told Lori the magistrate was

there, but she wasn't ready. She was always someone who liked to look her part, and looking disheveled was not what she had in mind. She heard unintelligible voices in the hallway; this only meant they were now inside waiting for her. Flustered by having to rush, she finally gave in and grunted, "Screw it." She took a scrunchy and pulled her long brown hair through it. "Looks like a ponytail will have to do."

She took one last look in the mirror before she headed out. "Don't be nervous. Just be yourself," she told herself. Having mentally walked through the meeting, she felt prepared. She left her room and walked to the front door.

Tiffany walked up and gave her a hug. "Congratulations, you're officially a part of our community."

Lori returned the hug and held it a second longer than she normally would. She liked Tiffany and had come to regard her as a genuinely sweet and tender young woman.

Brick stood like the towering figure he was in front of the door. He looked down at her and said, "Tiff is right. Congratulations are in order. I'll get Tiff to make something special for dinner to celebrate when you get home."

The word home hit Lori. She hadn't called any place home for a long time. She had thought that the ranch she and Travis had found might be that, but just when she called it that, they no sooner fled. She wasn't quite sure if home was the best description for Brick and Tiffany's house, but she'd keep her opinions to herself. "Thanks, Brick, and thank you, Tiffany. I look forward to anything you make. You're such a wonderful cook."

"My momma taught me everything."

Her hands shaking ever so gently, she turned the doorknob and opened the door. Out in the driveway was a large black SUV. She looked at Brick and Tiffany one more time, the nervousness dripping from her face. “See you later,” she said and marched towards the vehicle.

Martin got out of the front passenger side and opened the rear door.

Lori walked over, greeted him and climbed in. When the door shut, she looked at the person sitting next to her. “Mr. Magistrate, hello.”

“Hi, Lori.”

“This was quite a surprise,” she said with an anxious smile.

“I think I can do one better, Lori. I believe you know the man behind you.”

Lori shifted in her seat and looked. Her eyes bulged when she saw it was Travis. She tried to hide her shock, but somehow the magistrate knew.

“Um, who?” Lori asked, trying to be coy.

The magistrate laughed and said, “Lori, Captain Priddy, it’s fine. Don’t sweat it. I know you two know each other.”

“Magistrate, I think you’re mistaken,” Travis responded.

“Martin, take us to Area 29,” the magistrate ordered.

The SUV backed out of the driveway and sped down the street heading north out of town.

“Please stop playing like you don’t know one another. Captain, I told you I know everything about you because I do. After I cut off your hand, I contacted some sources I have back at the DIA. I asked if they knew a rogue Marine captain. Their answer, yes, a Captain Priddy had escaped, but what made it more exciting was that you had escaped with a woman, a fugitive by the name of Lori Roberts.”

Lori’s instinct to fight was stopped just then when Travis

said, "It was my idea to steal the car. She had nothing to do with it. Please don't hurt her."

Unsure of where the situation was going, Lori put her hands in her jacket pocket and found the cold steel crochet hook. She had taken it just in case she needed a weapon. She gripped it tightly and was ready at any moment to pull it out and plunge it into the magistrate's head.

"No, no, no, you've got me all wrong. Captain Priddy, I know we got off on the wrong foot, with the hand-cutting thing, but had I known who you were, then I wouldn't have done it at all. But like I said, I had to do something or else."

"You cut off his fucking hand!" Lori snapped.

"Aren't you a piss fire?" the magistrate blared.

"You call cutting off his hand getting off on the wrong foot?" Lori bellowed.

"Let me explain, please."

"What's there to explain?" Lori asked, her hand gripping the hook tighter.

"Are you taking us back to the chancellor?" Travis asked.

"Ha, ha, God no."

"Why not?" Lori asked.

"Why would I? You two are my ace in the hole to destroy that homicidal maniac."

Travis and Lori gave each other a confused look.

"I'll explain everything when we get to where we're going."

North Topsail Beach, North Carolina

The burial of Brady's older sister reminded Devin of his cousin and family's burial six weeks ago. Looking back, that moment seemed like a lifetime ago. In fact, many times when he thought back, his life seemed to be chopped up into different lives altogether. As the days turned to weeks and months after the Death arrived, the number of 'lives' seemed to accelerate. He sometimes wondered if this was all a nightmare and one morning he'd wake up in his midtown apartment. He could only hope, but no matter how often he convinced himself that it was all some sick dream, he knew it wasn't. The world was gone, Cassidy was gone, and now for Brady, his big sister was gone.

They had managed to coerce Brady out of the room and down to the front yard, but once he saw the open grave, he screamed and ran back inside. Devin didn't think it was the shock of seeing his sister dead; it was the reality that the last remaining person in his family was gone. The one last person that connected him to the past was no more, and he was alone.

Devin made a note to himself to not let Brady feel that way. As he, Tess and Brianna had done, they pledged themselves to each other and in essence became family, even Brando was part of that pact. The definition of what it meant to be family was different now; it would just take Brady a little longer to understand.

Tess's hair fluttered in the ocean wind as she smoothed out the silty dirt.

Megan and three of the boys walked over and placed

flowers on the freshly dug dirt.

Alex ran up panting, a small cross under his arm. “Here, I found some nails and paint in the garage,” he said, handing it to Tess.

Tess winked at him and said, “That was sweet.” She took it and placed it at the head of the gravesite while Devin hammered it into the ground.

One by one each child left and went back to the house, with Brianna coming last.

Tess, Devin, and Brando remained, all standing over the site as if in a trance.

“When I find the fuckers who did this, I’ll slit them open,” Tess grumbled.

“I’ll be right behind you, if I don’t beat you to it,” Devin said.

“Let’s find the kids so we can get the hell out of here. This place is definitely not my home anymore,” Tess said.

The sound of a truck engine hit their ears.

Acting on pure instinct and adrenaline, they all bolted towards it, but not before grabbing their weapons that had been stacked just a few feet away.

Devin was leading the way, but Tess accelerated past him as if he were standing still.

Her heart was pounding, and the look of revenge was in her eyes. With no concern for her own safety and acting like a crazy person, she bolted onto the street, with her rifle at the ready.

Devin made the street only to see Tess now stopped in the middle of the road, taking a stand against a large Toyota truck.

The doors of the truck opened, and two men stepped

out, both carrying weapons.

Tess didn't ask a question much less say a word; she let go a volley of fire that took both men down to the ground. However, her aim wasn't at their chests or heads but at their legs.

The men hit the ground, wailing and screaming in pain.

Devin watched her with amazement. Every time she acted so decisively, he was in awe and his attraction towards her grew.

She strutted over to the driver, who reached for his pistol.

Again, Tess didn't say a word; she raised the rifle and shot his hand.

The man yelled out in pain.

"Whoa, lady, calm down!" the second man said, his hands up.

Tess walked over to the driver, who was rolling around on the pavement, and put the muzzle of the rifle against his head and finally asked, "Where are the teenagers?"

"What teenagers?" he bellowed.

She pressed the rifle harder against his head and asked, "Where's your boat?"

Devin wasn't sure about this tactic, nor was he sure these men had anything to do with it.

The crack of the rifle had drawn all the children and Brianna out of the house.

Alex came sprinting down and gave Devin the confirmation he needed, "That man there, I know him. He was one of the guys who came before."

"I'll ask you one more time, where is your boat?"

Brando was standing next to the second man, growling,

ready to pounce.

"I don't know what you're talking about," he cried out.

"Wrong answer!" Tess said and pulled the trigger.

The back of the man's head exploded.

Not flinching, she marched towards the other man.

"No, don't. I'll tell you. I'll tell you everything!"

Tess was on a roll.

Devin had seen her act out, but she was a few notches above her old ruthless self. He figured it had to be the murder of Brady's sister, Becky which had sent her over the edge.

The man had told them everything he claimed he knew. He described a situation that sounded like it came from a horror movie. Renfield and his people didn't have a land base of operations but were operating off a container ship. Apparently Renfield was the captain of the ship before the Death. After the Death ravaged the world and killed his family, he took the ship out with what crew he could muster and had now fashioned himself a modern-day pirate. He would sail up and down the Atlantic seaboard, sending his marauding parties into shore. This made for a logical explanation as to why Alex claimed to not see them but every few weeks. The man further explained how Renfield's passion for flamboyance coupled with his insanity had driven him to declare himself the overlord of the coast from Atlantic City to Miami. The man told them that all the teens but one, Becky were still alive the last time he was on board. The teen boys were put to work while the girls had been sold off as sex slaves.

Hearing the sex slave part drove Tess crazy. The moment

after he mentioned it, she reflexively punched him in the face.

It took a lot of Devin's strength to pull her off of the man and to calm her down.

With a detailed explanation of where the kids were, they now needed a plan. This was the hard part and Devin knew it.

By the time they were finished with their interrogation of the man, they secured him to a large heavy workbench in the garage, taped his mouth shut, and closed the door, leaving him to whimper and bleed through the night.

Following a few steps behind, Devin called out to Tess, "Let's discuss a strategy."

"We will. I'm hungry; let's get a bite first," Tess replied and went into the house.

All eyes were on her when she walked in. The children other than Alex had never seen the Tess who showed herself today, and it scared them.

Tess noticed the stares but chose to ignore them. She walked into the kitchen and grabbed a liter bottle of water and a can of Chef Boyardee. Like a zombie she sauntered over to the couch and sat next to Meagan. She reached out, touched her leg and asked, "Hey, Megs, how's Melody?"

Meagan recoiled from her touch. "Fine."

Again noticing the stares and Meagan's negative response to her, she said, "I'm not a crazy person. I did what I had to do so I can get the teens back."

"And we are thankful," Alex said.

The other kids kept staring.

"Brianna, you've had an opinion on a lot lately. Anything from you?" Tess asked, her intention was only to spark a debate.

"I'm good, but I will say, that was some crazy stuff."

Tess peeled back the lid and dipped a spoon into the can.

"You cease to surprise me. I had my doubts at first but well done," Devin said.

"Glad you approve," she said sarcastically.

"So tomorrow, we'll have him take us to the boat. If our luck holds out, the other boat will be there," Devin said.

"Getting the boats is the easy part. It's how do we get on the ship full of fifty crazy men without getting shot up before we take our first step onto the deck?" Tess asked.

"That's why we're here discussing," Brianna said.

"People, I'm sorry, but this rescue mission is going to be a fucking bitch, straight up. First thing is we just don't motor up and step on. You heard him, Dev, once they get positive ID, they lower that davit thing and haul the boat out of the water. Say we get on without anyone noticing, just how are we going to locate and get the kids? I'm sure they're all over that ship, and you heard that douche bag downstairs, the ship is huge. I'm sorry, but one of the reasons I have a fucking attitude right now is because the minute he told me it was a ship, I just about exploded with anger."

Devin grinned, walked over and plopped himself on the couch next to her.

"What's that stupid grin for?" Tess asked.

Devin looked around the candlelit room and said, "I want you all to remember this moment."

"You're such a dork," Tess said, jabbing him with an elbow.

"Okay, here it is. All ships need to refuel, so they must pull into a port somewhere. We find that and make sure we're there when they go to top off."

Tess shoved a spoonful of raviolis in her mouth and

mumbled, "You're a smart dork."

Devin brought his hand to his beard and began to rub. Pride that he had come up with a brilliant solution to their problem filled him.

Tess took another spoonful of raviolis and playfully smeared it on his face.

"What was that?" he asked, shocked and amused.

"Oh, you looked hungry." She laughed.

The kids all laughed loudly seeing Tess and Devin act playful.

He cleaned his face off and said, "Stuff still tastes like dog food with tomato sauce."

"Better eat something. We gotta big day tomorrow," Tess said.

Outside Pine Bluffs

Travis knew exactly where they were when they pulled through the tall chain-link fence gate. It wasn't the signage on the gate that told him; he'd seen enough photos of these types of installations to know. In front of them were two small tan-colored cinder-block buildings with similar colored roofs.

They stepped out and stretched.

Lori looked around; in the far distance was another facility just at the edge of the horizon. She turned and asked, "What is this place?"

"It's a nuke silo," Travis answered.

The magistrate grinned and replied, "Correct. Very good, Captain."

Martin led the way and opened a door to one of the small buildings.

"Right this way," the magistrate said, pointing towards the door.

They all went inside and stopped before walking down from the platform.

Lori looked over the railing. She was amazed at how deep it went.

"Let's not be shy," the magistrate said, passing by them and descending into the building.

Down they went; one concrete step after another took them farther into the earth.

Lori clung to the cold steel railing. She wasn't nervous, just being cautious.

Travis got beside her and whispered, "How ya' been?"

"I should be asking you," Lori replied.

They reached the landing, a large concrete floor platform that sat four stories below the entrance.

The magistrate unlocked a massive blast door and opened it.

Lori was impressed by the size of it. In some ways it reminded her of a bank safe door.

They stepped through into a dimly lit circular shaft that spanned forty feet. The concrete floors had a sealant that shined and reflected the fluorescent tube lights. The shaft had an eight-foot diameter and was nothing more than a large corrugated metal tube.

"Let's see where this goes, shall we?" the magistrate said playfully and began walking.

Lori sniffed and scrunched her face at the smell. "What is that?"

"Dead people," Travis guessed.

"Unfortunately the men who operated this facility didn't make it. We discovered their corpses a few weeks after they had died. We cleaned it up, but the smell still lingers," the magistrate answered.

"I would have thought the U.S. military would have been securing these sites," Travis mentioned.

"The Order is not as sophisticated and organized as you might think."

At the end of the shaft was a large metal door.

The magistrate pulled out another key and unlocked the door. He opened it and waved them through.

Travis stepped into the dark room first; his senses told him the space was open and large. Cool air enveloped him, and by the sound of his footfall he could tell he was standing on a metal grate.

"All in, step further. Don't worry, you won't fall," the magistrate teased.

Lori came in followed by Martin.

"You're one for theatrics, aren't you?" Lori commented.

"Ms. Roberts, I've found that appearances are a big part of life," he replied as he stepped in and closed the door. He reached his right hand out, touched the wall, and found a large light panel. He started clicking.

Each click turned on a panel of lights. As the lights turned on, they began to show what was hidden in the darkness, an intercontinental ballistic missile.

"Oh my God," Lori gasped. She looked over the railing down to the floor. Her eyes then scanned the entire sixty-foot length of the huge white missile. What was missing for her was the black stenciled letters UNITED STATES AIR

FORCE or USA, like she had seen on popular images.

"That's a Minuteman missile, right?" Travis asked.

"A LGM-30 Minuteman III to be exact. It has an operational range of 8,100 miles and is equipped with a W78 thermonuclear warhead," the magistrate said, clearly happy about his possession of the weapon.

"You're scaring me. What exactly are you planning on doing with this?" Lori asked.

"Unfortunately, I can't do much in the way they were meant to be used, but I have some plans for them."

"Them?" Lori asked.

He turned to face her and answered, "Imagine you're standing in the middle of a field surrounded by corn. Well, we're standing in the middle of a field of nuclear missiles. This is one of over forty we've found unmanned."

"What?" Lori asked, her mouth wide open in shock.

"Like I said, the Order isn't as organized as you might have imagined."

"But what are you planning on doing with these weapons?" Travis asked.

"That's where you and your friend here will help. Come with me," the magistrate answered and left the silo.

They walked to a small break room and took a seat at a table. From the looks of it, they had been there more than once.

"Take a seat and I'll tell you exactly what is happening. What you thought you knew is only the half of it."

Lori and Travis took seats in the plastic chairs. Martin came in last and closed the door; he then sat at the head of the long table.

The magistrate began to pace the room for a moment,

then said, "Years ago I was a member of the Order. I believed in making our planet a better place, but when the plan to create the Death was passed, that was it for me. I protested, but a man whom you know as Chancellor Horton had me removed. I knew their plans were to kill me, so I fled. I went into hiding, off gird and as far away as I possibly could."

"Wait a minute. I was with the chancellor, and I saw these tablets with inscriptions. The Order clearly stated their intentions. You're not that old."

"I'm a bit older than you think I am, but yes, I'm aware of the so-called Georgia Guidestones. When they were made, I was not yet a part of the Order, but my father was. I was only a young boy when they were erected. I looked at those as more hyperbole than a realistic plan for a new world. When I came of age, my father had me initiated into the Order, and he went into retirement and died not long after. Only once I was working with them did I learn the truth behind what their plans were. I was horrified, and not long after I complained to Horton, I was expelled. I knew my life would be in danger, so I took off. Pretty much end of story with my involvement with them, but it was the beginning of the resistance for me. I knew they'd achieve their plan; it was only a matter of time. They had large sums of money, in the trillions, and effectively kept their plans hidden by buying politicians, planting people in places of power around the world, and destroying anyone who got wind of their plans. You want to hear the irony of ironies; Chancellor Horton was the director of the CDC before the Death broke out. He used his position to ensure the virus spread and was the man who personally killed the president and vice president."

"How can you resist them? They control what is left of

the armed forces," Travis said.

"Ha, that's where you're not entirely up to speed, Captain. There's no shortage of commanders that are in doubt and outright against what is happening. However, my sources tell me the chancellor is aware of these disgruntled officers and plans to move quickly to remove them. But this is not the worst of what I have to share. A deep source has told me that the chancellor is working on another virus, something more lethal and efficient than the Death. I don't know why he wants this, but I can only assume to kill off more people, even those of us that are immune."

Hearing this, Lori sank into her chair in despair.

The magistrate continued, "We have to stop him."

"The nukes, you're going to use the nukes!" Travis exclaimed.

"Yes, but not how you think I am. I don't plan on some sort of massive strike. Hell, I couldn't do one even if I wanted to, but the idea to use them is only part of the plan, and the other part is where I need you, Mrs. Roberts."

Lori perked up hearing this and sat straighter in her chair. "Me?"

"Once I found out who you were to the chancellor, I knew you were the piece to the puzzle I had been seeking. Do you want your baby to live past birth?" the magistrate asked.

"How do you know I'm pregnant?"

"Can the both of you stop asking me how I know things and just figure I know everything. Why is it people never take you at your word?" the magistrate asked rhetorically.

"You have a vaccine?" Lori asked.

The magistrate looked at Martin, then back to Lori. "Yes, I have a supply of it."

Travis chirped up, "I guess I'm immune."

"Don't be so sure, but you're fine now. The moment I found out who you were I had one of my people give you the R-59."

"You did?"

"Yes, I knew the military assets were only being given the old temporary shots with monthly boosters. I found out you'd fled around the time you'd need your monthly, so I gave you the R-59."

"That's what those shots were?" Travis asked.

"One was, the other was an antibiotic. I didn't want the arm to get infected."

Travis rubbed his stub and felt lucky in some ways that he was now vaccinated against the Death. It had been in the back of his mind whether he was truly immune. As the days had ticked down, he stressed, and when he went past, he breathed a sigh of relief and counted himself lucky, but now he knew the truth.

"I think that's twice I saved your life," the magistrate said.

Travis gave the magistrate a glare but declined to comment.

"You mentioned Chancellor Horton was doing something else," Lori said.

"Yes, let's get back on track. Chancellor Horton was given a directive by the Order to expand the cleansing. He has implemented that plan and is killing millions more people. The wholesale slaughter of civilians is underway across the continent."

"This is what I was telling you I overheard," Lori blurted out to Travis.

Travis nodded and said, "I just can't believe Marines much less soldiers or other military officers would carry out such plans."

"Believe it. Because they are, and if anyone refuses to help, they get eliminated immediately. Also, the threat of not giving them their monthly booster is hung over their heads. I know you like to think that all military people are honorable to the last man or woman, but some aren't. It's a hard lesson."

Travis grimaced.

"But let me get back on track. Besides everything else that is happening, the chancellor wishes to take total control, and in order to do that he has to kill off the Order. This new virus is incredibly deadlier than the Death, and we have to stop it. If we want a world for that baby to be born in where they have a chance at surviving, I need you two to help me."

Lori's earlier despair over the news shook her, but now she felt a fighting spirit. She had control over this, unlike when the Death was released. She didn't know if she trusted the magistrate completely, but what were her options right now? She could sit and wait for it to happen, or sit and wait to die at the hands of someone. Regardless, she had to do something, and if this was how she and her baby would die, then she had to do it. Sitting straighter in her chair, she said, "I'm in."

"You haven't heard what he wants you to do," Travis shot back at her.

"Does it matter?" Lori asked.

"She's right," the magistrate said, looking smug.

Travis thought, and Lori was right, did it matter? If everything the magistrate said was true, they would die soon. If you had to die, why not die trying to save the world. How crazy, he thought, did that sound? How strange was it that he could be instrumental in saving the world from further catastrophe? He looked at Lori, who sat pensively waiting for him to answer, and then to the magistrate, who stood with his arms crossed, looking for an answer. "I'm going with her," Travis insisted.

"Captain, I need you for something else."

"No, I need to go with her, to protect her."

"Captain, I appreciate your valor, but it will be in vain. The first step you make in there, you'll be taken down and ushered off to your death. I need you for something else. I need those skills as a battlefield commander."

"The chancellor might kill her. I don't know," Travis protested.

Lori raised her hand to silence Travis. "It's fine. What am I doing?"

"No, Lori, you don't know what the chancellor will do," Travis said.

"The magistrate is right. You won't last a second. I'll be fine, trust me."

"I like hearing how right I am so often," the magistrate commented.

"I can't let her go by herself," Travis said, still pressing the issue.

"Travis, you need to listen to him but, more importantly, to me. I don't want you there," Lori said.

This coming from her hit him hard. He recoiled and fell back in his chair, frustrated.

The magistrate unbuttoned the top breast pocket of his flannel shirt and pulled out a small vial. He placed it on a piece of paper and slid it over for Lori to examine. "This is what you'll be taking with you."

She leaned in to look at it. The vial was the size of a cigarette filter and contained a white powder. "What is it?"

"That, my dear, came at a high price, but as soon as I knew who you were, I knew there was only one way for you to get the chancellor. A gun is too crude, but let's be honest, he'll never let you within a mile of him if you had a weapon of any kind."

"Poison, I assume?" she asked.

"Yes, but something very special. It's polonium-210. It's very rare but extremely lethal. It's guaranteed to kill, no ifs, ands or buts."

"How do I give it to him?" she asked.

"Slip it into a drink or mix it with food. Whatever you do, don't drink or eat after him."

"How soon will it kill him?" Lori asked.

"This amount, just a day or two. His death will be agonizing and painful. It will come on like he has the flu, so they'll probably think he has some type of virus like the Death. I'm betting they'll quarantine him, and by then, he'll be dead. Upon his death, things will go crazy there. That's when my sources will come to the surface and extract you out of there, which is also when Mr. Martin here will deliver a nuclear device."

"What am I doing?" Travis asked.

"Captain, you'll be leading a force of Scraps in an assault from the west. We've been sending small unit-sized forces into Denver for weeks now so as not to draw attention. By our counts we have about five thousand men and women ready to fight."

"Wait a minute, the Scraps, you lead those people?" Lori asked, now suspicious.

"Yes, they're good people who want their country back like you and I do," the magistrate said.

"They attacked me and my colleagues and killed one of them."

"Martin is better suited to talk about the Scraps. He's one of their leaders," the magistrate said.

"Lori, we don't kill people unless we have to. We'd rather convert people to our cause."

"Why attack us?" she declared.

"You only just arrived and you're judging us. Have we hanged people? Yes, but we don't want to. We have a system that people have chosen to live by. You don't like it, leave, we say to anyone who comes, otherwise live by the covenant. It has restored order for us. The Scraps are good people; that name was given to those fighters by the chancellor. Like the magistrate said, they are men and women like you who want to stop what's happening to them and restore what they had," Martin said.

Lori stewed on what he said.

"I understand having allegiances with groups or people that aren't the best in order to achieve what you want," Travis added.

"You're wrong. This isn't a compromise; these are good people," Martin challenged.

"They killed an innocent and defenseless woman, I saw it," Lori countered.

"What was her name?" the magistrate asked.

"Margaret, I believe, but she went by Maggie. She was in her fifties—"

"And from California, right?" the magistrate said, cutting her off.

"How…"

"Once again with the *how*. She lives with us now. In fact, she helped design and work on some of our greenhouses. You see, Lori, we didn't kill her, we liberated her," the magistrate said. He had stopped pacing and placed his hands on the table and leaned in.

"When do you want to start this operation?" Travis asked.

"Two weeks ago, that's how far behind I think we are," Martin answered.

"He's right. We need to move fast," the magistrate added.

Having moved past her concerns about the Scraps, she decided to get details on her participation. "Can I handle this stuff?" she asked, referencing the polonium-210.

"Yes, it's harmless like it is, but if ingested, you've got a problem."

She picked up the small vial but fumbled it. Her eyes widened when she heard it hit the table. Nervous, she leaned away from it. After a moment she leaned back in to examine it and saw the vial was intact and not cracked or broken.

"Be careful with that stuff. I meant it when I said it was hard to come by. I had a team of people extract it from Fort Carson Nuclear Power Plant. It's very rare. That's all I have."

"When do I leave?" Lori asked.

"Right after this meeting," the magistrate said, then looked at Martin and nodded.

Martin stood and left.

"He's getting you a vehicle, a map, and a weapon, and we'll provide a chase car till just outside the first checkpoint. From there you'll go by yourself. Your cover story should be easy; you're coming back for your baby. You will plead, beg, cry, do whatever you need to do to get back in his good graces."

"Why are you so sure he'll take me back?" Lori asked.

"Trust me. He's put a lot on the line to have you and find you. He wants you back."

"What assurances do you have for her safety?" Travis asked.

"Little, this could be a suicide mission, but if it goes like I think it will, we'll extract her."

"Who's the source on the inside?" she asked.

"I can't tell you," the magistrate answered.

"Why not?" she asked.

"If I'm wrong and he suspects something, he's liable to torture you. I can't give you my people's names; it puts them in harm's way."

She nodded; that made sense to her. "Where should I hide this?" she asked.

The magistrate cocked his head, raised his eyebrow, and said, "They're probably going to strip-search you. Where do you think you should hide it?"

"Say no more," she replied.

They finished with some minor details and left the silo. On the surface, they were welcomed by a picture-perfect vanilla sky to the west.

So often in her life before, Lori had taken for granted the natural beauty of the Earth. She, like others now, was starting to notice the small but precious things that life and the world had to offer. She took an extra few seconds to mentally capture the moment before walking to the white sedan they had acquired for her long journey.

The magistrate walked up and said, "I can't thank you

enough for your willingness to do this on such a short time frame. I have to admit I thought it would take days to convince you. I was wrong about you."

"Most people are."

He put his hand out and she took it.

"Be safe. I hope to see you again."

"Me too," she said.

He walked away and Travis came forward. "I can't believe this is happening."

"I have to admit, I wouldn't have been on board with this crazy idea, but when he said something about another virus, I knew he wasn't lying. Chancellor Horton is a maniac and will do anything. He has to be stopped."

"I just wish there was another way."

She touched his arm and asked, "How bad is it?"

"My stock answer usually is, 'I've been through worse.' This time that doesn't work."

"You're a good man, Captain Travis Priddy, you really are. You're strong, sweet and funny. I mean, look at you, making a joke about your amputated hand. Who does that?"

"Come here," he said and drew her in close with a strong embrace.

"I was so scared for you. I wanted to say something. I'm sorry I didn't," she whispered as tears formed in her eyes.

He caressed her hair and whispered back, "You got my message not to say anything."

"So I wasn't seeing things."

"Nope," he replied, embracing her tighter. Her body felt good to him, and for one of the first times he had a strong urge to kiss her.

As if sensing where his intentions might be going, she

pulled away, but not before kissing him on the cheek. She jumped into the car and started it.

He didn't move, he just watched. He wanted to stop her and tell her something deeper, more profound, but he just didn't know what to say.

She gripped the steering wheel tightly, put the car into gear and drove away.

Day 226

May 14, 2021
Ten Miles North of Denver International Airport

Lori didn't feel alone or scared until the chase car left. Having them just behind her gave her a comfort that, while she knew was temporary, was there nonetheless. She got out of the car and watched them leave; they quickly disappeared as the darkness swallowed them.

She leaned back against the cold door of the car and looked up into the brilliant star-studded sky. Her mind quickly raced to that night with Travis a couple weeks ago when they were gazing up at these same stars. She smiled when she thought about how he had traced out the constellations with her finger to better show her where they were. The touch of his strong hand was so gentle. Compared to hers, his was like a giant to a child's. She liked his strong build and solid frame; it was one thing that attracted her to him, but she couldn't deny that his ability to make her feel safe because of his abilities was an attractive trait. However, this was not the look or man she had gone for in the past. David was not that type, nor was the man she had the affair with. Before she went for a man who was, as she put in her own words, 'cerebral'; she ignorantly imagined that men like Travis were too into themselves or ignorant. She sometimes found herself at cocktail or dinner parties ridiculing men such as Travis, specifically demeaning his service to the country as shallow. She now regretted those feelings and didn't recognize the woman she had become. The events that had befallen her over the past seven and half months were so inconceivable that if she could warn herself of the impending doom, she would have laughed herself out of the room or tried to commit herself.

Lori then realized that she was nothing more than a survivor and had been her entire life. It was natural before for her to want a man who could discuss the finer points of string theory or debate the consequences the Compromise of 1850 had on eventually igniting the Civil War. Then she didn't need a man who could physically protect her or had the skills to fight. She had lived in a world and a society where everyone for the most part lived by under and by the rule of law. She had taken for granted the men who were protecting her then, but somehow didn't really understand what they were doing or who they were protecting society from. She had become blinded by the safety net given her, so therefore her innate survival instincts told her it was fine to be with a man for his intellect and his income. Money had replaced muscle, glamour had replaced grit. She was nothing more than surviving in the modern world. She, like many before, had never seen hardship, war, poverty, or crime, so when she would criticize and critique the system, it was from a basis of ignorance. When she really started to process her past life, she came to realize she and many others had a normalcy bias, but the hardest thing for her to accept was that she was the ignorant one.

This epiphany brought David and Eric to the forefront of her mind. She cared for them both, and part of her journey back was to also save them if she could. However, she now could say that she didn't love David anymore. This was tough for her to admit. She did love him but not in a passionate way. She had known this for a long time but fought it to keep her family together.

A meteor suddenly streaked across the sky. She closed her eyes and made a wish that her mission would go exactly as planned, that she'd bring David and Eric to safety, and upon her return she'd tell Travis that she had fallen in love with him.

Large swaths of light splashed across her little car as she crept towards the first checkpoint a few miles outside of the DIA.

Lori could feel her body tense as she made her way into the single-lane channel. The floodlights were glaring and made it difficult for her to see. Her hands began to hurt from how tight her grip was on the steering wheel. She kept repeating, "Please God," like a mantra until she reached the guard shack and was stopped by a uniformed man.

The guard walked over to her window and tapped.

She rolled it down.

He turned on a flashlight and shined it on her face and inside the vehicle. "Where are you going?"

"I'm Lori Roberts; I'm here to turn myself in. I'm a fugitive," she blurted out.

The guard flashed his light in her face and stepped back. "Wait one minute," he said and walked away.

Moments later three other men came. One of them

approached her and asked, "You're who you say?"

She looked at this young man and said, "I'm Lori Roberts. I'm a fugitive. I'm here to turn myself in."

The man took out a square device that had an eye portal at the end and said, "Put your right eye against here."

She leaned over and put her eye on the soft rubber and looked at a small screen inside the device.

He hit a button; a quick flash was emitted towards her eye. He pulled the device back and tapped on an exterior screen. He must have seen something that validated her statements because he handed the device to the man next to him and ordered, "Get out of the car. Hands where I can see them."

"How do I open the door?" she asked.

One of the other guards opened the door.

With her hands up and palms facing them, she stepped out of the car and knelt down immediately.

The first man took her hands in one hand and with the other took out a set of handcuffs. He pulled her arms back and placed the handcuffs on, then stood her up and laid her over the hood of the car. He patted her down thoroughly and professionally. "She's clean. Check the car," he ordered.

The two other men, with flashlights in hand, began to rip the car apart. "Nothing here, sir."

"I'm going to take her back myself," the first guard said and escorted her to a white SUV. He put her in the back and got in the driver's seat.

Everything happened so fast that it almost seemed like a blur.

Just before they were coming to the main gate of the DIA, he slowed down, adjusted the rearview mirror and said,

"Lori, you okay?"

"Huh?"

"Are you okay?"

"Yes, thank you."

"You'll be fine. We've got your back," he said.

His comment surprised her; according to the magistrate, she wouldn't know any of the sources or her allies once there. Apparently, she thought, this man had just broken protocol. However, she didn't play along for fear she'd give something away. "Thank you."

They drove up to the main gate but were waved through.

Once inside the main area on the tarmac, she looked around. It all looked like it had when she had arrived before. Men, women and machines were coming and going; it was always nonstop there.

He took her to the security headquarters, where he transferred custody to another man. This man was wearing the black uniform of the DIA agents, but missing were the flags and patches she had seen before; they were replaced with the strange logo Travis had mentioned.

They sat her in a corner while they discussed what to do with her. Suddenly the phone rang. The agent answered it and quickly hung up. "You two, take her topside."

Two agents grabbed her and took her through the underbelly of the airport until they reached the elevators. They got in and went to the main floor. When the door opened a young, handsome man was standing there, his arms crossed. "I'll take her from here, and please remove the handcuffs," he said.

The two guards followed his instructions and released her to him.

The young man turned around and began to walk away. "Follow me," he ordered.

She did.

As they made turns through the hallways, she began to recognize where she was. Confirmation of where she was going came after the last turn. At the end of the hall stood a single door and two guards.

The man stopped and held his arm out, pointing towards the door farther down. "Please go."

She looked at him sheepishly, yearning to see if he was someone on her side. However, he gave no indication of that.

"Go," he ordered.

She slowly made her way down the hall. The last time she was there she had just murdered a man and was making her escape. Now here she was, voluntarily stepping back into the viper's nest. She prayed that she could fulfill her plan and kill him. She prayed that she'd be able to see Travis again. She reached the door, the guards opened it without question, and she stepped across the threshold into the vestibule.

The guards closed the door behind her.

She wished just then that she could turn and run away again. Her body was shaking uncontrollably. The determination the magistrate had given her was now gone. Horton did more than scare her, he terrified her to a point that no other had ever done before. Resting in him was pure evil, she thought. She knew she had been in the presence of bad people before, but this man was the embodiment of all that was wrong in mankind.

The dead bolt clicked, causing her heart to skip. The doorknob turned, and instinctually she took a half step back. The door began to open but at a torturously slow pace until she saw him.

"Hello, Lori, nice to see you. Would you please come in? We have a lot of catching up to do."

Outside Charleston, South Carolina

After Devin had brought it to her attention that the ship had to come into port now and then, she went to go visit their captive in the garage. As before, he offered up all the information he claimed he knew and promised upon his life that it was true. When he told them Charleston was the port where they were making landfall, she calculated the travel time and set to packing the Humvee so all they had to do was get up and leave.

Tess was an optimist, but she had a streak of reality that coursed through her, and it showed in what she unloaded from the Humvee and how much she did take.

Devin had questioned her about the packing, but she grumbled and he didn't want to waste time or energy arguing with her, especially after her display of anger earlier. Gone was most of the food; she only packed a case of MREs and a variety of different canned foods. She left most of their weapons and ammunition but kept the .50 caliber and all the rounds for it. She hoped that again would be the weapon that could help turn the tide.

The man appeared to be forthright with his information and told them the specific port in Charleston they routinely pulled into. He described in detail the refueling procedures and how many men they could expect to engage. It was the information about manpower that gave Devin a scare. According to their captive, there were fifty men on board the ship, but that number grew when they hit port.

Renfield, while going insane, was still a rational man. The one place he kept a formidable-size group of armed men was at the port.

Their captive told them that the port had over twenty-five men guarding it.

For Devin the mission was starting to sound impossible, but for Tess, any ability to gain access to the ship without sailing out to it was better than that type of plan. She wasn't a foolish person and knew they had a huge disadvantage. However, she had no choice; she had to go get those kids.

Their departure from Topsail Beach was a sad affair. Alex had begged to go, but she refused to allow that. She told him a half-dozen times that his place was there with Brianna protecting the other smaller children.

Melody, who had been suffering from tetanus, had almost recovered to a hundred percent. Her successful recovery gave Tess hope that things were turning in their favor. Tess still remembered little Meagan coming out calling her name. Had she not done that, most or all of these kids would be dead or, worse, in captivity with Renfield.

When Devin pressed her on just how they were going to make the mission a success, she would only answer 'of course we are'.

Just as the sun was rising, she, Devin and their captive set off, heading south along the coast. As always, they prepared for the worst but found the drive uneventful.

Their captive, who Devin finally got to give them his name, was called Morgan, and he claimed to be a native of

Charleston. Neither Tess nor Devin had been there, so this could be beneficial, if he were honest.

They had parked in a residential neighborhood a half mile from the south tip of Wando Welch Terminal, a large container loading and offloading dock. Wando Welch was massive for a city the size of Charleston. It had four container berths, eleven container cranes and over ninety acres of container storage, which now served as Renfield's onshore base of operations. From their position they'd be able to see the ship coming in from the south, and with dozens of small personal boat docks nearby, they could find one to use if need be.

They had arrived in plenty of time, as Morgan said they should expect the ship to be pulling into dock for refueling in the next day or two. He told them that Renfield was returning from pirating up north.

With the Humvee tucked away in a hide position and Morgan tied to a tree, Tess and Devin walked towards Hobcaw Creek, a small inlet off the Wando River.

Tess stopped at the water's edge and looked out, her mind deep in thought.

Devin walked up beside her and said, "So far so good."

"This was the easy part."

Devin saw a flat rock and picked it up. He cleaned off the mud by wiping it on his pants, then ran his thumb over the smooth sides.

Tess exhaled deeply.

Sensing a tension in her, he said, "Whatever happens, we did the right thing, the good thing."

"I know, I just don't know how we're going to get these kids. We're outnumbered a hundred to one."

"We've bested those odds before," Devin said in an attempt to reassure an extremely skeptical Tess.

"I know, but this just feels impossible, and I hate to use that word."

"If it's impossible, then what are we doing?"

"We're doing what must be done."

"But if we die, don't we fail the little ones we left with Brianna. Don't we fail Brianna by leaving her all alone?"

Tess craned her head at Devin and was about to snap but took a second to reflect. "You have a point, but we can't leave these kids in their hands. I couldn't sleep at night knowing we didn't try."

"I agree with you, but we have to look at the real possibility that this just might be impossible, and if it truly is, this is nothing more than a suicide mission and we accomplish nothing."

Tess looked at the rock he was holding and snatched it out of his hands. She ran her fingers over the smooth surface. She recoiled and threw it at an angle in an attempt to skip it across the water; it sank upon first strike.

Devin looked for another rock and found one. He quickly snapped his arm and the rock zinged and skipped five times before disappearing in the dark waters. He bent over and grabbed a few more and handed her one. "Here, this is a good one."

She took it and tried again, but like before, it went right in the water.

"You're doing it wrong; don't throw it that way. It's a sideways snap of the arm like this," he said and tossed another rock that skipped a few times.

She studied his technique.

"Try this one," he said, handing her another.

She tried to duplicate him, but it failed.

"Didn't you ever skip rocks as a kid up in the wilds of the Dakotas?" he asked. "My dad used to take me to Central Park almost every day after school, and we'd skip rocks, run around, play hide and seek, you know, kids' stuff. The best was our rock-skipping competitions. If I bested him, he'd buy me an ice cream cone from this little shop on 88th. They had the best soft serve. I personally loved vanilla. I know that can be kinda bland or boring to some, but theirs was so creamy…"

Frustrated, she turned around and stormed off.

Devin was confused by her reaction, but things were stressful so it could be anything, he thought. He jogged up to her and said, "Hey, what's wrong?"

"Just leave me alone for a bit."

"No, now's not the time to be leaving each other alone. We don't have much time to figure this out."

She stopped and barked, "Just let me be."

"Was it about the rock skipping or are you pissed about something else? If it's about the rescue attempt, then we need to talk because we need to make a plan."

She folded her arms in a defiant manner and held firm.

"You're pissed because I could skip rocks and you couldn't? You're so good at everything and here I go skipping rocks and that pisses you off?"

She lowered her head and confessed, "It's not that but is that."

"What?"

"Maybe I'm beginning to have PTSD or something, but I'm having a hard time coming to grips with everything. I came back to find a message from Travis only to find these children alone, scared and in need; then we find out more have been taken, no doubt tortured and raped. Then back in Reed we tried with all our might to find Daryl's son and we failed—we failed! All we have to show for it are scars and nightmares! This whole fucking world is just fucked up!"

"Like you said, we're the good guys, and we'll do what we can to make things right."

"You mentioned two things over there that really got me here," she said, pointing to her chest. "One was about not trying to save them because if we die, who takes care of the little ones? I want so much to disagree with you, but it makes sense. This just seems so impossible to do, and we'd just be racing towards our death." She stopped talking and began to cry.

For Devin seeing a woman cry was tough for him. His male instinct to protect her kicked in as he stepped into her, and she rested her head on his chest.

"You asked me if I ever skipped rocks as a kid. No, I didn't skip rocks, I sat locked away in a children's home. My real parents didn't want me. The other kids in the home picked on me because I had an ugly tumor on my face. I'd see adults come, and they wouldn't take me, they'd take the mean and horrible kids who picked on me and called me names. For years I sat and watched as a new crop of kids would come, they'd pick on me, and then leave. I grew hard there, I grew resentful of others. I once had a foster home, but those parents were sick. The man touched me. He hurt me. I was only twelve." Tess stopped talking and looked down. Tears fell from her face. She had rattled off in rapid-fire succession this long list of issues from her childhood that Devin never knew and had no experience himself.

He brought her in closer, and she allowed it. Soon they were embracing.

She began to sob heavier now as she just let go. It was hard for her to be vulnerable, especially since she always wanted to portray the strong one. Travis had known about her past, but he had never seen her like this. His only experience of her was the beautiful tough-as-nails woman he had met in high school. Besides the harrowing adventures and the near death situations she and Devin had experienced together, Devin had gotten to see a private and vulnerable side of her that Travis had never seen. This made her feel exceptionally close to Devin, a closeness that surpassed her feelings for Travis.

They lost themselves in each other's arms. It was Morgan's cries that brought them back from the emotional sanctuary they felt in the other's embrace.

"I wonder what he wants," Tess griped.

"Who cares?" Devin replied. He pulled up her head and said, "I'm sorry your childhood was shit. I really am."

"Now I hope you can fully understand my personal connection to all of these kids. I know what it means to be abandoned and not to have family."

"I get it."

"I hope you do, but I also get conflicted like I am now. I can't stand the thought of knowing those older kids are suffering, but leaving the little's all alone frightens me just as much."

Morgan cried out again.

"We should go see what he's whining about," Tess said and stepped away from Devin. She brushed her hair back and wiped her moist cheeks.

"Can I ask one more question?"

"Sure."

"Where was the tumor on your face?"

"You haven't seen the scar right here before?" she asked, pointing to a faint line that ran from the bottom of her right nostril two inches down at a forty-five-degree angle.

"Yeah, I've seen that but didn't think anything of it."

"I had a hemangioma, was born with it. It grew to be about the size of a quarter on my face. It was removed when I was eight years old."

"I think you're beautiful," Devin said.

Hearing him say this made her blush. He'd never been so sweet before.

"I don't know about that."

"Help, hurry!" Morgan cried louder.

"Let's go," Tess said, her tone showed her lack of concern.

They walked over to Morgan, who was tied to a tree, and saw the reason for his cries. A large snake was near his feet.

"Kill it, hurry. It's a cottonmouth."

"Aren't those poisonous?" Devin asked jokingly.

"Yeah, I think so, very poisonous."

"Please!" Morgan pleaded.

The snake inched closer and lifted its head to begin moving up Morgan's leg.

"Are you scared of snakes?" Devin asked Morgan.

"Come on, man, please?"

"Here's what's going to happen. You're going to tell us the best way to get into the shipyard and onto the ship," Tess said.

"Okay, okay, but kill this fucking thing."

"Nope, not till you tell us," Tess pressed.

"Oh, c'mon, that ain't fair."

"Fine, let's go back to scouting. What do you say, Dev?" Tess asked.

"Sure," Devin replied and turned around.

"Stop. Okay, fine," Morgan replied, his dark brown eyes as wide as saucers as sweat was sliding down his face and dripping from his thick bushy brown beard. His greasy dark hair clung partially to his face. He wanted to shake his head to move it, but fear the snake would bite prevented him from moving.

"Jump across the creek there. The south end of the shipyard isn't heavily guarded. There's a roving patrol but no real presence. You can cut through the chain-link fence there. It's easy to hide behind the Conex containers. Oh, man, the snake is getting closer. C'mon, I told you."

"How do we get on the ship? That's where the kids are, right?"

"Um, yes, but whoever owns them might take them off. I don't know if all the kids will be on there."

"Own?" Tess asked.

"Yeah, the girls are traded and purchased. The boys are trained to fight and be part of the crew."

Tess looked at Devin and shook her head.

Devin could see the rage building in her.

"Who owns the girls we're looking for?"

Morgan wouldn't stop looking at the snake; it had slithered over his boot and was lying on his right calf.

"I don't know, c'mon, I really don't know. You gotta believe me, there's like a shit load of guys on Renfield's crew. I don't know who has them specifically."

Tess believed him, but she didn't want to stop the snake just yet, as she enjoyed the terror it gave him.

Devin asked, "When they arrive back in port, is there a big party, something that draws everyone?"

"Are you serious?" Tess asked.

"Yes, yes, there is. It's always the first night back in port. There's a huge bonfire, lots of drinking, fucking, crazy shit happens."

"You see, I guess it pays to watch old pirate movies."

"You're such a dork," she joked.

"Hey, pirates always party when they pull into port. At least the ones in the movies do."

The snake edged closer to Morgan's crotch.

"Right now, mister water moccasin is about to bite your junk. This is your chance to tell us anything that's critical. Anything that will help us rescue all those kids," Tess pointedly said.

"I told you. I told you. Please!"

"More details!" Tess stressed.

"You'll never get all the kids. Some of them are just fucking brainwashed now, you know, children soldiers, tough as nails."

"The ship the night of the party, is it heavily guarded?" Devin asked.

"No, no one is on it but maybe a couple kids."

"Where can we find the kids?"

"If they're recent captures, we hold them in the aft berthing, fourth level."

The snake's forked tongue was jetting in and out of its mouth as it now curled up just under his groin.

"Goddamn it, do something!" Morgan screamed.

"Okay," Tess said, then grabbed his legs and closed them around the snake.

"Hey, what are you doing? Stop!" Morgan screamed.

"You told me to do something, and this is what I do to fucking pieces of shit!" she hollered back. With all her strength she squished the snake between his thighs and groin.

The snake reacted by biting him rapidly, one bite after another along his thighs and one last one in his crotch.

Morgan cried out in fear and pain.

Tess stood up quickly as the snake squirmed out. The last thing she wanted to do was get bit.

"Why, why? I told you everything you asked of me," Morgan asked as he began to cry.

"Because you're nothing but a fucking animal and a coward," Tess yelled, then spit at him.

"Tess, enough, he's done," Devin said, taking her arm.

Her eyes were wide and dilated.

He could see the rage of years past coming through them.

"He's subhuman trash and got what was coming to him," Tess proclaimed.

Morgan started sobbing.

She kicked him hard and said, "Stop crying, you fucking baby!"

"That's it. Let's go and let him die in peace," Devin insisted. He took greater hold of her arm and pulled her away.

Once a good distance away he stopped and asked, "Did that feel good? What the hell, Madam Sadistic?"

"As a matter of fact, it did feel good."

He stared at her and didn't know whether to just kiss her then or smack her for killing the one man who could've provided more answers to questions he knew surely would come.

Her chest heaved and she could feel a tingling from the encounter. She pulled her hair back and readjusted her ponytail and straightened out her shirt.

Morgan sobbed and begged for help, but no one was coming, his fate was sealed. A bite from a water moccasin didn't mean death, but without antivenom his chances of survival were not high, and until then he'd experience great pain and suffering. She preferred that for a man such as him who preyed upon the weak and abused the innocent.

"I really do feel better. I think I'm going to go practice skipping rocks. Care to join me?" Tess said and marched back towards the creek, a spring in her step.

Pine Bluffs, Wyoming

Having purpose and a mission gave Travis something to look forward to. His night had been spent lying in bed going over the different scenarios of how it would go down. Many of those had him dying in a fiery nuclear blast, so he would reassess and start over. With Lori gone risking all, he was committed to assuring he would be successful so that she might come home. He found himself feeling guilty as he tossed and turned throughout the night. The more he thought of Lori in a romantic way, the less he thought of Tess. He had thought it but couldn't speak it out loud, but that moment was coming soon. The reality of seeing Tess again was receding as a possibility. He hated thinking that way, but his world was on a path that was impossible to get off of.

To complicate matters for him, when he returned last night, Janine had greeted him happily with a large meal. He was proud of his new responsibility, and she could see it. He told her as much as he thought prudent. It was then that she shared her story and the story of the town. When the lights went out, she came to him in his bedroom. He found her attractive, but with Tess out there and Lori on his mind, he couldn't. This rejection sent her back to her room in tears.

When he had risen for the day, he couldn't find her, and the breakfast he had become accustomed to being ready for him wasn't there. His intention wasn't to hurt her, but he wanted to explain to her that lying with her would do greater harm than not. But the chance of explanation hadn't been given to him, and if it had, he wasn't sure it would have mattered. He had given up trying to explain the actions of women long ago.

He finished brushing his teeth and grinned widely to inspect afterward. Dental care was something that one did not want to overlook, he thought. The alarm sounded on his watch, telling him that it was time to go meet the magistrate and begin the planning for his part in the operation.

When he stepped onto the front porch, he found everything exactly how he had left it. Like Lori's caretakers, Brick and Tiffany, Janine also lived outside the walls. He understood the nostalgia or sentiment they had, but practically it was insane, he thought. Had he been a murderer, he could have killed Janine that night. The magistrate did provide exterior security in the means of patrols, but they were random and had a lot of area to cover.

Janine's explanation went a bit further than Brick's.

Besides not wanting to leave the house they had shared with their loved ones, Janine didn't quite like or trust the townspeople. They had killed her husband and son early after the Death outbreak during a period called the Chaos. She told him their crime was similar to his, but what they didn't have was the magistrate to appeal to or the covenant to call upon. The covenant could be perceived as harsh, but if someone examined it closely, they would find fairness in judgment. Not long after she had lost her family, the magistrate appeared with his small entourage. Their appearance didn't come easy, she explained to Travis. There was resistance, but once those people were subdued, the magistrate took control. He ushered in a new life for all, the mob rule was replaced with the rule of law, and soon after that security and safety became prominent.

Travis took in a deep breath, filling his lungs with the morning's cool air. He trotted over to the SUV they had given him and headed to meet the magistrate and Martin.

"How is your man going to get past the eye scanners?" Travis asked his first question of many.

The magistrate and Martin had given him the orders and the plan of attack. Like Lori's mission, his also had uncontrollable moving parts that if one were out of alignment, the entire operation would fail.

Travis was smart and could adapt to changes in missions, which from his experience happened more often than not. His major obstacle was getting all those forces together and operating in a coordinated manner. He did have his doubts, though, once the military assets at the DIA saw their assault, they'd bring superior firepower to bear.

"You won't have to worry about the scanners. One of our people will be at the first checkpoint. He'll clear Martin and then jump in the vehicle with him," the magistrate answered.

"Do you have any questions that pertain to your mission?" Martin asked.

"You know, I was thinking about this while I lay up till the wee hours. Why is it that Lori has to kill him this way when you've all but assured me that you can deliver the bomb?" Travis asked.

Martin went to answer, but the magistrate cut him off. "We are fully aware of how difficult each operation is and that it may not work. So we want to have redundancies."

"Makes sense, but still it puts her at risk when all you needed to do was take a bomb in," Travis replied.

"Just so you know, the bomb is the one we want most to work. It will destroy everything, especially that new virus. I want to incinerate it along with everyone else there."

"I'm still not getting it; you could have delivered a bomb a while ago, why now?" Travis asked, still not convinced by their answers.

"Captain Priddy, are you up for this mission or not?" Martin asked.

"Hold on there, I just have questions. Do you fault me for that?" Travis countered.

"Captain Priddy is within his rights to ask; he's about to risk his life," the magistrate said.

"Why now? Why use Lori? What's up?" Travis asked, now becoming more suspicious.

The magistrate leaned on the table with a forlorn look on

his face. "Captain, I'll be honest."

"Are you telling me you weren't before?"

"Of course, we were just leaving out a little nugget of info."

Travis adjusted in his chair.

"We would have tried before, but we didn't have a weapon ready to use. In fact, we don't know if the weapon we have assembled will work. It's not as if we can go around and test it. I managed to assemble a team of people months ago, but they just don't know if what they've created will do what we want it to."

"So the nuclear weapon might be a dud?" Travis asked.

"Correct."

"We can't launch anything; we don't have codes. All we've been able to do is take a warhead out of the missile and configure a triggering device. My team thinks they have it, but we won't know for sure until you deliver it."

"There are so many ways for this to go sideways," Travis said.

"We're aware of the risks, but you don't need to be concerned about that end, yours is to lead the Scraps."

"What is his background?" Travis asked, referring to Martin.

"United States Army."

"Why not have him lead the Scraps?" Travis asked.

Martin raised his eyebrows at the question and looked at the magistrate.

"There are several reasons, but you're better equipped to handle the job as an officer," the magistrate answered.

This response rebuffed Martin, who slightly cut his eyes at the magistrate.

"Don't look at me that way. We discussed this," the magistrate said in response to the look he got from Martin.

"Wait a minute. You're the leader of the people, but you're not leading them? What's the rub?" Travis asked, peppering Martin with questions.

"I can answer that. Captain, Mr. Martin here is only an enlisted man; you're an officer."

"Hold on, what did you do in the Army?"

"11 Bravo."

"He's infantry too. What was your rank?"

"Staff sergeant."

"He totally could lead his people."

"Captain Priddy, you don't know some of the sources, and delivering the weapon is paramount over anything else other than Lori's success."

"There's no guarantee the Scraps will listen to me. They don't know me. You expect me to roll in there and take over," Travis protested.

Martin remained quiet as he watched the back and forth.

Travis then decided to put his foot down; he never liked the fact that Lori was there alone. He didn't trust anyone else to rescue her; he wanted that responsibility. "I'm not going to lead the Scraps, he is. I'm going to deliver the weapon, and I'm not budging on this."

Martin shifted even more in his chair.

The magistrate was not one who enjoyed being told how things would be. While he fashioned himself as a fair leader, he preferred being a leader more than being fair. As a test to Travis's resolve, he pressed him, "Not going to happen, Captain."

Now with the ball back in his corner, Travis was

determined to hold firm. One of the several reasons he was a good Marine had to do with his determination. If Lori was to die and he hadn't been there to rescue her, he might as well die himself. "It's that or nothing. You can kill me now."

The tension in the room was high. The magistrate didn't like Travis's take-it-or-leave-it attitude. He looked at his stub and thought that this man in front of him knew how he dealt justice, and if he was asking him to kill him, it wasn't a bluff. Travis might mean it.

The seconds passed like minutes as the two stared each other down.

Travis sat up right and placed his bandaged stub on the table. He placed his right hand on it and started tapping his fingers.

The magistrate remained still; he kept his eyes fixed on Travis.

Martin watched the showdown with excitement; he began to rock in his chair faster in anticipation of who was going to win this game of chicken.

The magistrate broke his stare and quickly stood up. He put on his jacket and said, "It's chilly in here."

Travis knew the comment was more him than the temperature.

"Captain Priddy, I understand your desire to help your friend. She's beautiful, I'll grant you that. I'm not going to sit and argue with you; we're running out of time. My goal was never personal. I wanted to place people where I thought they could do the best for our collective efforts. You can deliver the nuke, and Martin here can go back and lead his people in the assault."

Martin cracked a subtle smile and rubbed his hands

together, but kept quiet. For him the magistrate made his decision and it fell his way, no need to add something that could overturn it.

"Thank you," Travis said.

The magistrate looked at his watch, then back to the two men in the room. He gave a half smile and said, "If you'll excuse me, I have some city matters to attend to."

Travis gazed at Martin, who still sat, his eyes looking at the table. It appeared to Travis he was deep in thought.

The magistrate believed in never allowing disagreements to shatter protocol and manners. He walked over to Travis, his posture was upright and he held his head high. He straightened out his jacket before extending his hand.

Travis stood, looked him in the eyes and shook his hand firmly like his father taught him many years ago.

"Captain Priddy, I want to thank you, I know our relationship started out…difficult, but you've stepped up to the task. Mr. Martin here will get you set up with the vehicle and everything you need. I don't think I'll see you until you return. I wish you Godspeed."

Travis raised his stub. It was becoming almost a showpiece for him now. "I'll raise my hand to that, oh, yeah, you cut it off."

"I like a man with a sense of humor."

"What's the saying? Let's get the show started."

The magistrate nodded and stepped back; he turned to Martin and said, "I'll see you after you set up the captain."

Martin nodded.

The magistrate left the room and closed the door softly.

Martin faced him and let out a huge grin. "I don't think I've ever seen anyone challenge the magistrate before. That was…awesome."

"I have nothing to lose."

"That might be true, but it took balls."

"Or lack of brains."

"Since you're now replacing me, I think I ought to tell you just what you volunteered for," Martin warned.

"I'm sure it won't be easy."

"Leaving the bomb is only part of your job. You have a secondary mission as well."

Travis sat back down and leaned across the table. "I'm all ears."

"We're dropping something there but also picking up a package. That was my mission, and now it's yours," Martin warned.

"What am I picking up?"

"It's not what but a who."

"Go ahead, enough of the drama," Travis sniped.

"In the bowels of the airport is a laboratory. There you'll find a patient you need to bring back. All the info is in a packet I put together for myself, but I'll give it to you."

"A patient? Who is this person that is so important to the magistrate?"

"I don't think it's because of who she was but who she is now. Her name is Cassidy Lange, and she was patient zero."

Denver International Airport

Lori's arrival had not turned into the horror that she imagined it could have. After he allowed her in, he was gracious and polite. He had taken her hand gently and walked her immediately to the couch to sit down. There he acted like the doting spouse or lover and queried about her time away. He had ordered his doctor to come and visit. She declined the medical attention, but he insisted, and there was no way to not have it done. This was his way of having her searched without appearing to be harsh.

The doctor had arrived promptly and performed his examination in the bedroom, to include a vaginal examination; this under the guise of ensuring her pregnancy was progressing. Lori was two steps ahead and had made sure the polonium-210 was tucked away nicely, but uncomfortably. After her medical exam she resumed reacquainting herself with Horton, and while he skillfully played his role, she played hers. He never asked about the night she had escaped. Even when she went to bring it up, he raised his hand and touched her lips softly in a gesture to remain silent. His gentleness would have seemed sincere to anyone but her. She knew the monster that resided behind that handsome face. Knowing everything he did was orchestrated, an act to deceive her, she played along and did exactly what he asked even going as far as sleeping with him. She applauded herself for showing strength during her sexual encounter with him because all she had wanted was to find something heavy and use it to smash in his face. Almost on queue he had fallen asleep afterward, his first snore was her signal to find refuge in the shower.

The hot water felt good on her skin, but no amount of water or soap could clean the grime she felt after having Horton lay with her. She cringed when she recalled each time he touched her. Her skin crawled when the memory of him being inside her came to the front of her mind. Being in the shower did bring back the memories of the first time he took her, but the difference was she refused to allow it to emotionally incapacitate her. She had one chance to finish this monster, so she couldn't allow her emotional side to win out.

Stepping out of the steaming shower, she was surprised to see him standing in the mist.

"You scared me," she said.

"Sorry," he replied. He had walked in there deliberately so as to do just what he did. His sole purpose now was to torture her; what he didn't realize was that she was ready for the mental combat. "I've arranged for a nice dinner tonight. My chef is preparing a beautiful pork loin in a truffle glaze."

"Sounds great."

"Seven tonight, feel free to walk freely. I've let the guards know you're safe to roam."

"Really?"

"Yes, of course. Why would you leave? You just came back."

Sensing a moment to capitalize on, she stepped up to him. Water still dripped from her legs and fell on to his polished leather boots. "I didn't tell you, but thank you for letting me come back with no questions asked." She leaned in and kissed him.

He returned her kiss and said, "You have a good day. We'll discuss everything tonight." He turned and exited, but neglected to close the door. Just outside was one of his guards; he whispered in his ear and gave her a wink.

Before this would have frightened her, but she now felt she had the upper hand. She walked to the door, stuck her head out and said, "I'm such an airhead, have a great day too." She closed and locked the door.

She approached the steamed mirror and with a swipe of the thick towel wiped it clear. She disrobed and looked at her body. Her hand caressed the obvious baby bump that now protruded slightly. "Good morning, baby, how are you?" she softly said. "Momma loves you."

This baby was her world right now, and if she wanted it born into a world where it could have a chance, she had to complete the task ahead.

She leaned closer to the mirror until her face was inches away. "Lori, you can do this. You WILL do this," she said. This was an old mantra she'd use just before she'd have a meeting with clients. Before the outbreak she had taken self-help courses. She attributed the lessons in those classes to her professional success; however she routinely faltered when it came to her personal life. For whatever reason, her personal life was always *complicated*; she often told herself it was the cross she bore.

With her self-improvement incantations complete, she whisked herself from the bathroom to the bedroom and dressed herself. As she put on each article of clothing, she did so with greater care and focus. This too was an old ritual.

Back in the bathroom she finished getting ready for the day. Each time the brush coursed through her hair she pressed down ever so slightly so it would massage her scalp. Taking advantage of the fact she didn't have to hurry, she enjoyed the primping.

As she was putting the brush and detangling spray back in the medicine cabinet, she saw her bottle of red nail polish.

She smiled and picked up the bottle. On the back was the price tag from CVS, which took her back to that day she'd bought it. She was returning home after meeting her lover, the

Denver councilman, for the first time. Needing to pick up her refill of her birth control, she made a quick pit stop. As she stood waiting for the prescription, she saw the cosmetics. Glancing through the various assortments of eyeliner, blush and lipsticks, she had found this bottle. On a whim she picked it up and purchased it. She wasn't one to wear nail polish, but for some unknown reason she felt she needed it. Sitting in the car outside the pharmacy, she applied it. Seeing her nails glistening with the ruby red color made her feel sexy; it was a departure from her stale life with David. Painting her nails was one way she could tell the world she felt sexy again. That affair radically changed her life; its effects still rippled. If she had not made the decision and violated David's trust, he would not have fled the DIA so quickly or may have fought for her to be with him at Camp Sierra. Wanting to mark another pivotal day, she exited the bathroom and walked into the den with its cozy leather chairs.

"This will be perfect," she said, looking at the oversized chair and ottoman. She placed the nail polish down on the table but didn't sit. "A drink sounds good right now," she said out loud.

She walked into his study and went right for the far cabinet. She opened the doors, and there sat Horton's collection of alcohol, all perfectly organized in different-size decanters. She lifted the lid from his favorite whiskey, and in the palm of her other hand was the small vial of polonium-210. She pulled the plug and dumped the entire contents inside. She swished it and replaced the top. She grabbed a glass, then took a bottle of tonic and filled her glass with ice from the small ice freezer.

Turning around, she raised her glass, took a sip and

looked directly at the security camera for a second.

"God, I wish this had vodka in it," she said, and then headed back to the den to apply the nail polish.

Charleston, South Carolina

Tess's brutality towards the two men had made Devin a bit cautious in how he treated her. He wasn't fearful for his own life but wanted to ensure he didn't upset her.

As they were coming back from a patrol of the area, he made only pleasant conversation and agreed to anything she proposed. It did help that she was right a lot, but where he might have had a slight disagreement, he decided to just let it go.

The patrol gave them a good sense of the area. They had also found two small boats that could take them across the creek to the southern perimeter and bring them and the teens back.

They discussed their options and again openly talked about the risk factor. The risk was there for anything they did, but they would make an attempt. However, they did give themselves permission to call the operation off without any judgment.

They drew closer to the Humvee and could hear a slight moan coming from Morgan.

"Sshh, you hear that?" Tess asked and put out her arm to stop Devin.

He cocked his head and pointed his best ear forward.

Another moan came from the other side of the Humvee.

It was definitely Morgan.

"The son of a bitch is still alive," Tess said, a sadistic smile on her face.

"You think that's funny?"

"Kinda."

"Wow, remind me never to piss you off."

"That looks like a good rock," Tess said. She squatted down and picked up a flat smooth gray rock. As her fingers ran over the stone, she imagined skipping it across the creek.

Devin hadn't stopped; he continued on. He cornered the Humvee and jumped back at what he saw. "Oh shit." He raised his rifle, and his right thumb flipped the selector switch.

In front of him were two feral hogs. Blood covered their faces, and they grunted as they devoured parts of a half-conscious Morgan.

Tess jogged up when she saw Devin's reaction.

"Holy fuck!" she exclaimed as she pulled her Glock 17 from her shoulder holster.

"Should we shoot them?" Devin asked.

Tess had heard that pigs and hogs ate people, but to see it was something straight out of a horror movie. "Don't shoot unless they charge us."

"Poor bastard," Devin commented.

"He's had a bad day for sure," Tess said, taking a couple steps back. "Walk back. They're so focused on eating him they don't know we're here."

Devin slowly placed one foot behind the other. Before long he and Tess were on the opposite side of the Humvee.

"Are we just going to let them eat him? The guy's still alive," Devin said.

"He probably doesn't feel anything because of the

multiple snake bites."

"Tess, c'mon, stop the hardcore stuff. That's just screwed up. We need to put the guy out of his misery," Devin implored.

She chewed her lip and rolled her eyes. The idea of allowing him not to suffer ran contradictory to how she felt. For her, Morgan was paying the price for the crimes her foster father had committed against her. While Morgan had pleaded innocence from molesting or raping any of the teens or children, she just didn't believe it. Anyone who ran with such a barbaric group of people was guilty.

"Think of something," Devin said. He kept looking over his shoulder for fear one of the hogs might come looking for dessert and he would be on the menu.

Tess pushed past him and opened the driver's side rear door. She removed the seat bottom and pulled out a long black cylinder approximately six inches in length and an inch and a half in diameter. On one end was a small threaded stub.

Devin had never seen it before and asked, "What's that?"

She placed her Glock in her left hand and stuck the threaded stub into the barrel and turned clockwise.

"I got this Glock from one of those Turner Raiders back in Reed. The silencer here, well, I found that digging through the Hummer one day a couple weeks ago. Now it's coming in handy." She turned it till it stopped, gripped the pistol back in her right hand, and put a foot on the driver's rear tire. With her left hand, she grabbed the long exhaust line that extended up and pulled herself on top of the Humvee.

The hogs were still oblivious.

Carefully she aimed and squeezed off the first shot. The hog to the left let out a grunt and fell to the ground dead. Her sights now turned to the hog on the right. Sight alignment, trigger control and squeeze. Second shot hit the pig in the top of its head; it collapsed in place.

Devin moved around the Humvee and saw the carnage.

Tess leaped like a superhero from the top of the Humvee, pistol still in hand.

Morgan mumbled something neither could understand.

Blood, flesh and guts were everywhere.

To Devin it looked like a slaughterhouse.

Tess leveled the pistol at Morgan's head and squeezed the third and final shot. It hit him in the head.

"There, happy?" Tess asked and walked away.

"It was the decent thing to do," he replied as he followed her back to the driver's side.

A few quick turns and the silencer popped off.

"Nice to know we have one of those," Devin remarked. "It's louder than I thought they'd be."

She finished storing it and said, "I thought the same thing when I first shot it."

"When was that?" he asked.

"Just then."

"I'd say pork was on the menu, but after seeing what's in their diet, I think I'll pass."

She turned around and tossed an MRE at him. "My exact thoughts."

"Never thought one of these would sound more appealing."

"Let's move this. I don't want to be smelling that later," she said, pointing to the other side.

They moved the Humvee closer to the small boat docks about a quarter mile away. The air quality was better but not enough to make up for the loss of concealment.

Tess chuckled every time she watched Devin eat an MRE.

He'd pull each packet from the tan sleeve and arrange it on the ground or table in order of how he'd eat it. On the left the entrée, snack in the middle and dessert on the right. He'd delicately pull the main entrée from the box and knead the package. With steady care he'd take his knife and cut it open horizontally. This way he could eat it easier than the traditional vertical position.

"I think I have an idea of how we can get in and out," Tess said, her eyes still enjoying the MRE show he was starring in.

"And what's the master plan?"

"A diversion, just like Reed."

"I don't know. It might have worked in Reed, but if I have to take on a flash mob of pissed-off pirates, I would say no."

"No one's asking you to."

"I'm all ears," he said, taking a large heaping spoonful of his meal and stuffing it in his mouth.

"Just a few blocks east of the main gate I saw a petrochemical facility. I say we strap on a bit of C-4 and blow it. The explosion should be immense, and there's no doubt they'll have all eyes that way. We'll get to the boats, cruise over, cut our way in and make for the ship, all under the cover of night."

"It's better than what I had in mind."

"Oh yeah, what was that?"

"Trust me, yours is better."

Finished with her entrée, she tossed the packet on the

ground.

"I'm going to be the devil's advocate. Say this all works, we get on the ship with zero issues. How do you want to conduct the search?"

"Easy, find the berthing spaces and state rooms first. If I were a dirty pirate, I'd keep my sex slaves where I sleep."

"I'd imagine the sleeping quarters are all in the same place."

"Probably not, officers will be on the high decks. I'd normally say we split up, but it's not advisable."

"I agree," Devin said, still maintaining his agreeable attitude.

"Score," she cheered, holding up a bag of M&Ms.

"Oh, that, I got one too. Must be the newer cases have them."

Tess tore open the wrapper and poured a few of the multicolored hard-shelled candies in her hand.

"Now I suppose we wait?" Devin asked.

Her mouth full as she chomped away on the candies, she replied, "More time to skip rocks."

Denver International Airport

Lori admired her nails; the bright red color now symbolized hope for her. Not only had she done her fingers but she painted her toes too. As she wiggled them, her memory catapulted her back to a time when she had just met David.

He was bright, enthusiastic but lacked charm. What she liked most about him then was he was stable. Then she believed he would be going places. He had just received his master's degree in American History, but what excited her was that a book he had written on Abraham Lincoln was selling and selling big. She imagined herself a wife of a writer, traveling, cocktail parties and the like. She had only started working in her field, and it was tough. Her creative suggestions weren't getting the traction she had hoped, and dealing with her overbearing boss was painful. A life full of nice things, a big house and expensive car filled her dreams then, so she hitched herself to a man she loved but now realized she wasn't passionate about. When the books sales dropped and his second book flopped, David gave up writing and pursued a career as a teacher. For her she respected it, but it wasn't the glamorous life. By then it was too late to reconsider. They were married, but she was also pregnant with Eric.

Not wanting to sit and ponder the past, she stood and walked over to the row of pictures Horton had on a shelf. These were the same photographs that had piqued her curiosity and skepticism of what was really happening at the DIA and around the country. She picked each framed photo up and studied it. All the photos had one common theme; they showed Horton with the men of the Order. She looked at each man's face in hopes of seeing the magistrate.

The dead bolt on the front door clacked followed by the door opening.

Feeling like a child that has been caught with her hand in the cookie jar, she almost dropped the picture as she placed it back on the shelf. Almost tripping over the coffee table, she plopped down on the couch and picked up the tablet she had been reading a book on.

Horton walked in a moment later.

To her, he looked a bit happier than he had when he left this morning.

Normally he was one who hid his emotions well, but Horton didn't mind letting her see how happy he was. "Good afternoon, evening, whatever it is."

"Hi."

"So what you been up to today?"

"Relaxing, reading and I did my nails," she said, holding out her hand.

"Red, very nice. Say, I've got some guests coming over for dinner in an hour. I'm going to freshen up; you might want to put on something sexier."

"Funny, I don't have anything here that I'd call sexy in the closet."

The doorbell chimed.

"Now you do," he said, a devilish grin on his face. Taking this as his queue, he walked into the bedroom.

Lori made her way to the door, a bit freaked out by how well timed that was. She opened the door, and there was a man she'd never met, holding a dress she'd never seen.

"Here you go, ma'am," the man said, holding out the dress and a small bag.

"What's in there?"

"Lingerie and shoes."

"Thank you," she said and took the items. Holding them as if she was holding a dead mouse, she went to the bedroom to change.

The dress fit perfectly. She hated to admit it, but she liked it.

Standing in front of the long mirror, she turned side to side, admiring how good it looked on her. Running her hands down her hips, she turned around and craned her head back to see her butt. The pink on the soles of the shoes was the thing she loved the most; she didn't want to walk on the hardwood floors for fear of scuffing them up.

"The table is set. Hurry, we have special guests coming," Horton hollered from the hall.

She rushed out of the bedroom. The aroma of the pork loin hit her, causing her mouth to water. In the dining room, the table was set for four. In the corner Horton was standing, a glass of whiskey in his hand. The sight of the glass and its contents excited her. Is he drinking the one I poisoned? she asked herself.

"Our guests should be arriving soon. Let's go into the den and wait for them."

He took her hand and walked her into the den. No sooner had they sat down than they heard a knock on the door.

Horton looked at his watch and said, "Looks like our special guests are early." He jumped up and swaggered to the door.

Lori took the time to look at herself in the hall mirror one last time.

Horton walked back into the den, flanked by the last people she expected to see, David and Eric.

"Lori, our guests have arrived," Horton said and gave her a wink.

Her knees trembled and almost buckled. "David, Eric, it's you. You're here?'

"Mom," Eric sang and ran into her arms.

David approached her too, but allowed Eric to take his time.

She embraced Eric tightly, kissing him on the head and face.

David fidgeted as he waited for his turn to greet his estranged wife.

"Get in here," she said, insisting David just step in and create a circle of love.

Encouraged by her insistence, he stepped forward, arms open, and embraced her.

She cocked her head to kiss him, but he cocked his head, and her lips made contact with his cheek.

"I was very worried about you. So glad you're safe," David said.

"It's so good to see you," she replied. She meant that but wished it wasn't here. Having them here complicated her mission.

Like a voyeur, Horton stood and watched with pleasure the three get reacquainted. "So sweet, I love family reunions."

Lori put her eyes on his and leered.

This look from her gave him greater pleasure, as he had struck first and hard in their battle. "Why don't we all sit and talk at the dinner table. You can catch up there."

With the three sitting and chatting, Horton wheeled in a cart. The clanging glass got everyone's attention.

"Drink anyone?" Horton asked.

"Yes, I'll have one," David said, his eyes fawning over the assortment of decanters.

Lori felt her gut tense when she saw the decanters. Her instinct was to tell David not to drink, but that would seem alarming. The last thing she wanted was to draw attention that something might be wrong with the alcohol. So she chose to steer David. "Go ahead. I'd suggest the vodka. It's good, and I know you love vodka martinis."

David raised his head, intrigued to try the vodka. Also the suggestion of a martini sounded so good to him. "Lori knows me like no one else. I'll have a vodka martini with olives, if you have any."

"We do have olives, but are you a whiskey man at all?" Horton asked.

"Years ago, but I prefer vodka."

Lori put her hand on David's and said, "Ole reliable."

Those were the opposite words David needed to hear. He found them disrespectful and degrading coming from her. For him it was like her again telling him he was boring, and that word had come up when he first confronted her about the affair years ago. "You know, I do like to step out of the box now and then."

"I like a man who lives a little," Horton said. He grasped the decanter of whiskey and held it up. "This is one of my favorites, and I'm sure you'll enjoy it too. I prefer to drink it over a handful of ice."

The sight of the poisoned bottle of whiskey almost sent Lori into a full-fledged panic. Her heart was pounding, and she searched for a way to prevent David from drinking it. "David, I've had it; it's just okay. I'd really suggest the vodka."

"No, I think I'll go with the whiskey. Sometimes I don't want to be 'ole reliable'."

Hearing the words come back at her made her cringe.

Horton poured a glass and handed it to David. He looked at Eric and asked, "How about Eric? You want a taste?"

"Absolutely not, he's just a boy," Lori exclaimed.

"Oh, come on, I'm a man in this world," Eric protested, sitting straighter in his chair.

"Last I checked, you weren't even old enough to vote," Lori countered.

"Vote and old enough sound like constructs of the past. Let the young man have a man's drink," Horton said.

"Yeah, Eric is a man in my eyes. Plus we're not going to get drunk here, just enjoy a cocktail," David said.

Feeling outnumbered but undeterred, she continued to resist Eric having a drink. She didn't want David to drink, but how could she really stop him. Eric, on the other hand, she had a say in his upbringing. "I insist, Eric will not be drinking."

"This is stupid; I'm no longer a kid. If you were ever around, you'd see that!" Eric said, his face flush with anger.

"I'm still your mother, and I say no."

"Mother, ha. Some mother you are," Eric blasted her.

Lori dug her nails into her right thigh. Her mouth opened, but nothing came out. She fought the urge to smack him in the mouth and send him to his room.

David watched the dustup and didn't get involved. He wanted her to hear how Eric felt about her. Deep down he wanted her to feel the pain he felt; he wanted her to know what it was like to know someone you love has pulled away from you.

"Chancellor, if I can have a little, that would be nice," Eric said boldly in an attempt to be manly.

Lori just shut down and didn't know what to do; then a drastic idea came to mind. She stopped digging in her leg and placed her right hand on the steak knife. Her fingers folded around the handle and she held it firmly. If she had to die saving her son, then so be it. Frozen in place as she convinced herself that killing Horton now was the only way, a warm hand touched hers.

Horton bent over and whispered, "This isn't the whiskey you think it is."

The blood drained out of her face.

He patted her hand and said for all to hear, "You know, this knife looks dirty. Let me get you a new one." He unrolled her closed fist and removed the blade.

David and Eric weren't paying much attention as they chitchatted about the whiskey.

Lori barely ate her salad, using her fork more for pushing around the food than eating it.

David and Eric gushed about each bite.

Eric had even taken a second drink, and its effects were starting to show as he became more vocal with an occasional word slurred.

The chef appeared from the kitchen with four plates. Around the table he went placing them, starting with Lori.

She looked at the plate, and the food looked amazing. Several slices of loin lay perfectly presented in the center with roasted Brussel sprouts at the top of the plate and a creamy polenta at the bottom. Her appetite was still absent following Horton's admission that he was aware of her poisoning the whiskey.

"Bon appétit, everyone," Horton said.

"Oh my God, this is amazing," David raved as he took his knife, sliced another piece of loin and dipped it into the thick sauce that accompanied it.

"This is so good," Eric added.

"I'm so glad you're enjoying it. As Lori knows, my chef is one of the best," Horton bragged.

"Is that so?" David smirked with his mouth full, looking at Lori.

Lori had tried to eat but found it impossible. Her appetite was completely gone. She caught David's hateful gaze but ignored it.

The dinner finished with shallow but pleasant conversation between Horton, David and Eric. Lori stayed quiet except for the few times she acknowledged a question, and then it was just a yes or no answer.

A range of emotions ran through her as she watched her husband and son. They seemed like strangers in some ways. A distance she hadn't felt before was between them, and she hated it.

The chef appeared one more time but now presented a cake. The three-tiered cake was covered in a thick chocolate frosting, and on the very top written in icing was 'Welcome Home, Lori'.

Seeing the cake and inscription, Lori clenched her jaw.

"Who wants a piece of cake?" Horton asked.

"I do, I do!" Eric said, sounding like a kid.

"Why not? It looks delicious," David said.

Lori sat speechless, and when Horton insisted, she shook her head.

"Very well, two slices of cake," Horton said and nodded to the chef, who promptly cut the cake and laid it on small plates in front of David and Eric.

Like the dinner, Lori remained quiet while David, Eric and Horton chatted.

For Lori, the time seemed to drag on forever. With the attempt to poison him gone, she needed to find a way to do it but how and when. His suspicions were raised now that he knew she had made an attempt.

David patted his belly and leaned back against the tall dining chair. "That was so good. What was the sauce on the pork?"

"It was a truffle reduction sauce, but I had the chef add a surprise ingredient tonight courtesy of Lori."

"What was it?" David asked.

Lori looked at David, and then pivoted towards Horton, her brow curled and skin ashen.

Horton looked at Lori and said, "Please, Lori, share with us all, what was the special ingredient?"

She didn't need to ask him what he was referring to, she knew. Her body grew rigid, and tears began to stream down her face.

Horton abruptly stood and signaled to a camera in the corner.

A half-dozen armed guards burst through the front door and ran into the dining room.

David and Eric looked all around, confused by what was happening. David looked at Lori and asked, "What did you do?"

Horton loved these types of moments; he had always enjoyed the big reveals. So often the things he and the Order had done went without anyone's knowledge, and he disliked that. He knew why he enjoyed these reveals, it was because he loved to show off just how smart or cunning he was. He walked around the table once and took his place at the head of the table before speaking. "I had the best time tonight.

Getting to know you and your wonderfully bright son was a treat," he said to David. "However, in all things there is so often collateral damage that is done. One cannot build a new world without destroying the old, and one cannot have a new relationship without one ending."

"Chancellor, you're scaring us. You're scaring my son," David said, his arm outstretched across Eric's torso.

"Mr. Roberts, you and your son have been nothing but pawns on my chessboard. I brought you here so I could keep you close so that when Lori returned, she could watch what remains of her family die."

Lori had heard enough. She pounced from the table and lunged at Horton with a fork in her hand.

Two guards grabbed her quickly and forced her back in her seat.

"Damn you, Goddamn you!" she screamed.

Horton laughed and continued, "Earlier today, Lori put poison in this decanter." He pulled an empty decanter from the tray and placed it on the table. "I don't know what it was, but I figured it would be fun to see just what it did, hence our little dinner party tonight."

"Damn you to hell!" Lori screamed.

"That wonderful loin had a truffle and whiskey reduction sauce, and dessert looked magnificent. That was a whiskey-infused chocolate cake."

"What have you done?" David asked, first looking at Horton then to Lori.

"All I did was give you the poison that your lovely wife gave me. If there's an antidote, you look to her for that," Horton explained.

"Lori, what was it?" David asked.

"I'm so sorry. Believe me, I'm so sorry," she cried, tears freely flowing from her eyes.

"Lori, what was the poison?" David asked, his face gripped with fear.

Eric bent over and began to puke.

Horton looked repulsed when Eric began to throw up. He turned to one of his men and ordered, "Get them out of here; send them to the lab. Tell Doctor Mueller to monitor them."

Four guards grabbed them and pulled them forcibly out of their chairs.

Lori struggled to free herself, but it was futile, the two men easily overpowered her.

"Don't hurt them, please; I'll do whatever you want!" Lori pleaded.

"I'm not hurting them, Lori, you are. I only used the whiskey you poisoned in our meal. Now if you have an antidote, then I'll let you give it to them."

"I don't have anything, I don't know if there's an antidote or not," she answered, her eyes begging for mercy.

David and Eric cried out as they were rushed off towards their fate.

Horton walked over to Lori and looked down. "What exactly did you put in the whiskey?"

"I can't remember exactly, polonium something."

"Hmm, polonium, never heard of it," Horton snapped.

"Please, I'll do anything, anything at all, just try to help them."

He leaned over till he was just a few inches from her face and said, "You had your chance to live in the new world but gave it all away. You think I want you back? I only wanted you back to punish you. Guards, take her away."

"Where to?" one guard asked.

"To the lab with her family, let her witness what her actions have caused."

The guards hauled her up by her arms and dragged her away.

Horton sauntered from the dining room into his office and picked up the phone. It rang several times until someone answered it.

"Doctor Mueller here."

"Doctor, Chancellor Horton. I have some new test subjects coming your way. The man and boy have been poisoned with polonium; put them in a space together. I also have a woman coming down too. Sedate her, then—"

Mueller interrupted him and asked, "Where did you get the polonium-210? That is extremely rare."

"Never mind that, let's get back to the woman. Listen carefully; I need you to do exactly as I say."

Pine Bluffs, Wyoming

The magistrate hit the red button on the satellite phone handset and placed it on his desk. He chewed on his lip and leaned back in the thick leather office chair and began to rock. The call had come from a source inside the DIA, and the report was not what he had wanted to hear.

He picked up the phone again and touched a couple keys but stopped short of pressing the green call button. His eyes rolled in his head as he pondered whether he should make the call or not. The other parts of his plan were in motion. It had taken him a long time to get to this point, but if Lori had been found out, then the plan might not come together at all. He had to assume he had been compromised and the other parts would also fall apart as well. His thumb still hovered over the green call button. If he hit the button, he'd call off the operation and order his forces to fall back to a predetermined rally point and regroup. They knew her part of the operation could be a failure, so they had made a contingency just in case. However, he didn't want to stop it, the wheels were in motion and they could still be successful. He pressed the green button, and the phone clicked then began to ring.

"Martin here."

"This is the magistrate. What's your location?"

"An hour outside of the drop-off for Captain Priddy."

"How long before you're in place?"

"Three hours. Have we gotten word from Ms. Roberts?"

The magistrate paused. His natural desire was to tell him the truth, but to do so would force him to question the operation's success. He needed Martin and Travis still moving towards their objectives, but he didn't want to sacrifice his Scraps. They were good people and he needed them.

"We haven't gotten word from her, but a source there has told me she failed. I need you to contact your second in command in Denver. Tell everyone to fall back to their secondary rendezvous points and wait further instructions."

"Roger that," Martin said. "I'll contact Captain Priddy and have him wave off too."

"No, he needs to proceed."

"But, sir, that was not part of our contingency."

"The bomb needs to go forward. We always talked about

doing this, so let's do it."

Martin was silent as he contemplated this shift in the plan.

"Are you there?" the magistrate asked.

"I'm here, sir. I'll contact my people, but I'm requesting I go forward with Captain Priddy."

"No, I can't lose you now."

"If you want this to happen, then me going with him helps ensure that. Remember, he only has one hand."

The magistrate gripped the phone tighter, he hated to be questioned, but Martin was right and he couldn't argue with him. "Go with him. Priority is to plant the bomb, secondary is getting patient zero and third is reclaiming Ms. Roberts. Keep Captain Priddy under control and focused on the priorities."

"I'll try, sir, but I can't guarantee I'll be successful."

"And you know what to do if you get caught?"

"Yes, sir, I realize what I'm risking here."

"Very well, good luck. We're going to evacuate the town and move towards our secondary location. I hope to see you there soon."

"Take care, sir," Martin said and hung up.

The magistrate put the satellite phone down and stood up. He walked around his large desk and exited his office. In a small waiting room just outside, his aide was busy writing. "Get in touch with Carolyn and Franklin. Order an evac. We're falling back to our secondary. This is a priority evac; we leave in an hour."

Hour North of Denver International Airport

Travis took the helmet from inside the Humvee and began to slam it against the hood violently.

Martin had asked once for him to stop but soon realized he needed to vent. Knowing he cared for her made him resist pressing the issue.

One hard slam after another Travis brought the helmet down until he heard the fiberglass hood crack and splinter. He inspected the damage but still hadn't exhausted his fury and hit the hood three more times before stopping.

"Can we get down the road now?" Martin asked.

Travis walked back and forth the length of the Humvee. He stopped when he caught a glimpse of himself reflected in the rear driver's side window. He looked at himself sporting the green camouflage uniform of the Marine Corps but with a different name tab sewn above the angled top right pocket. Disgusted by himself and everything, he took the helmet and slammed it into the window. The impact from his Kevlar helmet did nothing to the inches-thick ballistic glass. Angry that his attempt failed to break it, he swung his arm back to hit it again.

Martin had seen enough. He grabbed his arm and said, "Enough. Take your anger out on our mutual enemy not our vehicle."

Travis pulled his arm away and said, "Get off of me."

"Listen, we don't have time for this bullshit. Let's ride."

Looking at the helmet in his hand, he thought about what Martin just said. His anger was piqued, and all he wanted to do was smash things.

"It's just you and me. Now go jump in the passenger side. I'm driving us in."

Travis brought his gaze back up and said, "Okay."

Martin walked around him and got behind the wheel. As he closed the door, he heard a loud impact. He turned around and saw that Travis had hit the window again.

"Sorry, couldn't resist."

"Get your ass in the vehicle; we got a job to do."

The remaining forty-five minutes it took to get to the first checkpoint was filled with rehearsing just exactly what they were going to do.

After much discussion, it was decided that after the bomb was set in place they split up. Martin argued that doing so jeopardized the second part, but there was no convincing Travis. He was dead set on finding Lori even though he didn't know where she was. His first assumption was the brig, and that would be guarded heavily; just how he'd get in and get her, well, he thought he'd just have to play it by ear.

While Travis was doing that, Martin would be attempting to recover patient zero.

When the first checkpoint came into view, both men sat up straighter and tried to look the part. They zigzagged through the S curve of jersey walls and sandbags until they stopped at the fortified guard station.

Martin looked for their man but didn't see him. "Shit, where is he?"

"This is going to be fun," Travis smirked, pulling out his pistol and resting it between his legs.

A black uniformed guard walked up and said, "Who are

you, and what's your business here?"

Looking around, Travis could see the military was not manning the checkpoint like they had when he had been there. Now DHS agents were all they saw milling around. This development must have just happened, or their source's intelligence was horribly wrong.

"We're coming in from Camp 19; I'm transporting Captain Miller here. He has orders to be the new supply commanding officer at the DIA," Martin said.

The guard looked at Martin clad in his army uniform and then cocked his head and examined Travis. "Do you have paperwork?"

Travis buried the pistol in his lap, opened his right cargo pocket and removed a set of papers. He handed the folded stack across the wide console to the guard's waiting hands.

The expressionless guard flipped through the paperwork, then raised his eyebrow; he looked back in and said, "Looks good."

For an instant both Travis and Martin felt at ease, but the guard's next request shattered that.

"Hold here for positive ID. I'll get the scanner." The guard walked away, chatted with another guard and disappeared into the small structure.

"I'm not going to pass the retinal scan; you do know that?" Travis commented with his jaw clenched.

"I'm not either," Martin said, looking at Travis, a dour look on his face. He unsnapped his shoulder holster and pulled out his H&K pistol. "Not what I imagined would happen, but if we're going to have to fight our way out of this, let's not screw around."

Several men exited the shack and walked over. One was

wearing a military uniform.

"That's our guy, right there, that's him," Martin said, a tone of excitement in his voice.

The military-uniformed man walked up with a small black box and said, "Good evening, gentlemen, I'm Staff Sergeant Gomez. Sorry to keep you waiting. Let's get you to ID yourselves here." Staff Sergeant Gomez, a large man with broad shoulders, handed the scanner to Martin.

Martin obliged, and after a second of looking into the eyepiece, a loud beep sounded.

"Looks good, Staff Sergeant Smith, thank you. Please hand the scanner to the captain."

Martin did as he said when another man walked up. He was wearing black fatigues and had a pissed-off look on his face. "Staff Sergeant Gomez, you know we're under a lockdown. Orders are to not allow anyone in till further notice."

"But this man is supposed to report to supply."

"Supply? You think supply is critical?" the man barked.

"Not sure who you are, but I was requested specifically by the chancellor himself. I'm here to help with logistics for the lab."

The black-fatigued man peered in and grimaced at Travis. "I don't care where you're going. We're under strict orders; no one is allowed in."

"How about I escort them in?" Gomez said.

The man looked at Gomez and said, "No."

"Can I make a call to my commanding officer?" Travis blurted out. He was now just winging it.

The man answered him with disdain, "We can do that. Pull over there and park; stay in your vehicle."

Martin looked at Travis with a concerned look. He wanted some sort of direction.

"How many have you counted?" Travis asked.

Martin looked and said, "Upon approach, about a dozen."

Gomez pointed to a small gravel space a dozen feet just past the shack for them to park.

Slowly Martin pulled the vehicle there and stopped.

"I tried," Gomez said, looking inside at Martin and Travis.

"Hi, I'm Martin, and this is—"

"Captain Priddy, I know. You're a wanted man," Gomez said.

"Any suggestions?" Travis asked.

"Well, unless you have a contact at the office, your orders will come back as bullshit," Gomez answered.

Not needing to hear anymore, Travis got out and stood. He looked back at Martin and ordered, "Grab a grenade. I've got these three. After the spoon flies, hold it for a count of two before tossing it into the window."

"Roger that," Martin said and promptly followed his instructions. He grabbed his rucksack and pulled a high-explosive grenade out of a pouch on the outside.

"So this is how it's going down?" Gomez asked.

Martin gave him a look and shrugged his shoulders. "I don't think we have a choice."

Travis's hard-soled boots crunched on the gravel as he approached the shack.

He took long strides and was almost there when a guard yelled, "Stop right there."

"Is there a head in there? I gotta piss," Travis said.

"Get back in your vehicle," the guard ordered.

"Can't a guy take a piss?" Travis barked.

"Wilkens, chill out, man," Gomez said as he walked up to the guard and stood next to him.

"But you heard the commander," the guard said and repeated the last orders he had received, "These men must stay in the vehicle."

While Gomez kept the guard's attention focused on him, Travis walked within a foot of him and stopped while Martin swung around to a few feet of the southernmost window of the twenty-foot-by-twenty-foot building.

"Your name is Wilkens?" Travis asked.

"Yes, sir."

"Where you from?"

"I'm an Arcadian."

"Well, would you look at that, he's an Arcadian," Travis said as he drew his pistol, placed it under the man's chin and pressed the trigger.

The man's head exploded and he dropped straight to the ground.

Travis stepped over him, pistol out in front of him. He leveled the sights on the first man he saw and squeezed another round off.

The startled guard didn't have time to react and took the bullet in the chest.

Gomez also sprang into action and fired off several rounds from his M-4 rifle into the other gate guard.

While this was happening, Martin had pulled the pin, and the spoon from the grenade popped off with a clang. "One one thousand, two one thousand," he said to himself and tossed the grenade through the window.

Two seconds later an explosion shook the ground. The other windows blew out followed by black billowing smoke.

Travis ran up the wooden ramp that led to the front door. The door had been blown off from the explosion. With no concern for his own safety, he entered the smoldering building.

Martin ran up and entered just a moment behind him. His eyes tried to adjust to the minimal light and smoke, but it was almost impossible. The deafening crack of gunfire hurt his ears and made him jump. He pivoted and walked into Travis. As his eyes focused, he saw Travis standing over the commander, who was still holding a handset. The glow from small fires inside illuminated his bloodied face.

"Think we were too late?" Martin asked.

"Not sure, but there's no turning back. Make sure they're all dead," Travis said and stepped to his right.

Another loud crack sounded followed by three more.

Martin did as Travis ordered, and he found two men, their bodies twisted in the debris. They looked dead, but just to make sure, he aimed his pistol and squeezed off a round into each one's head. When he walked out of the smoke, he saw Travis and Gomez waiting.

"What took you so long?" Travis asked.

Martin coughed and replied, "I didn't realize I took that long."

"Well, gentlemen, it's on. I don't know where it goes from here, but we are fully committed," Travis said.

"Just a short drive to the secondary gate and we'll be inside. Do you think he made contact?" Gomez asked.

"Right now we have to assume so," Travis answered.

The small fires inside had grown and now enveloped the

entire building in an intense blaze. The orange glow of the fire cast long shadows of the three men.

They all looked and knew what they had done and what it meant. Travis was right; there was no turning back now.

Charleston, South Carolina

A horn blared loudly three times. The sound carried across the river and echoed over the city and beyond.

Devin shot straight up and looked around, awoken by the loud blast. The night was pitch dark; with no moon, it made it impossible to see. His eyes slowly adjusted but could only make out some shapes. "Tess, what was that?"

No response.

He jumped up and whispered, "Tess, you there?"

Still no response.

Devin walked a few feet and whispered again, "Tess, where are you?"

A dark shadow moved in the distance.

"Tess, is that you?"

The shadow drew closer.

"Tess," he said loudly.

"Yeah, it's me. Why are you shouting?"

"I'm not. I couldn't find you."

"Thank God for these things," she said, pulling off the pair of night-vision goggles.

"Was that horn what I think it was?" Devin asked.

"Yep, a ship is coming in now. I'd say they'll be mooring up in a half an hour to an hour. Our window of opportunity will come a bit after that."

The sounds of men yelling bounced off the creek and hit their ears.

"Looks like they're coming to life," Devin said.

"Hey, this might be the last time I get to say it, and I want to get this off my chest."

The soft tone in Tess's voice grabbed him, and he leaned in to listen.

"I don't know what's going to happen tonight, but I think we're going into the fucking hornets' nest. I know I can be a hard-ass, foul-mouthed bitch sometimes, but please believe me when I say that you're a good guy. I like you, Devin Chase, I really do," she finished and grasped two of his fingers on his right hand.

Devin sensed this might be his moment to kiss her; he leaned a bit closer.

She didn't pull back but seemed to wait.

He leaned even farther, closing the gap between their lips. He could now smell her breath, a sweet spearmint from her favorite gum. He chuckled to himself that only she had the best apocalyptic breath. Somehow she had found a stash of gum that would last a lifetime. For him, he loved it; he just hoped his breath wasn't repulsive.

She hovered, waiting for him.

He was about to close the gap when a large glow erupted to the north.

They both looked and saw flames licking the sky. Music followed right after, and they could see shadowy figures dancing around a huge bonfire.

Frustrated by the interruption, he put his mind back to the task of kissing her, but Tess's attention was gone, focused on the fire and the task ahead. She released his fingers and said, "Come, time to put the diversion in play." She briskly walked away towards the Humvee.

"Damn it," he muttered under his breath.

"C'mon, let's go," she barked.

Devin turned and laughed to himself. His timing was sometimes the worst but not always. He asked himself why it had to be bad just then, why then.

The first part of their rescue attempt required a diversion, and they had one. There was no doubt what they had in mind would work; what they were concerned about was how long it would occupy their attention.

Devin had identified some large hundred-thousand-gallon tanks of chemicals located a quarter mile away from the loading dock's main gate. They'd set the explosives, blow the tank, and watch the fireworks commence.

They arrived at the facility and found it wide open. The gate was a twisted piece of metal on the ground. Clearly someone had gone in looking for things of value.

Devin was driving and headed directly for the tank he thought would work.

The darkness was their friend and enemy. It provided them the cover they'd need, but it slowed them down at the same time.

They parked on the far side of the tank from the shipyard's gate and went to work.

Devin had set C-4 only once before, and then he had Daryl to help him. Wanting to ensure the diversion worked, he allowed Tess to set the charges while he kept watch.

With just a headlamp, she approached the first tank and looked around for anything that told her this tank was suitable.

Nothing.

In the distance she saw thirty-six-inch pipes coming out of the tank and disappearing into the pavement. A large valve came off the pipe and was marked with a large red square sign marked 'Highly flammable'. This was it. She didn't know what it was, but it would more than likely cause the blast they were looking for. Her little fingers worked diligently and swiftly, inserting blasting caps into the five bricks of C-4 they had.

The only issue she saw for them was detonation. They couldn't do it remotely or by a timer; they had to blow it from a short distance away. First, she didn't know exactly how large the blast would be, and second, they'd have to flee south in a hurry and get their boats launched for phase two.

The commotion grew louder from the shipyard. Screams, howls and yelling continued to boom out across the area. It was obvious they didn't fear anyone, and for Tess and Devin, that might be to their advantage.

Devin watched the huge glow to the west and patiently waited.

"All set. You ready to blow this bitch?" Tess asked.

"There's not a better time than now. I heard the ship blare its horn a few more times, and I can see lights from the superstructure. The ship is definitely moored up," Devin answered.

"I think we have a few seconds," Tess said.

"For what?"

"This," she said, then planted a kiss on his lips and pressed her body against his.

Devin was shocked by the kiss, as there was no warning. He adjusted in a split second and returned the kiss and embrace.

They held the kiss for a few seconds before she pulled away.

"I know you meant to do that earlier. I wanted to let you know that," she said.

"I did want to, but the ship distracted us."

"I know," she said and caressed his bearded cheek.

"Tess, I have something to say too."

She put her index finger on his lips and said, "Don't tell me now, tell me on our way back home. I want something to look forward to."

"But I want to tell you now."

"No, later," she said. There was no doubt in her mind what he was going to say, and hearing a man tell her that he loved her was not something she was prepared to hear at that moment.

"I let you talk," he protested.

"You'll just have to wait. I like a man who has patience," she teased, then continued, "And I don't just mean waiting to talk."

Devin got the hint, and wanting to explore what she meant later, he kept his mouth shut.

She pulled him down to the ground behind the Humvee, took the firing device in one hand and said, "Let's go get those kids." She pressed the handle down several times. There was a brief pause, then an explosion erupted that was like none they had ever seen.

Denver International Airport

Martin and Gomez used the short time between checkpoints to get some assets on the inside to the secondary checkpoint. If the commander at the first one had managed to get a call out, they'd have a hell of a time getting through.

"You know exactly where we're taking this thing?" Travis asked.

"Yes, but you should too. This was supposed to be your job, remember?"

"I know, just making sure you know," Travis joked.

"Just be ready to do some damage when we get up there."

Martin leaned across the steering wheel and squinted. "Is that muzzle blasts I see up ahead?"

Travis looked carefully as well to confirm.

The checkpoint was less than a quarter mile away. There they were seeing small flashes.

"Why didn't you get us a Humvee with a gun on it? That would have been helpful right about now," Travis chided him.

"Well, excuse me. I didn't think we'd be going into a fucking firefight."

Travis didn't need to press check his weapons; he was loaded and ready to fight. He wasn't thrilled that shooting his rifle would be cumbersome, but he'd just have to adapt.

Martin pressed the accelerator down hard. They closed on the gate quickly but didn't see anyone manning it; however, they did see people running around in what was definitely a gun battle.

"What are you doing?" Travis asked. He pushed himself

back into the seat cushion and braced himself for impact.

The arm of the gate was down and they were closing fast. Three hundred feet, two hundred feet, one hundred, fifty, twenty-five, impact! The Humvee plowed through the metal gate arm.

Out the window Travis saw bodies lying on the ground.

Martin made the hard turn right and onto the tarmac.

The gun battle at the gate had drawn an army of soldiers and DHS agents out of the terminal buildings. None of them seemed to notice as they sped past them.

Another sharp left and they drove into the lower parking structure and deep into the bowels of the airport.

Travis knew exactly where he was. "Stop, drop me right here!"

"No, we have to set up the device!" Martin yelled.

"Drop me here. The brig is just a level up, over there," he hollered.

"No, you're coming with me to set up the bomb. This is our mission."

"Stop the fucking vehicle!"

Martin slammed on the brakes. The Humvee howled as it slid to a stop. "Get the fuck out! Just don't be late for the extraction; I'm not waiting for your ass!"

Travis grabbed his radio and jumped out.

Martin hit the accelerator and sped off deeper into the airport underground levels.

A single door stood calling Travis. Through here, he'd find an elevator, and just past that, he'd find Lori, or so he hoped.

"Wake her up," Horton ordered Mueller.

Mueller slowly injected the contents of a needle into an IV that sprouted from her left arm. The audible beeps on Lori's heart monitor increased in tempo as he continued to inject the clear fluid into the line.

Horton clapped his hands loudly several times, trying to wake her up.

Her head began to bob around and she slowly opened her eyes.

"Wake up, Lori. Get up!" Horton yelled.

The intercom kept repeating over and over again that the base was under attack.

Horton was concerned about the incident, but he wasn't about to allow it to stop him from the pleasure he was about to experience.

She opened her eyes wide each time he yelled at her, but quickly closed them.

"Wake her up, damn it!" Horton ordered.

"Not everyone responds to sedation the same way. It might take her a few minutes," Mueller said, standing to the side in his white lab coat.

"Give her more, get her up!"

"But that might not be safe," Mueller foolishly said.

"Might not be safe, are you joking? Look at what you just did. Do you think I care?"

Mueller grabbed a small vial and inserted the needle.

"What is…where…?" Lori mumbled.

"Hi, sweetheart, how are you feeling?" Horton asked mockingly.

She forced her eyes open and looked at him. "What…?"

Horton snapped his thick fingers in her face.

She opened her eyes again and blinked repeatedly to focus. Her vision was blurry but coming back after each blink. When he came into focus, her facial expression changed from confusion to anger, with the heart monitor registering the change for all to hear. The straps on her arms prevented her from reflexively striking out at him.

"Settle down," he said.

"What are you doing?" she asked.

"I've got a couple questions for you," Horton said.

"I'm not telling you anything," she said angrily.

"Why don't you hear what I have to offer you?"

"What do you want?"

"I'm so sorry we never had a chance to talk, you know, to see why you came back."

"Where's my family?"

"I'll make you a deal. You tell me everything I need to know and I'll reconnect you with your family. You'll be free to be with them."

"What did you do to me? I feel numb; my legs are numb."

"Do you want to be with your family again?" he asked.

"Yes."

"Then tell me why you came back."

"To kill you."

"I guess that was an easy question, but you came here with the most unusual weapon to kill me. The great Dr. Mueller here said the substance you tried to poison me with is called polonium-210. That is a very rare substance. Who gave it to you?"

"I found it."

"Do you want to see your family again?"

"Let me see them now and I'll tell you where I got it."

"My dear Lori, you fail to see that I hold all the cards."

"Let me see my son and I'll tell you everything I know."

Horton curled his right eyebrow, intrigued by her offer. "That would be easy, for me to show you Eric, but you seemed to forget I'm the one in control here. Let me know what you know and I'll give him an antidote."

"You can save them?"

"Tell me who gave you the polonium."

"Let me see my son," she insisted.

He tensed up, clenching his fists, and walked towards the holding cells where he had seen the woman poisoned earlier in the week.

"Doctor, raise her up and wheel her over to the second window," Horton ordered and walked towards the small holding cells in the laboratory.

After raising her, Mueller wheeled her over to the darkened window. As she noticed her white hospital gown, she again asked, "What are you doing to me?"

"You clearly don't understand what's happening. Maybe you're a visual person. Dr. Mueller, turn on the lights."

Mueller flipped the light switch.

The light turned on in the room and revealed to her Horton's true evil.

When her eyes looked upon the horror in the room, she cried out, "No, no, no, ahhh, no!"

"Look hard, Lori, this is what happens to people who defy me. This is what you have brought upon yourself."

Tears burst from her eyes as she watched David and Eric crawl around on the floor, naked and covered in their own feces, urine and vomit. She looked at Eric and cringed as he shook violently after vomiting up bile and blood.

"Turn off the light," Horton ordered.

Mueller followed his command and the room went dark again.

"I can reunite you with them and ensure you're given an antidote; all you need to do is tell me where you got the polonium."

Lori slowed her breathing and thought about his offer. Inside she was experiencing an immense struggle. If she didn't tell him, her family would die for sure. If she did tell him, he'd kill many innocent people and quite possibly her and her family anyway. Trusting him to stand by his word was asking a lot, but allowing your child to die before your eyes was too much to deal with. "Pine Bluffs, Wyoming."

"Pine Bluffs, Wyoming. Where the hell is that?" he asked.

"A man runs the town, I don't know his name, but he goes by the name the magistrate."

"The magistrate? Hmm, I wonder who that is?"

"He asked me to do it. He knew everything about you."

Horton folded his arms and tapped his fingers on his mouth.

"Now please give them the antidote," she begged.

"Lori, do you believe in consequences?"

"Give them the antidote. I told you where and who I got the poison from."

"Who is this magistrate person? Tell me, tell me everything you know."

"I already did."

"Turn on the light."

Mueller flipped the switch again.

The scene in the room horrified her; she needed it to

stop. "I don't know his name, I swear, but he knows you. He used to be in the Order."

This shocked Horton. He leaned over her and asked, "What's his name?"

"I don't know, I never heard it, he only went by the magistrate."

"What does he look like?"

"Um, he's tall, dark hair, lean."

"That can be many people. Did he have something unique about him?"

Lori struggled to answer his question. She had given up on protecting Pine Bluffs and the magistrate; all she wanted now was to save her family. "I know, he spoke very proper, like he was from the last century, seemed like old proper."

That was the clue he needed. He knew who it was.

"Now help my family," she pleaded. "I told you everything I know."

"Lori, you're a fool. There is no antidote for polonium. There's nothing I can do, but I will honor my word and have you join them, *all* of them." Horton's inhumane behavior knew no end. He grabbed her by the neck, turned her head to the right and said, "Say goodbye to your entire family!"

"Ahhh!" Lori screamed when she saw the small bloody form on the floor near David. At first she had thought it nothing but a collection of blood and feces, but upon his insisting she focus on it, she knew exactly what it was, her unborn baby.

"Oh my God, no, no, no!" she screamed. With all her strength she tried to free herself, but the restraints were too strong.

With his grip still on her neck, he turned her head

towards his and said, "This is what happens when you mess with the chancellor!"

She spat at him and barked, "You'll get yours, you son of a bitch. You will burn in hell; that I promise."

"You're powerless against me," he taunted her.

"I didn't tell you everything; I didn't tell you that the second part of our plan was to blast you and this place to hell. While you're busy torturing me, you're not paying attention to what else is happening. This place will be nothing but a cinder by tomorrow and you along with it."

He grabbed her face and screamed, "You like to run your mouth."

"Right now a nuclear bomb sits, hidden, but soon it will go off and you will die when it does."

A thought crossed his mind that she was bluffing, but then he remembered Calvin. If there was a man who was smart enough to get polonium-210, then he could get a nuclear weapon.

"Where's this weapon?" he asked.

"You can torture me all you want; I don't know where it is. That was kept from me on purpose."

He pushed her face away and grunted.

The brutal show had even affected Mueller, who was purposely not looking.

"Doctor, give her the rest of that tainted whiskey and put her in with her beloved family. When you're done with that, grab the new virus, the Lazarus antidote and meet me topside at the helicopter pad," Horton ordered and walked away.

"Sir, what about patient zero?"

"You've gotten what you need from her, correct?"

Mueller nodded.

"Kill her."

As he walked the corridors back to his residence, Horton thought about the evening's events. Every word he had uttered tonight came from the heart, specifically the one about not crossing him.

Wiping out Lori and her family brought him great joy. After she embarrassed him, he could not put her and the thought of getting back at her out of his mind. Tonight also gave him greater confidence that he could be successful against his enemies.

Digging into his khaki pants, he pulled out his mobile phone and dialed a number. A voice suddenly appeared on the other end. "Wendell, listen carefully. Gather your family and meet me at the helicopter pad. We're leaving immediately; there's no time to discuss it."

Travis stood in the bright elevator carriage and wiped the sweat from his brow. He had his rifle slung and his pistol holstered. Running around like a madman was not the way he thought he should go now; drawing attention to oneself would not work.

The elevator shuddered and stopped, a bell rang and the doors opened. Ahead of him was a long hallway with several doors that entered onto it. At the very end was a large reinforced metal door. Beyond that door sat the brig and hopefully Lori. What was noticeably missing at the door was a guard.

He stepped out and hesitated for a moment. "Where is

everyone?" he asked under his breath.

A loudspeaker in the ceiling crackled to life. "Attention, attention all personnel. Code Red. Mandatory evacuations are underway. Repeat, mandatory evacuations are underway. Report to your nearest unit commander or supervisor for further instructions."

"That's where they are," he said out loud. He brought the M4 rifle to his shoulder and steadied it with his stump and moved down the hall. If anyone at all stepped out of one of those doors, he would put a round in them. No more talking or negotiation, this was now about killing and moving.

His radio boomed, "Priddy, this is Martin! Over."

Travis jumped for a nanosecond but kept proceeding. He had no time to talk and couldn't handle his rifle and respond anyway, the difficulties of having only one hand.

"Priddy, this is Martin. Come in! Over."

Travis reached the door; he lowered his rifle and tried the handle. With a loud click the handle moved right and the latch freed; it was unlocked.

"Priddy, Lori is not in the brig. She is in the lab. Come now!"

Travis's heart skipped a beat. He let go of the cold steel handle and grabbed the radio. "Where are you?"

"Lab."

"Where's that?"

"Too difficult to explain; go back to where I dropped you. Follow the parking structure down to the bottom. I'll meet you there, and hurry! Over."

Travis didn't respond. He raced as hard as his legs would take him to the elevator. After waiting what seemed like an eternity for the elevator car, the door chimed and opened, but now it wasn't empty. On board were two DHS guards, fully dressed in their black uniforms and masks.

Not expecting to run directly into anyone and not knowing if he would be their target, Travis broke leather and pulled out his pistol. He shot the man on the right in the face.

The other guard raised his H&K MP5, but Travis rushed him.

With his left elbow he jabbed the man in the throat and pinned him against the wall of the elevator. He jammed his pistol under the man's chin and pulled the trigger.

Parts of the man's skull, brains and Kevlar helmet erupted onto the ceiling.

Pulling his arm away, Travis let gravity take over, and the man dropped straight down.

Adjusting himself, he turned around, exhaled deeply, hit the desired button and said, "This is going to be a long night."

Charleston, South Carolina

The shockwave from the blast was intense; it hit Tess and Devin like a sledgehammer.

The explosive force from the tank had exceeded what was necessary for the effect.

Dazed from the enormity of the blast, they pulled themselves up and headed towards the creek to begin phase two.

In the Humvee, Devin couldn't stop laughing.

"What the hell is so funny?" Tess chided.

"That back there was crazy. I mean, c'mon, were you

expecting that? I think we're lucky to be alive."

"No, I wasn't expecting that. I think I almost had a heart attack."

"If that doesn't get their attention, I don't know what will."

Tess drove hard, making each turn without slowing down. The last thing they wanted was to run into any of Renfield's men. They wanted to make their introduction on their terms.

Without any encounters and moving as swiftly as the darkness would allow, they parked the Humvee at a small boat dock.

"Let's check our gear quickly," Tess said.

Devin took inventory of his equipment. He patted his tactical vest and felt for the grenades and extra rifle and pistol magazines. He hadn't used his pistol and knew it was in condition one, ready to fire, his rifle was the same. "You good to go?"

Tess was tense, but that was normal for her. She never displayed nervousness overtly, but if she were ever honest, she'd admit to being scared. "All good, let's go through the names of the kids one more time," she said and began to call off each name.

She'd say a name and he'd recite it, trying to burn it into his mind. They had been lucky enough to have gotten photos from the boys, but they knew the reality of finding them all was difficult if not outright impossible. Their long conversations and planning had settled on just bringing home any child they encountered.

Devin reached out and felt her chest.

She swatted him away and stepped back. "Just because

we kissed doesn't give you the right to grab my boobs."

"No, no, I was making sure you had your trauma plate in."

"I took it out. It's too big for me, uncomfortable."

"Please put it in."

"I hate it."

"For me."

"No."

"Then do it for the kids."

"C'mon, let's go," she said, brushing him off and walking briskly towards the boats.

He jogged up beside her and was about to talk when she stopped.

"Just wait, one sec." She turned around and went back to the Humvee.

He could hear her digging and talking to herself. Thirty seconds later she ran back. "Okay, I'm good. Let's do this."

"What did you forget?"

"Ah, nothing," she answered, then punched him in the arm.

As was typical in their relationship, she took control and he let her.

He sat at the bow, keeping watch as best he could in the darkness as she slowly navigated the creek.

With the tank on fire, it added a second glow to the northeastern sky. The hoots and hollering of a joyous and boisterous group were now replaced with yelling and screaming mixed with sounds of heavy equipment, men running, and vehicles driving to and fro.

She pulled the small boat right up on the shore.

Devin jumped out and pulled it farther and tied off the bow to a large tree. The second boat floated behind the first one, tied to the aft.

They hustled through the thick brush and uneven terrain for fifty feet before reaching the southwestern corner of the shipyard.

The ship sat moored not three hundred feet in front of them. Massive floodlights shined on the black hulking sides, and all the lights on board were on. More sounds of people coming and going with urgency, no doubt in response to their explosion. The music that had been blasting was gone; the events for the evening were put on hold, no doubt making some of Renfield's men unhappy.

Devin and Tess each had a pair of bolt cutters and were quickly clipping away at the chain-link fence. In no time, they had cut an opening five feet tall and four feet wide.

Just before they slipped through, Devin stopped her. "Remember we said we'd check in before we went ahead with this?"

"Yes, I remember."

"This is that time. Once we go through there, we may not come back. That's the hornets' nest right there," he said, pointing to the ship.

"I know."

"So we're a go? I'm a go, are you?"

"Well, if you're a go, then I'm with you," she replied.

He hugged her one last time.

She returned his embrace and said, "Let's hope we run into the queen bee, because I'm gonna squash him."

Denver International Airport

Martin and Gomez were waiting at the very end of the underground parking lot next to a parked white van.

Travis sprinted up to them, his chest heaving and sweat pouring off his flush face. "Where is she?"

"Down in the lab," Martin said.

"Why didn't you bring her up?" Travis asked, looking in the van. "Who's that?"

"That's our package, patient zero," Martin said. "Listen, man, you don't want to go down there."

"What do you mean? Is she dead?" Travis asked. A look of panic gripped his face.

Martin looked at Gomez, but neither answered.

"Take me to her, now!" Travis urged.

Martin touched his arm and said, "Look, man, it's not good. I'm sure you don't want to see her this way."

"What the fuck are you talking about? Take me there now, and if you won't, tell me how to get there!"

The loudspeaker sounded again, repeating the base-wide mandatory evacuation notice.

"You have fifteen minutes, tops; if you're not back here, we have to leave you. The bomb has been set; it goes off in forty-five minutes. We're pushing it by waiting for you."

"Where is she?"

"Fuck it, I'll go with you. Gomez, you got this. If we're not back in fifteen, go," Martin ordered, then took off for a door twenty feet away.

Travis was on his heels. "I thought we had a bird?"

"Not anymore, just us and that Ford Econoline," Martin

replied.

They burst into the stairwell, and swiftly they ran down the concrete stairs, skipping several at a time. At the bottom they stopped at a door.

"On the other side of the door is a hallway, goes left or right. We're going left, straight down, end of hall and into another set of stairs, then down two more flights."

"What are we waiting for?" Travis said as he opened the door, peered both ways and bolted out.

As they ran, Martin looked at his watch. Almost three minutes had gone by. They'd reach the lab in two more. They had only five minutes in the lab, no more.

Martin's timing was correct; at the five-minute mark they had reached the entrance to the lab. Bodies lay strewn and twisted on the floor; the massive steel door was nothing more than a charred piece of metal.

"Your calling card, I imagine," Travis joked.

"Army strong."

Stepping over bodies, debris, broken glass and equipment, Travis surveyed the laboratory. "Where is she?"

Martin pushed by him towards the hall. He stopped just before the second window and put his arm out.

"Why are you stopping me?"

"One last time, are you sure you want to see?"

Travis pushed his arm and Martin aside and walked up to the window. He looked in and was horrified by what he saw.

Lori had managed to gather her entire family together, including the fetus, around her.

Eric's head was resting on her lap, with David leaning against her and the baby in her arms, wrapped in a bloody cloth taken from her hospital gown.

The handle of the door wouldn't budge. Travis frantically tried, and when he couldn't get it to budge, he pushed hard against the door. "Help me!" he ordered Martin.

Martin was no good; he felt sorry for her and him. He had gone through the same exercise Travis was going through when he first discovered her. It was hard for him, and he knew it would be almost impossible for Travis to come to grips with the reality of the situation.

Travis found a chair and began to slam it against the glass, but to no avail. Each hit produced the same result, the chair just bounced off the inches-thick safety glass.

Lori saw Travis. Tears again began to flow from her face. There stood the man she should have been with many years before but never allowed herself to see. In her last moments she had total clarity. While her life had been full of successes, she had never truly loved. Yes, there was the love of her children, but she had never fully known the love of an equal, someone she could share her life with. The moments she and Travis shared, especially the weeks after her escape, had given her a glimpse of a man that would have been that love. Now it was too late, a life squandered on things that now she didn't think of. All she wanted now was to have her family back and to be in Travis's arms. So much time wasted, she thought, on such trivial things. Things she thought then brought happiness but didn't. She remembered an old saying that referenced the truly important things in life, and none of them included money or material items. People…people and the positive and loving relationships with them equaled happiness.

As she watched Travis bang away on the glass and door, she was saddened that not until now did she have the full understanding of what the world meant. She asked herself why God played tricks on people and only opened their eyes at the end, but she knew that wasn't true. God had given her the message a long time ago; she had just refused to take it to heart. Was she responsible for all of the carnage around her? No, she thought, but she did own the parts in her life where her actions and reactions resulted in others' pain. She was sorry for that, but looking at how David reacted to her just before he died told her he had forgiven her.

She gently placed Eric's lifeless head on the floor and with all the care she could muster laid her dead baby in his arms. She stood and staggered to the window.

Outside, Travis was still attempting to get in, but every attempt was futile.

The glass was cold to her touch. She laid her hand fully out and spread her fingers.

He stopped and put his hand on the glass where hers was.

"I'm not sure you can hear me, but stop, there's no use!" she yelled.

Travis could hear her faintly. He replied, "I'll get you out, okay, just give me a minute."

"You only have two left," Martin reminded him.

"Travis, I was given the poison. I'm going to die."

"No, the magistrate can find a cure."

"There is no cure," Martin blurted out.

"Would you shut up!" Travis snapped at him.

"Please go. You have to go."

"No, give me another minute. I'll get you out!" Travis yelled and banged on the glass.

"I never told you and I should have, I love you. I only wish I could go back to our days at the ranch; I should have told you then."

"I love you too, Lori."

"Those weeks were special."

"Time's up!" Martin yelled.

"Travis, I love you, but you need to go. I'm with my family now. Go, leave me to die with them," she said, then kissed the glass.

"No, I can't let you die; no, this is not what happens!" Travis screamed and banged his fist on the glass. Tears freely streamed down his face, as no matter what he said to convince himself of the outcome, he knew it was over for her.

Lori turned away from the glass and went back to her place on the soiled floor. She picked up the bloody swaddle and held it close to her heart.

Travis repeatedly banged and banged.

She took one last look at him, lowered her head and closed her eyes.

Charleston, South Carolina

The diversion had worked. They moved quickly from the fence line to the gangway of the ship without running into anyone.

With everyone focused on the inferno still raging outside the gates, they slipped onto the ship unnoticed.

"You know the plan. You go up, I go down," Tess said once they stepped into the first hatch on the superstructure.

"No change of plan. We stay together."

Tess's instinct was to disagree but decided now wasn't

the time, and she liked having him by her side. "Then let's go up."

"Ladies first," Devin joked.

She turned left, saw a ladder well that went up, and began to climb.

A man appeared at the top, a thick long beard hung from his grungy face. He looked at Tess, then Devin strangely and asked, "Who the hell are you?"

Devin raised his rifle and squeezed off two rounds; both hit him in the chest.

The force of the shots sent him backwards into the passageway above them.

"Ugh, that was loud," Tess grunted as she pulled on her ear.

Devin had fired his rifle just over her shoulder.

The shots no doubt would bring others; the clock was ticking for them. At the top, they stepped over him and looked both ways. The passageway that went left traveled the width of the ship, another passageway to the right ended after a few feet, then headed towards the bow.

"This way," Devin said, motioning to the left.

"You take the doors on the left; I'll get the right," Tess ordered.

They swiftly and systematically made their way through every room, but nothing, not a soul, not a child.

At the end another stairwell beckoned for them to go higher.

Tess moved to the base of it but didn't get a chance to climb.

A volley of fire came down on her; one bullet ripped into her left arm.

Devin grabbed her by the back of her vest and pulled her back just in time as another volley of bullets rained down. Pinned against the wall, he plotted a way out or around.

"Fuck that hurts," Tess grunted as she looked at her bleeding arm.

"This will shut them up," Devin said as he pulled a pin on a grenade and tossed it up.

The grenade bounced off a couple walls, and whoever was up there went scrambling, their heavy footfalls running down the upper passageway before the explosion.

"Think that got them?" Tess asked.

"Let's find out." Devin bolted up to take a look. The white walls were now black from the grenade, and two men lay lifeless on the floor. "Looks clear."

Tess came up and stood beside him.

"Same as below, you left, me right," Tess said.

They didn't take three steps when the hatch at the end of the passageway burst open, and at least a dozen men came funneling through.

"We've got company!" Devin yelled. He raised his rifle and let loose a volley of fire.

Tess took a knee and did the same.

The men fell, as there was no place for them to go in the narrow passageway. As the first ones went down, the others tripped over their bodies. But the advantage Renfield's men had was numbers; as they fell, more came through the hatch.

Seeing they couldn't stay put, Tess ordered, "We have to get out of here!"

"I'll cover. You go first," Devin barked.

The few times she did listen to him, she did as he said. She stood and raced to the ladder well and slid down.

Devin fired until his magazine emptied. This was his cue to make haste. He came down just as fast as she did.

"Well, the hive has awakened," Devin joked, slapping another magazine in his rifle.

"Just one kid, any kid, I can't leave without saving one child," Tess moaned.

"Tess, I want to see the other kids at home. Let's get out of here before we're swarmed," Devin said and opened the hatch near them. He stuck his head out and saw no one. Over the railing and below the river coursed by. "If we go out this way, we have to make our way around to the dock side."

The opposite hatch opened, and men came running in, effectively shutting down other options.

Tess fired a few rounds at them before jumping through the open hatch.

Devin slammed it shut and said, "This way." He ran at full speed and came to a set of stairs that led down. It was then he noticed Tess was not with him. He turned to see her standing where they had exited. She was facing the aft of the ship with her arms out.

"Little boy, come here. I'm here to save you."

The boy wasn't more than twelve. He stood like a statue, frozen to the spot. The gunfire and shouting had drawn him out. Curiosity had gotten the better of him, and now he was standing face-to-face with who he thought was the enemy.

"My name is Tess; I'm here to help you. I'll take you away from these bad men," Tess said softly, her arms still outstretched.

Devin began to make his way back to help her when the boy raised his right arm.

"No! I'm here to help you. Put the gun down!" Tess

ordered in a subdued tone.

The butt of Devin's rifle found its way to his shoulder as he marched towards Tess.

Crouched down and her arms still out, showing she meant no harm, Tess took three steps towards the boy. "My name is Tess; I'm here to save you."

"Tess, back away. I don't trust this kid," Devin said. He was a foot behind her now.

"Devin, be quiet. He's just a boy."

The small pistol shook in the boy's grip as he processed just how to deal with the strangers before him.

Tess took a few more steps.

Three shots rang out.

Tess stumbled backwards and fell down; one of the bullets had hit her in the chest.

Devin, in shock, lowered his rifle and went to her aid.

The boy yelled out, "They're over here! They're over here!"

Devin grabbed her under the arm and brought her to her feet. "Tess, you okay? Please tell me you're okay."

"Um, the little fucker shot me," Tess said, a look of surprise on her face.

Another series of shots rang out; one hit Devin in his left shoulder. The other hit Tess, but the bullet ripped through her right arm.

She grunted loudly and fell back against the railing.

The shot that hit Devin made him spin and lose his grasp on her.

The boy walked a few feet closer to Tess. He took aim on her.

On wobbly feet she took a step, looked at him and asked,

"Why? I'm one of the good ones. I'm here to help save you."

The boy cocked his head, confused by her comment, and pulled the trigger again. The bullet hit her center mass. The force of this impact slammed her back against the rail and over.

"No, Tess!" Devin cried out as he watched the bullet slam into her. He lunged for her but just missed grabbing her. He watched her disappear into the darkness then into the black of the water below.

"Hey, mister," the boy said, walking up to him.

Devin, distraught after losing Tess, looked at the boy.

The boy grinned devilishly and pulled the trigger.

Denver International Airport

It took everything to pull Travis from the lab and back up to the van. They were two minutes late, and fortunately for them, Gomez had decided to give them another five.

Pushing him inside, Martin yelled, "You damn fool, you're lucky Gomez gave us more time."

Gomez didn't wait for Martin's door to close; he hit the accelerator and sped off. Each turn through the parking structure put stress on the tires, causing them to squeal with every quick left. They weren't the only ones moving rapidly to flee. When they came out of the darkened garage and onto the tarmac, they saw hundreds of people making their way to their evacuation stations.

The reverberating sounds of propellers drowned out volumes of people racing, yelling and screaming as they hastily made for their transportation out of the airport. The blinking lights from Ospreys and helicopters that were airborne lit the night sky like the twinkling lights on a Christmas tree. Their destination was Dulce, New Mexico, a secret base used by the military and virtually an unknown location to most people.

Travis was in a fog as he sat in the back of the van next to patient zero. He could hear Martin and Gomez talking, but their voices sounded like he was listening to them underwater. The reality of what had just happened was too hard for him to fathom. His memory raced to the day he first met Lori in the cafeteria. The first thing he noticed about her was her backside. He wasn't a pervert, he claimed, he was just being a guy. As she made her way through the chow line, he kept a close eye on her. He saw his moment when she stood looking for a place to sit in the crowded space. Using this as his in, he had called her over. For him personality was critical for him to have lasting feelings for anyone. He was attracted to a strong woman, not because he lacked in his own masculinity but because he respected a woman who had strength but maintained beauty. His intention initially wasn't to fall for her but to flirt. The rest was history, and now he was a man who had lost everything. He had lost so much over the past seven months; now he could add losing someone he had fallen in love with, a woman that could have been the only one who could replace the loss of Tess.

Gomez put the van to the test and drove as fast as it could go north.

Martin kept his eyes glued to his watch as the seconds melted into minutes and grew closer to the detonation.

Lost in his sorrow, Travis had his head buried in his hands. A tap on his head brought him out of his haze. He looked up and saw a small delicate hand. Thinking it had just slipped off the gurney because of the turbulent driving, he softly laid it back on her stomach and went back to sulking.

Another tap on his head.

He looked, but this time patient zero was looking at him, her eyes half open and her hand beckoning him to come closer.

"Guys, she's awake," Travis advised. He sat up and leaned in closer to hear the whispers coming from her mouth.

"Thirsty," she said.

"Yeah, water, I have some. Guys, I need some water."

Martin tossed him bottled water.

"Here," Travis said, giving her a few sips.

She drank cautiously.

"Good?" he asked.

She nodded and waved to signal she was done.

"Can I get you anything else?" he asked.

She nodded and again waved for him to come closer.

He leaned in again.

"Devin, please find Devin."

Charleston, South Carolina

The pistol clicked, signaling the boy was out of ammunition.

Devin's range of emotions swung rapidly from fear to anger. His rifle hung from his body on the two-point sling, but he didn't go for that. He stepped towards the boy, knocked the gun out of his hand and smacked him across the face.

The boy fell and cried out.

Devin whipped out his pistol and pointed it at the boy.

"Don't shoot, please," the boy begged.

The anger turned to rage as he thought of Tess and what this boy had done to the woman he cared for.

"Please, I'm just a kid. Don't shoot me."

"You're not a kid, you're a fucking monster," Devin coldly said and pressed the trigger.

After shooting the boy, Devin stood over his body, tempted to shoot him again, but he refrained.

Several exterior doors opened.

Devin looked behind him. There were dozens of men pouring out of the ship, and he was their target. He knew he couldn't take them, he'd surely die, but if he jumped, he just might survive the forty-foot fall. Desperate and with no place to go, he hurled himself over the railing and into the dark water below. As he fell, he had just one moment to ponder if the impact would hurt. When he hit, he found his answer; it did hurt.

The pain from his gunshot was aggravating, but he soon forgot about it as he held his breath and swam as hard and long as he could. He heard the muffled sounds of guns firing and bullets hitting the water. All he could do was pray that he'd not get hit again. His life was literally on the line, and if he came up once, that would be enough for them to zero in on him. When he impacted the water, he hadn't paid attention to the direction he was swimming, he had just started to swim with all his might. Luckily for him he had picked the best direction and found cover under the curvature of the ship. He came up, caught his breath and continued swimming towards the aft. From there he swam until he reached the inlet of the creek and river.

He had made it, but the success of his jump was dampened by the fact that he had lost Tess. His right hand was the first to warn him he had reached the muddy shore of the creek. On his hands and knees he crawled out of the creek and rested on the grassy mud just a few feet out of the water. His chest burned from overexerting himself, and his shoulder was numb now. Still lying on his back, he reached over and inspected his shoulder; just his touch brought searing pain. He thought about getting up and moving, but he was exhausted. Grabbing a handful of mud, he stuffed it into the bullet hole. He had no idea when he'd be able to give the wound the attention it needed, and this for now would stop it from bleeding, or so he hoped.

Large floodlights blasted the river and surrounding area of the shipyard. Renfield's men were looking for him no doubt, he thought, but he was also sure they were looking for others that might have been with him.

His body screamed out in pain as he sat up. From his shoulder to his back, his body told him to stay put, but he knew that was impossible. Soon, he knew, they'd be looking outside the shipyard. Ignoring his body, he grunted and moaned until he reached his feet. Based upon where the ship was behind him, he figured the Humvee wasn't far. Slogging through the tall grasses, he walked east until he found the small gravel road; there he knew he was close. The sounds of vehicles leaving the shipyard echoed over the trees and creek. This gave him the encouragement to walk faster. His assumptions and innate sense of direction were proven correct; the Humvee was exactly where he'd thought it was.

After a slight struggle to get his racked body inside the vehicle, he hesitated before starting it. He peered through the thick windshield glass towards the ship. The floodlights were still splashing across the area in a desperate hunt for him and Tess. It was Tess that gave him pause; he couldn't believe she was gone. He was tempted to stay and look for her body, but her voice popped in his head and scolded him for such a dumb idea.

With deep regret and sadness, he started the Humvee and pulled out of the boat docks and headed towards North Carolina.

Fifty-seven miles north of Denver International Airport

They still sped north, headed towards their new home, the missile silos of Wyoming.

Martin had kept in satellite phone contact with his Scraps in Denver. They reported back that their mission had been a success. They had pulled it off. They had destroyed the DIA, Horton's lab and taken patient zero, but what they failed to find was any vials that had contained the new virus. In Martin and Gomez's search of the laboratory, they had collected trash bags of hard drives and paperwork. Their hope was they'd be able to reconstruct or find something useful.

For Travis the mission was an utter failure. Losing Lori was something he'd never recover from, and when he heard that the bomb had gone off, he hoped that it provided her relief. Upon his return he planned to set out and find Tess. He had waited too long, and with nothing holding him down, he was free to go. Guilt entered his mind when he thought of his fiancée, but he quickly dismissed it. He decided then that he wouldn't plague his mind or conscience with such useless emotions. He was a man who needed missions, who needed purpose, and now he had one.

Cassidy was now awake and asking an endless stream of questions. For her the entire seven months was a dream. Her last memories were of the hospital in Indianapolis and being sick. As Travis and Martin explained the world, she couldn't believe it. She thought that it all must be some sort of dream or a nightmare. She was important for the magistrate, as she could save the world or kill the world. However, all she cared about was finding Devin wherever he might be. Her life had been a challenge since she was a little girl, but she always found a way to survive and succeed. She would have to tap into this internal strength to find her place in this new world.

The van crested a small hill and past the old imaginary line that separated Colorado and Wyoming. In a few hours the light of a new day would break the horizon. For all of them any tomorrow was not a guarantee but an opportunity and a blessing. Their struggle was far from over, but they could take heart that they had secured a victory in a war that had only begun.

Day 227

North Topsail Beach, North Carolina
May 15, 2021

Devin's aches and pains had slowed him down considerably, but he persevered and completed the six-hour drive. Stopping just short of the house, he couldn't decide on how to tell the kids they had failed and in that failure lost Tess. He still couldn't believe it himself. The long drive found him pulling over several times to stretch and cry. Imagining a world without her was unspeakable, yet he had to go on. He didn't do it for himself or the kids but for her; that was what she would want. He would have to be strong and lead Brianna and the kids out of there and to a new home. Where that would be was still unknown, but he would find a way.

Finally gathering the strength, he put the Humvee in gear and drove the remaining distance to the house.

Brianna was the first to spot him; she called out to the children, who all came rushing out of the house and into the driveway.

He parked and looked at the happy faces on all the little ones, as she called them. Even Melody was outside eager to greet them. It broke his heart to have to tell them she was dead and they had failed to rescue anyone.

Brianna knew something was wrong. She could see it was

only him behind the wheel and saw the pain written all over his face.

"Okay, kids, back inside, you're probably scaring them with all these squeals of excitement."

"No, we want to see them, welcome them home," Alex said with a large smile.

Devin couldn't let them wait anymore; he opened the door and slowly stepped out.

When the children saw the condition he was in, they stopped their celebratory laughter and cheers.

Meagan ran up to him and gave him a hug. "Uncle Devin, you're hurt."

Devin couldn't stop the tears and didn't want to; he broke down. He placed his hand on her head and said, "Yeah, I got a bit banged up."

"Where's Tess?" Alex asked. He had walked to the passenger side and looked in. "Where is everyone? Are they coming behind you in another car?"

Devin began to sob and tried to talk, but the words wouldn't come.

"Kids, give him some space, please," Brianna ordered.

Meagan wouldn't let go and held onto his hand.

"No, Alex, there isn't another car. No one else is coming."

"What?" he asked, shocked.

The joyous occasion took a dramatic turn and became somber.

"I'm so sorry, but we couldn't rescue your brothers or sisters. We tried, but there were too many."

"Where's Tess?" Alex asked with anger in his voice.

Devin sobbed again and tried hard to stop, but seeing the

kids and Brianna made it impossible.

"Where is she?" Alex again asked, almost yelling.

"She was killed. She's not coming back," Devin said, finally getting out what everyone already knew.

"No, no!" Alex screamed and ran off.

"Alex, come back!" Brianna hollered.

"I failed you all, but we tried. There were just too many," Devin cried. "There were just too many."

Brianna took control of the sad situation and brought Devin inside. She cleaned him up and put him to bed.

As he lay looking at the ceiling, all he could think of was Tess. He felt cheated. The world had taken Cassidy, and now it had taken Tess. Anger grew in him. Never again would he allow himself to fall victim to love, and never again would he allow anyone to victimize the innocent. Tess would live on in him through his new mission in life. He would be the champion of the weak and innocent. He would find these children a home, but he would go beyond that, he would create them a community to live in that was safe from the predators and marauders, but that all would begin after he woke. The fatigue of the past couple days caught up with him, and slowly he drifted off to sleep. Just before he dozed off, he muttered, "I love you, Tess."

Epilogue

Day 233

North Topsail Beach, North Carolina
May 21, 2021

Devin was excited to get back on the road. With Brianna's help, he had healed nicely from the gunshot wound. Thankfully for him it had been a clean shot straight through.

The children were also excited about the prospects of a new home and were being extremely helpful as he packed the Humvee and truck.

Devin was diligent and detailed, others would say he was anal, but he ignored those comments. Before he packed any vehicle, he took everything out and organized it, then repacked it so it had a place and he knew where to find it.

As he went through his inventory of protective equipment, he lined up his tactical vest and the spare Brianna had. He remembered Brianna didn't have a trauma plate, and after what happened to Tess, he wanted her to have the one Tess refused to wear.

He dug through the back but couldn't find it. He emptied every pocket of every pack, but it was gone. Frustrated, he ripped through every square inch. He tossed and threw every scrap out of the Humvee, but it was nowhere to be found.

"Arghh!" he grunted loudly.

"What are you getting pissed about?" Brianna asked.

"Tess's trauma plate, I can't find it. After losing her for not having one, I'm not going to let that happen to anyone else."

"You sure you looked in every spot?"

"Yes, I've looked everywhere. It's not in there."

"Bri, can you come here? Melody needs you," Meagan called from the house.

"I'll be right there," she replied to Meagan. She turned and headed back in, but stopped and asked, "Are you sure Tess didn't have it on?"

Devin thought. No was his initial answer. He distinctly remembered touching her chest and not feeling it. Annoyed, he dove back in the Humvee and looked again; then it struck him. His memory from that night came back. "Wait a minute, she went back to get something. Wait a minute!" Devin ran towards the house, yelling, "She had it on! She was wearing the plate!"

Brianna stopped what she was doing and looked at Devin. "Slow down. You're about to hyperventilate."

"Bri, we have to go back. We have to go look for her. She might be alive."

"But you said she was shot in the chest."

"She was, but she had the trauma plate on. It was a ballistics plate; it would have stopped the bullet!"

"Are you sure?"

"Yes, I remember she didn't have it on; then she went back and did something. Now I can't find it. Brianna, we have to go back. Tess might be alive!"

For more information on
John W. Vance
visit
www.jwvance.com
www.facebook.com/authorjohnwvance

If you have time please leave a review on Amazon.

Thank you,
John W. Vance

ABOUT THE AUTHOR

John W. Vance is a former Marine and retired Intelligence Analyst with the CIA. When not writing he spends as much time as he can either with his family or in the water. He lives in complete bliss somewhere where the waves meet the shore

Made in the USA
San Bernardino, CA
19 January 2016